S0-AXJ-278

"DO YOU EVER TAKE NO?"

"Not often," he said, leaning close enough for her to feel the impression of his body, sending strange sensations to the pit of her stomach. "I feel like I've been waiting on a precipice for months. Why don't we start with a kiss?"

Alyssa moaned.

Their faces were mere inches apart. He moved closer, but instead of kissing her fully on the lips, he touched the corner of her mouth, dotted kisses to her cheeks. His lips were cool against her heated skin, and unexpected pleasure rushed through her.

Alyssa sighed. She'd been dreaming about those lips touching hers. Her body ached for his touch. And even knowing she was making a decision she'd regret in the morning, she moved to kiss him fully.

Also by Candice Poarch
from Dafina Romance

Golden Night

Discarded Promises

Bittersweet

Long, Hot Nights

CANDICE POARCH

Kensington Publishing Corp.

http://www.kensingtonbooks.com

DAFINA BOOKS are published by

Kensington Publishing Corp.
850 Third Avenue
New York, NY 10022

Copyright © 2008 by Candice Poarch

All rights reserved. No part of this book may be reproduced in any form or by any means without the prior written consent of the Publisher, excepting brief quotes used in reviews.

If you purchased this book without a cover, you should be aware that this book is stolen property. It was reported as "unsold and destroyed" to the Publisher and neither the Author nor the Publisher has received any payment for this "stripped book."

All Kensington Titles, Imprints, and Distributed Lines are available at special quantity discounts for bulk purchases for sales promotions, premiums, fund-raising, and educational or institutional use. Special book excerpts or customized printings can also be created to fit specific needs. For details, write or phone the office of the Kensington special sales manager: Kensington Publishing Corp., 850 Third Avenue, New York, NY 10022, attn: Special Sales Department, Phone: 1-800-221-2647.

Dafina and the Dafina logo Reg. U.S. Pat. & TM Off.

ISBN-13: 978-0-7582-1978-7
ISBN-10: 0-7582-1978-4

First mass market printing: May 2008

10 9 8 7 6 5 4 3 2 1

Printed in the United States of America

Acknowledgments

My sincere thanks to readers, book clubs, book sellers, and librarians for their continued support. Thank you Larry Simmons, Jay Cey, Mary Porter, and Al Alston for background information.

As always profound thanks to my parents; my sister Evangeline, who travels with me to promote my books; and Sandy Rangel, Kate Duffy, and Karen Solem for their unswerving help. Most of all I'm deeply grateful to my husband's continued support for my writing. Thanks to my writer friends for keeping me sane.

Prologue

It was the year 1618, and Abiola had been married three months. She was in the family way.

As she worked, she let her mind roam. Abiola's father moved his family to England when she was a little girl. She spent most of her life there until she boarded a ship to sail with a group of men and women to the New World. But in a storm, they went off course and were tossed at sea for weeks before they were captured by pirates. All the men had been killed, but the women had been taken aboard the pirates' ship and the pirates sank their vessel. Then they sailed off to an unknown shore.

The pirates were in a celebratory mood, for they'd captured many riches from other raided ships. The women were forced to cook for everyone, and the captain had given them use of the spices. Abiola and the women had poisoned the men and managed to sail away. They had no idea where they were going. But they hadn't traveled nearly far enough before the ship had grounded on a sandbar. They were, however, lucky enough to make it to an island and row their provisions to shore before it sank.

The pirates had a voyage's worth of booty on board, and the women had split the riches among themselves. There were spices, seeds, and silk, in addition to Spanish coins, gold bullion, and four golden bowls. They'd salvaged the sails to make new clothes, for provisions were scarce and they had to make do with what they had.

When they had arrived a year ago, the island was deserted, and it looked as if a huge storm had ravaged it. It was fall, and they'd feared they'd never find another living soul, but in the spring two men in a fishing vessel who had been caught in a storm at sea came ashore. They were as surprised to see the women as the women were to see them.

One of them was now Abiola's husband. He'd traded for seeds from the Indians for them to plant. An Englishman who'd been indentured, he had already worked off his time. In the beginning, the English wouldn't adapt the Indian ways for survival, and many of them had perished. Since he'd gained his freedom, he'd learned much about survival in this land from the Indians.

It was now fall again, and her husband was fast at work, building a new home for them before winter settled in. He'd gotten a couple of men to help him build a root cellar first. At least the new house was near a stream so fresh water was close by.

Abiola was busily preserving vegetables from the garden as best she could for the winter months. She also had four mouths to feed for the noontime meal.

Life was not like it would have been in Africa or England. This was a different world. She would never see her family again. But she was lucky to be alive. She had her own land now, and she could raise cattle, chickens, and pigs, and she'd have a garden where she'd grow corn and other things to feed them.

Her husband had recently returned from Jamestown and told her tobacco would be a priority to sell. Come spring, he'd plant a crop.

They would have children to tend to the land one day

when she was gone. Three other families lived on the island, too, and this land would grow and prosper. They had something to build from.

She glanced at her husband. His muscles strained as he worked to cut down a tree to build their new home. He'd gone fishing before daybreak and brought back enough for their main meal at noon. She'd cleaned the fish after they had broken their fast. She would cook them after she ground the corn for skillet bread. Thank goodness there had been cookware on the ship.

It was a beautiful day. A brisk sea breeze blew over her heated skin. Trees and wild flowers grew in abundance. Even the precious sassafras she brewed for tea and used for medicine grew wild. And a hundred feet away was the ocean beckoning her with its coolness. What a beautiful place. They had aptly named it Paradise Island.

Abiola had hidden the golden bowl, a couple of bars of gold bullion, and a few coins. The rest she shared with her husband. He'd used some to buy tobacco plants from the West Indies. The riches she'd hidden would be saved for a rainy day. And if they didn't need it, she'd pass it all down to one of her female children.

Abiola had always lived in villages. But the island was too large for the four families to reach their fields from one location each day. They wanted to make the best use of the land, so the women who had remained on the island divided the land among themselves and spread out with their new husbands. As women were scarce in the New World, finding husbands was easy. Three of the seven women from the ship had settled on the mainland.

Her greatest fear was that armed men would come one day to take their land from them, or worse, murder them.

Abiola swallowed her fear. She had too many chores to complete to worry about that. But she still wondered how long the land and gold would stay in the family.

Chapter 1

In a heavily wooded area of Virginia's Blue Ridge
Mountains, several members of the all-female Hampton
Roads' High Tides Motorcycle Club were camped out,
most with husbands or dates. Alyssa Claxton had invited
Reginald Jones, but he'd canceled at the last minute. They
were friends, not lovers, and since neither of them was
dating anyone special, they often substituted as each
other's date when either one needed an escort.

"You should give *him* a try," Melinda Easton said, tip-
ping her head toward the man across the campfire. Melinda, five-eight with a rich milk chocolate complexion,
wore her hair scraped back in a ponytail.

Under attack by bloodsucking mosquitoes, Alyssa
sprayed herself liberally with insect repellent as she shifted
her gaze to Jordan Ellis. Six-five to her six feet even, he
sat at the picnic table, his long, long, jean-clad legs
stretched out in front of him. His arms were crossed over
his well-built chest, which was covered in a green designer
golf shirt that Alyssa freely admitted enhanced his walnut-
brown complexion. Although he conversed with the
people around him, his gaze constantly veered back to her.
And she couldn't help the flutter in her insides.

"I don't think so," Alyssa said almost reluctantly, coming back to the conversation. "Reg and I are considering kicking our relationship up a notch. Platonic doesn't do it anymore. Girl, I haven't had sex in so long . . ."

"Considering? Looks to me like you're desperate, but not for Reginald. Any man will do, is that it?" Melinda asked.

"That's not fair," Alyssa snapped. "Why would you say something like that?"

"I think you're doing Reginald wrong. And I can name a place that sells toys to take care of your problem."

"Forget your toys. They can't take the place of a hot-blooded man."

"Hot-blooded can't take his eyes off you. Just look at him. He's one determined man."

Alyssa looked. She'd looked all weekend. Heat rushed through her, spreading out like a slow drug. She fanned herself, but it didn't cool her.

"If something was going to happen between you and Reginald, it would have happened by now," Melinda continued.

Alyssa worked to bring her body under control. "We care for each other, and we have the same interests, like biking and boating—outdoors stuff," she said evenly.

"How do you think he's going to feel when he realizes he can't measure up to your ideal man?" Melinda continued doggedly. "He holds you back and frustrates the heck out of you. It's not fair to him for you to go out with him but wish you were with Jordan. He'll let you indulge your wild side. Reg is way too tame, too safe. Jordan is more unrestrained, like you. And you don't threaten him the way you do Reginald."

Alyssa barked out a disbelieving laugh. "I don't threaten Reg. We've been friends since . . ."

"I know, I know. Since kindergarten." Melinda waved a dismissive hand. "You're *friends*. He's not the love of your life. He could be with you right now, but where is he? He preferred to direct a funeral rather than to come on a trip with you."

"Why don't you just stick a knife in my gut and twist it?" The words hurt like acid. "The woman who died is a pillar of the community," Alyssa defended him, even though she'd used the same argument when he'd canceled. "He's trying to grow the business." The excuse sounded lame even to her.

"Stanley is a mortician, too, and he could have gone in Reginald's place. Jordan's a businessman with lots of deals pending, but he didn't let that stop him. He's here because you're here. I'm sure he could have found some work to do if he wanted to."

"Are you implying Reg chose the funeral because he didn't want to spend the weekend with me?"

Melinda slapped at a mosquito on her arm. "What do you want me to say? He's as confused as you are."

Anger bubbled to the surface, but Alyssa managed to contain it as she glanced at the object of her frustration. Jordan Ellis' eyes were trained on her, mocking her.

"You're not exactly unbiased. You've always hated Reg."

"I don't dislike him," Melinda said, losing the attitude. "I just think you two are mismatched. Unlike Jordan."

"Because he's wealthy?"

"Don't be a moron. Wealth wouldn't impress you. He's a good match for your fiery nature. You're attracted to Jordan, and I know you wouldn't admit it even if your ass was sitting on a bed of hot coals and your life depended on a confession."

"You think you could be little more dramatic?" Alyssa said with an uncomfortable chuckle. Everyone except Melinda thought she and Reginald were the perfect couple. "Are you on your period or something?"

"Go ahead. Be a smart ass, detective. You always have to be right."

"Right. I am the detective," Alyssa snapped. "None of your business anyway."

Melinda sighed just as Racine Hammerfield cut across Jordan's path, moving her well-trimmed body in slow motion.

She wore a knit top with half her paid for boobs hanging out. Gone were the cheerleading days when she stuffed socks into her bra. Obviously, she'd used a shoehorn to squeeze into those tight jeans. Bending over right in front of Jordan, she gave him an up close and personal view of her backside. Some women had no class.

"She's trying to push her fake boobs and big butt in his face, but he's still ignoring her."

"None of my business," Alyssa informed her. Racine had been a thorn in Alyssa's backside from elementary school, and things had only gone downhill in junior high and beyond. Early on, Alyssa sprouted up taller than the average boy in her class, and Racine had picked at her emotional wounds until Alyssa knocked her on her ass. Of course, Alyssa always got in trouble, but she never let the fact that it bothered her show. She had her mother to thank for that. There wasn't a day that went by that her mother hadn't told her how beautiful she was. And made sure her father got on the bandwagon.

Jordan cut Racine an irritated glance, and annoyed at being ignored, she finally moved on. Racine was recently divorced, and her search for husband number two had turned into a full-time job.

Alyssa sipped her Riesling. Jordan made her heart race. But the truth was she was sick to death of putting her heart and soul into relationships, only to come up on the short end of the stick. She'd heard, *"I don't make promises,"* so many times she could make a CD. Or worse, the new catchphrase was, *"No strings attached."*

A relationship was an investment. An investment of time, energy, catering to another's needs and fitting them into your schedule, and vice versa. It was filled with heartbreak and disappointment. Women always invested more than men. With Reginald, she knew her investment would net a sizable payout. They'd had a history. Not as lovers, but she trusted him.

The stakes were higher, too, because if things went sour, she could lose a valued friend.

Alyssa didn't let fear rule her life. She was willing to dive into almost anything headfirst. But she wasn't stupid. Who *didn't* know that Jordan lived by the *No Strings Attached* motto? Just ask the string of heartbroken women he'd left in his wake.

Besides, Alyssa had grown up with three brothers, and no one had to tell her a woman couldn't change a man.

But *was* she substituting Reginald for her ideal man? And would she eventually hurt him? Melinda was just ranting. She didn't know what she was talking about. Alyssa couldn't stand the idea of forcing Reginald into a disastrous situation—one that would cause him unhappiness—just because she was ready for another chapter in her life and he was willing to oblige. A woman should love the man she married, not dream of what could have been.

But she loved Reginald, didn't she?

Vanetta Claxton Frasier's plane touched down on her return from New York; she'd planned to spend the night with her college friend in Williamsburg and they were going to spend Monday at Busch Gardens. Vanetta, however, had bought some sexy lingerie at a Fifth Avenue boutique and she wanted to try it out on her husband.

Sex had been nonexistent lately, and Vanetta wanted to get that part of their lives back on track. She was in her mid-thirties while Matthew was in his fifties, but most men of that age still boasted a healthy sex life. Vanetta missed the closeness and intimacy most of all.

She took the ferry back home to Paradise Island. Only two other cars rode over with her. She stood at the railing alone, watching the star-filled night, thinking of the times she and Matthew had stood with his arms wrapped around her on balmy nights like this.

As a warm breeze blew over her, she remembered how for the first few years of their marriage, when she and Matthew had lived in Norfolk, she'd longed to return to her island. When he had landed his first big deal, they'd built an enormous house on the island.

The ferry docked, and giddy with anticipation, Vanetta drove home, barely ten minutes away.

Her bubble deflated a little when Matthew's car wasn't in the garage. Maybe he was visiting someone. But it was late. Who would he visit this time of night? Maybe he'd take the next ferry back.

Her home was one of the largest on the island, but that was changing. Jordan was building one so immense the islanders dubbed it "the castle."

She loved her six-bedroom home. They'd hired an architect to design it, and Matthew had given her free rein in decorating, so she'd chosen French Country. He was pleased with the effect. And although she'd wanted separate bathrooms in the master suite, he'd insisted on only one. He wanted the pleasure of watching her dress. But lately, he rarely watched her.

She rushed to the bathroom, turned on the water in the shower, and stepped out of her slacks. She reached into the drawer for her shower cap and spotted pills on the countertop. Curious, she picked up the bottle.

Viagra. Her heart gladdened. Of course he missed their intimacy as much as she did. According to the label, he had thirty pills. No time like the present to start trying them out. Vanetta opened the bottle. One, two, three, four tiny blue pills. Twenty-six of the little suckers were missing. He sure as heck hadn't used them on her—not even one. Come to think of it, why were the pills out when he wasn't expecting her back until tomorrow?

It didn't take a genius to answer that question. Damn him. Vanetta went weak with anger. She slid onto the little vanity stool to gather her wits. Anger started as a slow simmer and increased to a roaring rage. Damn him. Vanetta wasn't putting up with this crap.

Quickly, she reached down and pulled her slacks back on, remembered the running water, and turned it off.

She picked up the phone and dialed Matthew's cell. He didn't answer.

She wasn't waiting for him to show up at some ungodly hour. Chances were he wouldn't return until morning. Probably come rushing in an hour before she was due home. He was, more than likely, spending the night at The Cove, the upscale business club in Virginia Beach he owned with his two partners.

She grabbed her purse and headed to the ferry. On this ride back to Virginia Beach, she stayed in her car instead of getting out to catch the ocean breeze. As soon as the ferry docked, she headed to the club. She was going to catch that two-timer in the act.

She slammed to a stop and sailed inside the club, ignoring the elegant decor and old-world charm.

"May I have a key to Mr. Frasier's room, please?" she asked the front desk clerk.

"I don't believe he's here tonight, ma'am. He rarely stays here, especially now that Mr. Ellis is back," the middle-aged, coffee-complexioned man said.

"He told me he was staying here," Vanetta assured him. "Please give me the key."

"Let me check the guest list. Excuse me, please." He disappeared through a door. A minute later, the GM, Wade Ripley, approached her. He reminded her of a sleazy used car salesman. All false charm.

"It's good to see you, Vanetta. I'm sorry you made a fruitless trip, but Matthew isn't staying here tonight."

"He told me he was. I need to speak to him. It's urgent."

Wade gently took her arm and steered her to a private seating area, but they remained standing. "I'm sorry, Vanetta. He really isn't here. I don't know where he is. Did you try his cell phone?"

"Of course." Did she look like a moron? Vanetta sighed and left for her car. *Liar.* If Matthew wasn't there, he'd arrive eventually. She'd come over on the last ferry. Where else would he stay when he owned an exclusive business club with seventy rooms? Make that seventy-one. Jordan had insisted on having a suite available for the owners.

She parked across the street, turned off the engine, then the lights . . . and waited.

Alyssa drank the last of her wine and got up to refill her glass. Seconds later, Jordan was beside her.

"I know I've been away a lot working on the new clubs but still I've been trying to arrange a date with you since Valentine's Day. Why are you playing so hard to get? Why don't you give a guy some slack?"

"Why are you invading my space?" Alyssa asked. "The average guy would have gotten the message by now. Your persistence borders on stalking."

"I'm trying to court you. There's a difference." He deftly uncorked the wine bottle and filled Alyssa's glass.

"Let's just put an end to this right now. I don't like you. I won't date you. So don't waste your time."

Jordan shook his head. "I don't understand. What do you have against me? I know you're attracted. I could feel the sizzle between us from way over there. So what's the problem?"

"It's lightning bugs." Alyssa held up her filled glass. "Thanks for the wine," she said before starting to return to her seat. But Jordan grasped her arm.

"No, no, no. Don't walk out on me like that. What have I done?"

"You have a lot of nerve. Do you really think I'll just close my eyes to the fact that you make it easy for Matthew to cheat on his wife?"

"What the hell are you talking about?" He looked genuinely shocked, but Alyssa wasn't buying it.

"Oh, come on. He brings his women to the club. Parades them right under your nose."

"Not when I'm there."

"Do you really expect me to believe that?"

"Matthew doesn't even stay at the club. At least, he hasn't since I returned. Listen, he's a grown man and a partner in the club. But there's no way in hell I'd let a partner carry on like that in our business environment. I don't control what he does on his own time. Like I said, he's a grown man."

Alyssa searched his eyes for the truth. Jordan was known for his integrity. Besides, he was right, darn him. Only Matthew could control his actions. She couldn't blame the world because Matthew was an asshole. Racine had deliberately let the news of Matthew's affairs slip with an, "Oops. Didn't know you were there." Alyssa had wanted to smack her.

"If I've misjudged you, then I apologize."

"Apology accepted." He kept a light grip on Alyssa's arm. "Does Vanetta know?"

Alyssa cast her gaze down. "I don't think so."

Jordan rubbed a hand behind his neck. "I'm sorry, Alyssa. Vanetta deserves better."

"You bet she does. And she needs to know. She has to protect herself from diseases. If it were me, I'd leave the son of a bitch," Alyssa said between her teeth. "How the hell do I tell my cousin her husband's a lying, cheating piece of scum?"

"I don't know," he said, releasing her to cross his arms, tucking his hands beneath his armpits as if to keep himself from touching her. "So that's what you've been holding against me all this time."

"For the last couple of hours, anyway."

His gaze roved lazily over her. "I haven't had sex since February, when I fell for you. And right now, I'm so needy I could pretty much drag you off into the bushes and . . ."

Alyssa held up a shaky hand. "Just stop right there." She did not need sexual images of Jordan crowding her mind. "Thanks for the wine," she said abruptly and made her way to the table, easing herself into the seat next to Melinda.

Jordan took a seat across the fire from her again. And he was still staring at her. Her defenses were down.

Melinda sighed.

"Tired?" Alyssa asked, still perturbed at her friend, but glad to focus on another topic.

"Not really."

"Other than my love life, what's wrong?"

Melinda frowned. "I touched a raw nerve, didn't I?"

Alyssa wouldn't dignify that with a response.

"I'm worried about Vicky." Vicky was Melinda's younger sister.

Alyssa sat her glass on the seat between them. "Is she taking the divorce hard?"

"I'm worried about the group she's hanging out with."

"What don't you like about them?"

"It's her. She's so secretive. That's what worries me."

"She has enough sense to stay out of trouble."

"With the law. But she's always skirting the edge. Always thinking up some scheme."

"What is she doing this time?" Alyssa asked.

"That's just it. I don't know. Like I said, she's secretive. Ever since Vicky was a child, when things got this quiet, something happened. She's going over to Norfolk every weekend."

"So what? A lot of islanders go there. There's not much entertainment on the island."

"She never says where she's going, and she makes a mess of everything. Despite the rumors about him, her husband is a good man, and look what happened. Maybe I should have stayed home and had a talk with her."

"It's not like you can tell her what to do. She's grown."

"Only in age. There's something to be said for maturity," Melinda said.

"If there's anything I can do, just say the word."

Melinda nodded. "I'm turning in," she said and rose from the bench.

Alyssa watched her friend make her way to her tent. What the heck was Vicky up to now? A few years ago, a rumor spread that her husband dabbled in necrophilia. Since he was a mortician, that did not go over well with the locals. Who wanted to wonder if a necrophiliac was handling a dearly departed loved one? He nearly lost his business, and he was finally forced to sell out to Reginald and Stanley.

It was only a rumor, but a powerful one. A rumor that made a difference. He now worked in some factory in Norfolk.

Alyssa made a mental note to ask around about Vicky when she returned to Paradise Island.

Including Alyssa, four people were left around the fire. Two other women and Jordan. Racine had disappeared.

Sighing, Alyssa sipped her Riesling. She'd turned thirty a couple of weeks ago. Thirty and single, her mother reminded her on a weekly basis. It was even more glaring here because nearly everyone was paired off, and one by one, they were leaving the campfire for their tents. Alyssa might shrug off her single state, but deep down, she, too, wanted to be part of a couple.

It was the group's last evening in the mountains. Tomorrow was Labor Day, and they were leaving early in the morning. Alyssa loved Paradise Island, but she was the only detective there, so it was hard to get down time unless she simply left.

"See you in the morning." Alyssa drank the last of her wine and bade everyone good night, making her way through the trees and picnic tables to her tent. The campground was full. Many campers were already asleep. Sounds carried in the night. One group several yards away was talking in whispered voices.

All of the bikers' tents were in the same general area, but Alyssa's was more isolated than the rest of them. She'd showered earlier, so she zipped her tent closed and changed into sweats before she climbed into her sleeping bag and zipped it up to her chin. It was already cold in the mountains at night. The mornings were so chilly she wanted to stay snuggled in the warmth of the sleeping bag as long as possible.

Finally, she dozed off, thinking how much more pleasant the trip would have been if Reginald was with her.

The group had gone hiking, horseback riding, boating, and fishing, and some had even performed stunts with their bikes. And through it all, Alyssa felt something was missing. It didn't help that the irritating Jordan had been front and center in her mind. Alyssa fell asleep perturbed that she was still thinking of him.

It was after one when Vanetta saw Wade's car pull out of the driveway. Only anger and the need to know pried her sleepy eyes open. When sufficient space was between them, she followed him. He was soon on I-64. It was difficult trailing someone at night without staying glued to his bumper. But she wasn't about to lose him.

She was probably running a fool's errand. If she had any sense, she would have hired a private investigator. Wade was more than likely on his way home after a long night's work. Then what was she going to do? She should have stayed at home. On second thought, she should have stayed in Williamsburg. At least she would have had a fun day at Busch Gardens. Now she was traipsing behind a man as if she was a hotshot PI. This was something Alyssa would do. It would shock the heck out of her family if they knew she was in hot pursuit of Matthew.

Wade signaled and took an exit that led to Sandbridge. What used to be cultivated fields of crops had given way to condos, townhomes, and upscale houses. Several minutes later, he pulled into a lavish estate. The house could not be seen from the road. Vanetta drove by and quickly turned around, debating whether she should drive down the lane or park on the street.

Who owned that house? Wade couldn't afford anything that expensive. Was he merely visiting friends? It was way too late just to visit friends.

Outside, lights lined the driveway. Vanetta turned her headlights off. As soon as she heard a door slam, she crept up the long lane and parked in a secluded area behind some trees. She opened the door, then closed it quietly.

She prayed there were no dogs running loose. If they were, she was in deep doo-doo.

You're crazy, she said to herself as she skulked around the corner of the house.

Matthew's car was parked in back, another car beside it. Her heart sank, but she pushed on. So this was where they met. If it was the last thing she did, she was going to find out who her husband was using those Viagra pills on while she'd been without a man for months. Anger hurried her footsteps.

Was this woman dallying with her husband while her own husband was out of town? She had to be wealthy to afford that house.

Vanetta crept around the patio searching for an opening. She hit pay dirt when she tried the door that led to the garage. She was quickly inside a space that could easily hold four cars. Hers was only a three-car garage. This home was much larger than hers. Matthew could afford this place, but he better not have purchased it for his slut. Not if he valued his life.

Vanetta inhaled a determined breath. She was going to confront her husband and his tramp.

Victoria Easton Michaels was spending the night in Norfolk. The party was finally over, and Matthew was waiting for her in the living room. She'd fixed him a glass of expensive bourbon before she disappeared into the master bathroom to shower and perfume herself. She had plans. But Matthew was waiting for Wade to stop by. Afterward, she thought with a secret smile, they'd settle down to business.

She got into the huge shower and took her time soaping her body. When she was through, she got out and dried off with a heated towel.

She glanced around the well-appointed room and shook her head in resignation and determination. What she wouldn't give to have the money to afford a place like this. One day, she *would* have a home like this. There were seven bedrooms upstairs, a master suite downstairs. She'd counted them all.

She smoothed a hand along the cool granite countertop. Pouring expensive lotion into her hands, she rubbed it over herself, enjoying the silky smoothness against her skin. After she had covered her entire body, she pulled on a silk blouse and slacks and dabbed on perfume. Matthew wasn't in a rush to get home—Vanetta was out of town.

She worked two jobs, and if she continued to work them for the rest of her life, she wouldn't make enough to buy anything nearly as luxurious as this. This was living large, and she wanted some of it. Since Vicky and her husband had separated a couple of years ago, she'd lived in a trailer. It was a nice double-wide with all the bells and whistles, but a trailer nonetheless.

She was moving out of that trailer soon. Her nice little windfall had brought her closer to her goal, but still not on the scale of this place.

She glanced around the lavish room again. There was a separate shower with several shower heads. A whirlpool tub. A separate room for the commode. The room was larger than her bedroom, and so was the huge walk-in closet. Her trailer didn't begin to compare with this.

No sense in stalling. Her benefactor could afford to keep her in the style she wished to ascend to.

With one last glance in the mirror, she left the room. Matthew had fallen asleep on the sofa. Wade must have already come and gone. Matthew was fifty with gray hair around the temples, but he wasn't so old he couldn't stay up past midnight. She had things to do.

She sat on the edge of the sofa next to Matthew, and the

cushions shifted. She tapped his arm. Why wouldn't he wake up?

"Matthew," she whispered softly. But he slept the sleep of the dead. "Matthew?" She shook him gently. He opened his eyes, but immediately closed them again.

"Come on, wake up. I can't stay long," she said. When he didn't awaken, she shook him harder. Was he drugged?

Suddenly, she heard a sound behind her and turned to see what it was.

She hopped off the sofa. "What are you doing here?" The look in the hate-filled eyes frightened her.

"You whore!" a gravely voice whispered as the intruder approached.

"Get out of here." Frightened, Vicky backed toward the wall. "Matthew! Get up." She threw a quick glance at Matthew, but he didn't move. It was then that she realized something was wrong with him. "What did you do to him?"

"Not as much as I'm going to do to you."

Vicky grabbed the bedside lamp, but it was knocked out of her hand. She screamed. A hand grabbed her by the throat and slammed her into the wall so hard stars flashed before her eyes. Still, she had the presence of mind to lash out with acrylic nails sharp as talons. Finally, blessed freedom.

Vicky stumbled away, but she took only a couple of steps before something whacked her in the back like a three-hundred-pound linebacker. She fell flat on her face. Her nose cracked, and pain shot through her. She lay stunned.

Her hands were jerked behind her, and by the time she thought to resist, her wrists were shackled. She kicked out, tried to crawl away, but it was a weak effort. She was easily subdued by the weight pressing on her. She was in so much pain. Suddenly, she was flipped over. With the weight of her body on her hands, they throbbed. She whispered "Matthew," but she knew no help was coming from him.

"You stupid whore. You will never betray me again."
Then strong hands pressed on her throat, cutting off
her breath.

She gagged . . . couldn't breathe. She tried to twist away
and thrash to no avail. *Oh God. Another ten seconds of
this, and I'm dead.* But there was no help for her. She
started praying for her sins.

As a child, her parents had taught her to pray every day.
Now she rarely remembered to pray when she went to bed.
It was funny, she thought as she felt herself fading away.
How quickly she turned to God now that she was in trouble,
when she hadn't gone to church in months.

Chapter 2

The fire had been extinguished, and the few stragglers remaining had gone to bed a half hour ago. It was dark as sin when Jordan made a beeline to Alyssa's tent. The wind rustling through the branches of trees blew a cool breeze, and he pulled his jacket tighter around him. His shoes crunched on fallen leaves as he tiptoed along the path. Hopefully, he would remain unnoticed as he passed by several tents.

I had better moves in high school, he thought, disgusted with himself. Since Alyssa made sure she was constantly surrounded by people, the weekend had been a complete disaster, but he intended to remedy that. She was alone now, he thought as he stood at her tent opening. Soon he'd have to return to California, but he wasn't leaving again until he'd made some headway with Alyssa.

"Alyssa," he called out softly, so as not to wake the campground. When she didn't respond, he unzipped her tent and crawled in, closing the opening behind him.

Maybe this was a huge mistake. She looked all soft and comfy snuggled up in the sleeping bag. Okay. Okay. Get your mind off climbing in the bag with her.

"Hey," he said.

Her eyes opened, and she caught a startled scream before it erupted.

"What the heck are you doing in my tent?"

"Sorry," he said. "Didn't mean to frighten you, but we need to talk."

"Get out," she hissed and pulled the covers tight beneath her chin.

"After we talk."

She glared at him. "Are you crazy?"

"Hey, the weekend's almost over. It's time we discuss this thing between us."

"There's no us," she said. "Go to your own tent."

"You're pissed. Why don't you tell me why?" It was warmer in the tent, and he pulled his jacket off and settled in to enjoy this time with her.

She turned her back to him.

"You've been unreasonable, you know. It's only fair to give me a chance to defend myself. I thought we'd cleared up the bit about Matthew."

Alyssa faced him again. "What do you want from me?"

"A date. A chance to get to know you better. I'd like to spend some time with you before I leave again."

"And then what?"

"We'll be in a solid relationship," he said with such certainty Alyssa debated whether to hit him or to laugh.

"Do you ever take no?"

"Not often," he said, leaning close enough for her to feel the impression of his body, sending strange sensations to the pit of her stomach. "I feel like I've been waiting on a precipice for months. Why don't we start with a kiss?"

Alyssa moaned.

Their faces were mere inches apart. He moved closer, but instead of kissing her fully on the lips, he touched the corner of her mouth, dotted kisses to her cheeks. His lips were cool against her heated skin, and unexpected pleasure rushed through her.

Alyssa sighed. She'd been dreaming about those lips touching hers. Her body ached for his touch. And even knowing she was making a decision she'd regret in the morning, she moved to kiss him fully.

Trying not to rush her, Jordan moved slowly, savoring her sweetness. She was all woman, but she was so different with her defenses down. It shocked him when her arm eased out of the sleeping bag to hold his neck in place.

The kiss deepened, quickly inching to the point of no return. He would, but . . . he pulled back, inhaling deeply. "Talk. Let's talk."

She pressed the sleeping bag open fully, motioning for him to join her.

"I don't want to talk," she whispered with that sleep-husky voice against his lips.

"Alyssa . . . Are you sure?" It seemed all those months of denial had been building up to this.

"Positive." Alyssa didn't know what had come over her.

Suddenly, he was springing soft kisses on her, and the temperature in the sleeping bag climbed a thousand degrees. Cool air rushed in a moment before his body eased in beside her, filling her with heat. He covered them with the unzipped bag and settled his weight next to her.

"God knows I want to be with you tonight," he said. "But I don't want you to regret it in the morning."

Alyssa couldn't think about tomorrow. She wanted him. In the back of her mind, something nagged at her that this was wrong, but when she felt the gentle touch of a warm hand moving down her arm and the warmth of his big body plastered against her, she lost all semblance of reason. He was as addictive as fine chocolate.

"Oh, Alyssa." Her name was a sigh on his lips. What woman could resist that?

He slid her sweats and her tiny scrap of panties down her hips and pressed her thighs apart. Her body humming with need, Alyssa reached up, dragged her hands beneath his shirt. Her fingers outlined strong muscles, slid down, clutched his butt cheeks in her hands. He ground his groin against her. His erection was solid proof that he wanted her.

Damn it. This was a dream, wasn't it? She might as well explore it to the fullest. She snagged his shirt and pulled it over his head.

Sliding lower, he nuzzled her shirt up until his lips closed around a nipple. He caressed her intimately. She moaned, deepening the kiss even more. Sinking her fingers into his shoulders, she dragged her hands down his back to his jeans. He rose slightly, and she unsnapped, unzipped, tugged until he was free.

Breath ragged, he dug into his pockets, emptied them, found what he needed. He was already down there, but she was still shocked at how much her body ached for his touch. And then his hot lips touched her thigh.

Skillfully caressing her with his hands, his tongue, his lips, he worked his magic on her body until she could stand it no longer. Then she pushed him flat on his back and rolled on top of him.

"My turn," she whispered with a ragged breath.

"I'm all yours."

And he was. Alyssa's strokes sent him soaring to a new high. He didn't know it was possible to need someone so desperately. She slid the condom on him slowly, and when they came together, the stars blasted across the night sky.

They tried to move slowly, to savor each stroke, but need drove them to a frenzied pace, and when their tumultuous release came, they felt as if the world had shifted.

Damn, Jordan thought, unable to cry out as he pleased.

Smothering their cries with their lips, they clung to each other as their bodies slowly came under control.

Alyssa awakened to birdsong, cicadas, and the sound of other campers moving about. She stretched, and when her nipples moved against the sleeping bag, memory crashed back with a vengeance.

She was naked beneath the covers—and Jordan had spent the night with her.

Oh, my gosh. How could she have let that happen? She and Reginald were thinking about themselves as a couple, and she'd slept with another man.

The bright light streaming on her brought on a headache. The memory of the night came back in vivid detail. The sneaky devil had invaded her space, but she'd been with him all the way. "No regrets in the morning," he'd said. And she'd agreed. It wasn't his fault, but all hers.

Alyssa dressed quickly and went out to the bathroom to shower and brush her teeth. By the time she applied a minimum of makeup and returned, Jordan was sitting at a table with others in the group. He stood as soon as she got there.

"May I get you a cup of coffee?" he asked.

Alyssa shook her head, got her own coffee, and took it with her to her tent to pack.

How the heck was she going to handle this with Reginald?

Jordan watched her stalk away. He wanted to follow her, but his business experience had taught him timing was everything. And this wasn't the time to invade Alyssa's space. Obviously, she was having second thoughts about last night. Maybe he hadn't used the smoothest, most sensible tactics, but she was playing damn hard to get. Maybe he hadn't planned to make love, but with her grabbing him the way she did, well, he was only human. He'd made sure to leave her tent long before daylight, before people started stirring.

Campers were early risers, and he wanted to preserve their privacy. At four-thirty A.M., when he'd left Alyssa's tent and went to the men's room, a couple of guys were already getting ready to pull out to go fishing. Jordan smiled. He'd gone fishing and caught Alyssa. He watched her as she deftly took her tent down. He wanted to help her but knew better. It was obvious she was quite capable on her own.

Damn if she didn't look good. Exactly six feet tall, she was one gorgeous female. The curvature of her body was perfection. Breasts, a perfect fit in his hands. The symmetrical flare of hips and long legs. And last night, for the first time, he'd touched every inch of her silky skin. He loved everything about Alyssa from her height to her attitude.

He just wished she wasn't so hard to get.

Jordan drank the last of his coffee. The annoying woman who had displayed her goods in front of him last night started whining about needing help with her tent. But he'd caught Alyssa's glare. He wasn't going to touch that with a ten-foot pole. He helped Melinda with her tent, storing it in the truck a club member's husband had driven to carry all their gear. Someone else finally took pity on Ms. Helpless.

With her don't-mess-with-me attitude, no one approached Alyssa as she carried her own tent and equipment to the truck and tossed it in the back.

Less than a half hour later, they mounted their bikes and started the trek back to Paradise Island.

Riding mountain hills and switchbacks was a thrilling and unique experience, a high unlike any other, Alyssa thought as she leaned into a curve. She was wild and free.

She only wished she could let loose and ride a little crazy sometimes, but her boss, the Sheriff of Paradise Island, had drilled her on responsibility in everything she did. She was a detective, he said, and a role model for the crazy SOBs who didn't know better. There were just too many motorcycle injuries and deaths. She didn't live anonymously in the big city. So she suited up in her leather boots, leather jacket, gloves, and chaps. She always wore her helmet and dark sunshades.

And she tried to drive sedately, but she didn't know what it was about those S curves where the road dipped between pine and poplar that stirred the tempest in her. The bike accelerated. The air flowed sweet and cool against her leather-covered body.

Jordan had the good sense not to mess with her, and Alyssa cast him from her mind and simply enjoyed the ride.

A couple of hours later, most of the riders parted company. Some lived in Norfolk, Virginia Beach, Suffolk, and Smithfield.

Alyssa boarded the ferry with the other islanders and lowered her kick plate. Melinda parked beside her.

They took off their helmets and jackets and stored them on the bikes.

"Did you ride out the anger?" Melinda asked.

Alyssa smiled. "It was a ride made in heaven," she said. A ride like that always calmed her.

When she left the ferry, the island breeze felt good on her skin as she traveled the familiar roads. She tooted at a couple of kids who raced toward the road and waved frantically at her.

Bidding her friends good-bye, she left everyone behind and drove the final isolated stretch to her house. The tiny stretch of land, no more than forty feet wide, had the ocean on each side.

She revved the motor, and the bike shot forward. Alyssa

threw back her head and laughed. Adrenalin rushed through her veins like a narcotic. Damn, she felt good.

Alyssa was going fast, but she kept her eyes glued to the road. That was the problem with Reginald. He was a cautious rider who always lectured her when she wanted to let loose and go.

Alyssa slowed just a little as she leaned into a sharp curve with a few scraggly trees obscuring the view. She anticipated speeding out of the curve.

"Damn it!" Alyssa came up on an obstruction so quickly it was only a blur as she swerved to keep from hitting it, her tires kicking up a wide arc of dirt on the shoulder. She nearly lost control of the bike, but wrestled it under control before she slowed. Swiveling around in a circle, she rode back to see what the heck had been left in the road.

A naked pair lay coupled, making love. *Stupid teenagers.* She was having somebody's ass over this. No one else would be idiot enough to make love in the damn road. The boy's friends had more than likely dared him—probably a football player—and some starstruck cheerleader had no more sense than to follow along. She wouldn't be surprised to see eyes peeking from the bushes on one side of the road, hands over mouths, smothering laughter. Did they take a class in stupid?

Alyssa parked her bike and whipped her helmet and shades off as she approached the couple. Something wasn't right. The very fact that they hadn't moved worried Alyssa. Even if they were up to mischief, with all the noise she'd made, they would have run for cover by now.

The woman's face was partially covered by the man's. His face was buried in the woman's neck, and one leg rested between hers. They still hadn't moved. Dread sank to the pit of Alyssa's stomach as she stooped beside them to verify what her instincts had already registered.

Discarding her gloves, her body tensed as she checked for

a pulse in the man's neck . . . and found none. She moved the man's face just a bit to see if she could identify him. He felt cold to the touch. It was Matthew Frasier, her cousin Vanetta's husband. Dread crept into her stomach, and cold sweat trickled down her back. Dear Lord. Was Vanetta buried under him? Quickly, she moved Matthew's face enough to identify the woman.

Jesus. She went numb from head to foot. She sank to her knees to keep from falling. The dark face staring back at her was beautiful. Victoria Easton Michaels' face should have been full of laughter and mischief. Alyssa couldn't detach as her mind rushed back to thirty years of memories of picnics and play, of school and dates. Vicky was Melinda's sister.

She remembered Matthew and Vanetta's wedding. The dark older man and the beautiful young Vanetta, almost a Hollywood couple. His temples were brushed with gray, but it only made him look more distinguished.

Alyssa moved away quickly to the water's edge and swallowed hard to keep from gagging. She'd seen corpses before—a lot of them on Baltimore's streets when she'd worked there for a couple of years. They were all strangers. Only evidence in a crime scene. Anonymous. But this was family and friends.

Alyssa inhaled several deep breaths. She had a job to do. She dug her cell phone out of her pocket and dialed the station. Then she began to check the bodies.

Already darkened areas on Vicky revealed several defensive bruises. She'd put up a fight. There were dark circles around her wrists and arms.

Alyssa looked closer at Matthew. He did not show similar bruising. There was no swelling on his head. Just darkened areas along his back where blood had settled.

The bodies had obviously been moved. This wasn't the scene of the crime.

Matthew was much larger and stronger than Vicky. He should have put up a bigger fight—unless he'd been drugged.

Alyssa closed her eyes briefly. She'd have the unwanted duty of telling her cousin that not only had her husband died, but also that his corpse had been found in the arms of another woman. That now *she,* the spouse, in this case the scorned wife, was the prime suspect.

There was always a story attached to a crime. What was the story here? Did a jealous boyfriend or soon to be ex-husband kill them both in a fit of anger?

This was a small island. The story would sweep through like a hurricane.

Vicky lived on the other side of the island. Matthew lived several miles away. Why were they on the narrow road to Alyssa's house? Cheating husbands were run-of-the-mill, but why do it under the wife's family's nose with a woman who was part of the island culture? Couldn't he find some anonymous woman in Norfolk or Virginia Beach?

Discoloration marked the side of Vicky's neck, possible signs of strangulation.

She called the coroner next. As soon as she hung up, she heard sirens in the distance. County cars began to roll into view. Harper Porterfield, the sheriff, was out of town, although he was due back later that day.

A younger officer, John Aldridge, came running toward her. "What's . . . Oh."

Alyssa tossed him her keys. She was in her element. Since she was in high school and had watched *Colombo,* she'd wanted to be a hotshot detective. "Drive to my house and get my car. Then help cordon off the area," she barked.

Her insides quivered with emotion. But she couldn't afford an emotional breakdown now.

Alyssa forcibly schooled her expression and slowed her heartbeat for the task ahead.

* * *

"Alyssa," the town's only reporter for the town's single newspaper called out less than fifty feet away. The woman, Tracy Moore, carried a tape recorder and clutched a pad beneath her arm. Her jeans were too large and partially twisted, as if she'd pulled them on too quickly.

"What is she doing here?" Alyssa asked John. Tracy was positioning her camera to take pictures. Alyssa snatched it out of her hand.

"What the hell do you think you're doing? Get the hell out of here."

"This is news," she started. "We have a right—"

"Get her out of here, now!" she snapped at John. "And stay the hell away from my crime scene."

"It's not fair. The people have a right to know."

"You'll get your interview when I'm ready."

John approached the woman and gently tugged her by the arm to get her moving.

"And make sure she doesn't compromise evidence. Tell those officers not to let anyone through, or they'll have me to deal with." The moment one died, all sense of propriety left. Here were two bodies laid out naked for the entire world to see. And Tracy wanted to take pictures to splash on the front page of her paper.

Alyssa focused her gaze on the coroner, the town's only doctor. Everyone called her Doc. The temperature had risen and it was getting hot, but she looked cool. "Find anything?"

"Looks like postmortem sex occurred."

"Killed in the act?"

She shrugged. "Can't tell. The medical examiner will do a more thorough examination."

Alyssa gazed at the discoloration on Vicky's skin, sweeping down from her head to her toe. There was a tiny piece of something white in her pubic hair. Alyssa pulled out an evidence bag and, with her gloved hands, picked it up. Doc had already moved on to Matthew's body.

Alyssa held the object closer for inspection. It looked like a rug fiber, but she couldn't be sure. She put it in the evidence bag, sealed and labeled it.

"It looks like he was killed with a single stab wound to the chest," Doc said. "There's no evidence of a struggle. No defensive wounds immediately evident, as if he was killed in his sleep."

"Or drugged."

"Maybe. The toxicologist will determine that. He was alive when he was stabbed." She zipped up the bag, and a couple of officers came over to load them into the van before the victims were taken away.

From the distance, she heard car doors slam and raised voices. Alyssa ignored them. One by one, the islanders would arrive. But she hadn't released the identity of the bodies yet. Only she, John, and Doc had actually seen them. But a double murder in this area was unknown—and unthinkable.

"Pull a couple more officers so we can walk off the area. We need to find the scene of the crime," Alyssa said to John.

As John walked away, Alyssa's phone rang. She retrieved it from her pocket and glanced at the number. It was Melinda. Obviously, she'd heard about the dead bodies. Alyssa had not reported the deaths as murders. She rubbed the tension out of her neck. She'd have to visit Melinda after they finished with the scene.

God. Her friend would be heartbroken.

John came trudging back with another officer and Harper Porterfield, the sheriff.

"What's going on?" Harper asked with his hands planted on his hips. A huge man with a rich dark brown complexion, he was one of the few who towered over Alyssa at six-five or six-six. He had played pro football but had hurt his knees in his first season. After working with the Baltimore police force for several years, he had returned to the island. He'd been sheriff for the last ten years. She guessed he was at least fifty.

"Looks like a double homicide. We sent the bodies to the medical examiner's office. We were just about to canvass the area. Try to find the scene of the crime," Alyssa said. "The bodies had been moved."

Harper asked a few more questions, and Alyssa answered them.

"I'll deal with the reporters while you work the scene," he finally said. "I take it the identities of the bodies haven't been revealed yet?"

"Not yet. As soon as I finish here, I'll visit Vanetta and then Melinda's parents."

He glanced at John, who was checking the area around the scene.

"He wants to get more involved. This is a good one for him to get his feet wet," Alyssa said.

He nodded. "Try not to piss off any more reporters."

"She was out of line. I have a scene to process, and she broke the line and came in with her camera at the ready."

Harper blew out a long breath and walked down the road to face the crowd.

Alyssa called John and the other officer over. They were just a few yards from the ocean. The three of them walked the beach side by side, searching for evidence.

They even checked Alyssa's house to see if the murders had occurred there. But her house looked exactly as it had when she'd left on Friday.

By the time Alyssa and John finished interviewing neighbors, it was after four. No one had seen anything unusual in the last twenty-four hours. No one had heard strange sounds in the middle of the night.

It was nearly dusk before they left the scene. Alyssa drove her bike to her house, and John parked her Crown Vic behind the bike. She took a few minutes to freshen up and change clothes.

John got into the passenger seat, and Alyssa slid behind the wheel with her shoulder holster tucked beneath her jacket.

"You know what?" Alyssa said aloud, although she'd been thinking it all day. She turned the car around and drove down the lane.

"What?" John asked.

"Why here? Why were the bodies dumped here? My house is the only one in the area."

"And you're our only detective."

"There are a million places the bodies could have been deposited. Why dump them practically in my front yard? What's my connection to this?"

"You think someone has a grudge against you?" John asked.

"If that's the case, why kill Matthew and Vicky? Why not come after me?"

John shrugged.

Harper had given the reporter his newsbyte, and she had left to print the story.

It was time to contact the families. Alyssa called her dad to find out if Vanetta had returned to town from her weekend trip to New York. Next, she headed to Vicky's parents' home.

Melissa's parents were having a barbecue. From the smell of the food roasting on the grill, they'd pulled out all the stops. *I wonder how they'd feel about barbecues after today?* Alyssa thought as she spied Melinda's car in the driveway. Several cars were lined beside the street.

Dread settled deep in Alyssa's chest as she and John climbed out of the car and walked around the side of the house, following the sound of laughter.

Bob Easton was flipping ribs on the grill. Hortense, his wife, set a plate of sliced tomatoes and lettuce on the table, picked up a napkin, and wiped the perspiration from her face.

She smiled when she saw Alyssa. "Glad you stopped by. We have plenty of food. Hear you've been working hard all day. I know you're tired and hungry," she said, pulling out a chair. "Just sit here."

"Another time. May I talk to you inside?"

Hortense stared at her. Her smile faltered. The tongs clattered onto the deck as Bob rushed over.

"What is it?" he asked.

"Let's move inside."

Melinda came to her side, but Alyssa just took her arm and steered her into the homey kitchen while John motioned a couple of relatives inside. The sunny kitchen of pale yellow and blue was lined by cute little chicks above the white cabinets.

Anxiously, Bob, Hortense, and Melinda gazed at her. Alyssa took a deep breath, knowing she was bearing news that would break their hearts.

"Let's have a seat."

"Just tell us," Bob said. "We know something happened. Vicky's not here yet, is she . . . ?"

"Vicky's dead."

Hortense wailed, "Not my baby!" and collapsed in her husband's arms. He held her tightly.

The most dreadful part of Alyssa's job was notifying a family that a loved one was gone. Even worse was telling your own family or friends. The shock hit like a thousand-pound weight. They wanted to know, why their loved ones, and what had happened?

"We won't know what killed her until after we have the autopsy done, but . . ."

She held Melissa in her arms as she wailed, "No! No. No, she can't be. Tell me it's not true."

"It's true, and it's bad how she died. She was murdered and . . ." As gently as possible, she told them what she could.

It was an hour before Alyssa and John could leave. The family was heartbroken. Melinda was inconsolable. But at least they weren't alone. Alyssa wished she could have stayed longer, but a killer was on the loose.

Vanetta's father and mother went with Alyssa to tell Vanetta about Matthew's death. Death, in itself, was bad enough, but having to tell her he was found in a compromising position with another woman was a "hard row to hoe," as her grandmother would say. She decided to wait to tell her about the tryst. It was too much to assimilate at once.

Now she approached Vicky's ex-husband's house. According to Melinda, the divorce should be final within a matter of days. She sure hoped Vicky had changed her will and insurance policies. People tended to forget the little details when more pressing matters were at hand.

"Do you think he did it?" John asked.

"I don't know."

Brit Michaels' car was parked in the yard. She rang the doorbell, but it took a couple of tries before he answered. He worked the night shift. At five-eight, he was Vicky's height, a lean man with a pleasing face. His eyes were red, as if he'd been crying.

"I already know," he said. "I got a call an hour ago."

"I'm sorry," Alyssa said. "May we come in?"

He stepped to the side. "Sure. Come on in." They entered

directly into the living room. It was relatively neat, as if this wasn't the center of family activity.

"I've seen enough *Law and Order* to know I'm your main suspect. That's why you're here, right?"

"We're gathering information," Alyssa said.

"I did a double shift yesterday. Worked from three in the afternoon to seven this morning."

He didn't realize that the information made him more suspect. If he had hired someone to kill Vicky and her lover, he'd make sure he had witnesses during the time his wife was murdered.

Alyssa retrieved her notebook from her jacket pocket. "Did Vicky have any enemies?"

He shook his head. "She was so easygoing. Besides always giving a man a hard time, I don't know. I don't understand this thing with Matthew. She was talking about us getting back together. I know something was going on, though."

"What?" John asked.

"Lately, she'd been giving me money. Asked me to save it for our future."

"Why wouldn't she put it in her own account?"

"Like I said, she said she had some news and she was going to tell me about it soon."

"Did she give you any clues?"

"She said I'll be getting my business back."

Three years ago, Brit had owned a prosperous island funeral home until a rumor spread that he was participating in necrophilia with some of the female bodies he was preparing. The business had literally shut down. Not one family would send their dearly departed to his funeral home.

Doc had said there were possible signs of necrophilia, which certainly made Brit a suspect.

"So the money was for you to start another funeral home?"

He shrugged. "I never considered it. It was Vicky's idea."

"We need all the help we can get to solve this case," Alyssa said.

"I loved Vicky." His voice broke. "Lately, we've been going out on dates. After all the mess, I never expected we'd get back together. I want you to find who killed her."

"How much money did Vicky give you?"

"Over the last month, about fifty."

"Fifty what?" John asked.

"Fifty thousand," Brit said.

"Where did she get that kind of money?"

"I don't know. And she wouldn't tell me when I asked."

"Why were you working a double shift?" Alyssa asked.

"My supervisor called me at the last minute when someone didn't show up. You can call him and ask him."

"I will," Alyssa assured him.

He searched for a piece of paper and wrote a name and phone number.

What was going on with Vicky and this man? Alyssa wondered. She'd always considered Brit a nice guy. Although Vicky was flashy and spoiled, she was pretty decent. Melinda certainly was.

Alyssa pulled out a card. "If you think of anything that might help us, no matter how small the details, call me."

"Why don't you talk to her sister? You're friends, and I'm sure she knows more about what was going on with Vicky. When Vicky and I were still married, Melinda and I used to talk. Still do sometimes."

"I will."

Melinda was always making remarks about Vicky getting her life together as an aside, but she never went into details.

Alyssa sighed. She would stop by Vanetta's place again, then visit Melinda . . . again.

Alyssa dialed the office and asked to speak to Harper. "Do you have the search warrants yet?" she asked.

"They're here. Have you informed the families yet?"

"Yes."

"I'll release the identities to the press," he said as if nobody knew who they were. "Then I'll help with the search. You might want to take a cursory look around Vanetta's place since it's so late. We'll do a thorough check tomorrow." He hung up. It was a small department. With a case this serious, everyone had to pitch in.

"Harper is going to meet us at Vanetta's with the search warrant," she told John after she hung up.

"You don't need a warrant," John said. "They're your family and friends. They'll let you search through her belongings."

"Murder is serious police business. We have to go by the book."

"You handle things differently from Graham." Graham was the old detective.

"Yes, I do," Alyssa said. "If Vicky was going to help Brit open a new funeral home, where would he open it?"

"He couldn't open it here," John said. "People have long memories. Besides, where was all that money coming from?"

"That's what I want to know," Alyssa said. "Damn it. I forgot to call Matthew's partners. He doesn't have family, but they're like his family."

"Harper has done his press conference by now. They already know."

Chapter 3

News flashes of two dead bodies found on Paradise Island had been running all day. Jordan had finally turned the TV off. He'd called an island friend who told him Alyssa was running the investigation and hadn't revealed anything yet.

Jordan glanced at his watch. Matthew was an hour late for their meeting. The last two weeks, it had been hard as heck tracking Matthew down. He usually hated involving himself with business, even wanted to be a silent partner like Curtis, but Jordan couldn't handle everything if they wanted to expand to other locations. Curtis was a doctor. Getting help from him was out of the question. This project required Jordan to move among California, New Orleans, and Virginia Beach for several months, but with the understanding Matthew would handle things on the East Coast. Their goal was to open five more clubs within the next four years.

Jordan was running into problems with a couple of large investors who wanted weekly updates and expected him to make regular flights to Colorado and Arizona where they lived.

"You see the news?" Wade came rushing into Jordan's office. "Oh, man."

"No. What's wrong?" Jordan asked.

"Turn on the news. It's Matthew. I can't believe it. I just can't believe it." Wade didn't wait for a response. He ran to the TV cabinet, thrust open the door, and flicked the tube on.

"Breaking news," the reporter said. "Two bodies were found on Paradise Island this morning. The police now believe it to be a double homicide." The screen flashed to a peaceful seaside area where the bodies were being carried away. A reporter interviewed a couple of locals standing around. Then another camera focused on the sheriff.

Jordan listened as Harper Porterfield revealed the names of the deceased and the reporter elaborated on how they were found.

"I can't believe it," Wade said again.

"Jesus. Unbelievable." Jordan's breath rushed from his lungs. He felt he had been punched.

"I just saw him last night. He stopped by here for a few minutes."

Matthew was more than a partner. He'd been a second father. Jordan sat in total shock. He couldn't believe Matthew was dead. The phone rang. It was Curtis Durant, his other partner.

"Can you believe it?" Curtis asked, clearly as stunned as Jordan was. "What the hell happened?"

"I'm just hearing about it, too," Jordan said, standing. "I'm leaving for the island. I'll let you know what I find out." Jordan shoved the folder he was working on into his desk drawer. "I'll see you tomorrow," he said to Wade.

"I'm sorry about Matthew."

"Yeah, me too. Have my car brought around."

Wade left, and suddenly, Jordan remembered Alyssa's anger the night before. She never mentioned who Matthew was having the affair with. Was it Vicky? My God. Had they really been murdered? Everybody certainly seemed to think so.

By the time Jordan reached the front door, his black Escalade was waiting for him.

Alyssa reached Vanetta's house the same time as Jordan and immediately came face-to-face with the night before. She'd gone to bed late. He'd sneaked into her tent, and the best sex she'd ever had followed. She'd betrayed Reginald. Even now, with his forehead creased in worry, Jordan looked damn good.

Jordan Ellis wasn't the man she wanted to see right now. Still, her body went hot, then cold. Alyssa knew she was on overdrive. Too much had happened. With two deaths front and center, her tired mind couldn't assimilate another thing. Her personal dilemma just had to wait, so she did her best to cast Jordan from her mind.

"You've heard," Alyssa said.

Jordan nodded. "A damn shame. Where were the bodies found?"

"Near my place."

"Your place? Were you there?" he asked with concern.

"The murders occurred last night."

"But why . . ."

"I can't answer any of your questions now. We're still investigating." She touched his arm. "I'm sorry for your loss. I know Matt was more than your partner. He was your friend."

"A damn good one. Can you tell me anything? My only source of information came from the news."

"He and Vicky were found coupled on the road leading to my house. They were both naked. You probably heard that much."

He stared at her. "Oh, hell. Then it's true." He swiped a hand across his face. "He was having an affair with Vicky?"

"I don't know that. I can only tell you what we found. I don't have anything more conclusive. We will release more information later."

"Damn it, don't talk to me like I'm the press. Matt was my friend." His voice cracked.

"I know. Truthfully, I don't know anything yet." She understood his grief and frustration and helplessness.

Jordan nodded and followed her inside. Alyssa didn't see Vanetta, but the family was in a huddle in the great room, discussing the situation.

"What do you have so far?" one of her uncles asked. "As far as I'm concerned, the SOB did us a favor."

"Uncle Abraham, you can't say those things around me."

"Why not? I wish he was alive so I could beat the crap out of him," Alyssa's dad, Cleveland Claxton, said. Both men towered to six-five.

"Dad . . ." Alyssa had an angry family on her hands. They couldn't take it out on Matthew. The worst had been done. He was already dead.

"And that trashy Vicky. Never knew how to keep her drawers up or her skirt tail down," her aunt said.

Alyssa rolled her eyes. "She didn't deserve to die."

She noticed Jordan had disappeared. He'd probably found Vanetta.

"I hope you aren't talking like this in Vanetta's hearing," Alyssa said. "She has enough to cope with."

"Do tell."

Lisa Claxton, Vanetta's younger sister, came in from the deck. She was shorter and more rough around the edges. Vanetta was culture to Lisa's coarseness. Lisa drew her fingers through her short hair.

"Where's Van?" Alyssa asked.

"She took Patience Kingsley to the deck," Alyssa's father said.

"To keep her from drinking the whole canister of bourbon. She's toasted," Lisa said. "Barely kept from hitting my car when she drove that huge Cadillac in here. Van's going to have to replenish her liquor cabinet by the time that woman leaves." Lisa sighed. "Lord knows, I could use a stiff one myself."

"Don't let Mrs. Kingsley drive home," Alyssa warned.

"Stop talking about Patience. She has a good heart," Vanetta's mother said. "There's plenty of food on the kitchen table if you're hungry, Alyssa. I bet you haven't taken time to eat today."

"You're right," Alyssa said, remembering she had skipped breakfast that morning. "I'll grab something on my way out." She made her way through the French door to the deck.

Jordan sat on a chair beside Vanetta and held her in his arms. Alyssa wanted to pull every strand of her hair out. Everywhere she turned, that man was present. And although she'd done this many times, witnessing grief was never easy.

Patience Kingsley wasn't the best advertisement for her husband's funeral home. She was slumped in a chair, nodding off, a shot glass still clutched in her hand. Any normal person would have dropped the glass by now, but not Patience.

"I'll take her home," Jordan said.

"Thank you." The woman had everything. An attentive husband, more money than Midas. But she still drank herself into a stupor. And her poor husband stood by her, giving her all the support a woman could ask for. It did no good. Nothing he did convinced Patience to quit her drinking. Patience was one lucky woman to have a man like Stanley Kingsley. He didn't allow people to make harsh remarks about her within his hearing. Not many men would support an alcoholic wife the way he did.

He must not have heard about the deaths yet. Otherwise, he would have beaten a path over here. He didn't leave anything to chance.

Alyssa approached Vanetta. She wore black slacks with a blue silk blouse. A weekly trip to the hair salon kept her hair always looking good, and she shopped at the finest stores. Usually made a couple of shopping trips to New York each year. She wore fashions that hadn't made it this far South yet. When she walked into church on Sundays, heads turned just to see what new outfit she was sporting.

Vanetta was Lisa's older sister by several years, and she was as sweet as Lisa was disagreeable. Grandma always said Lisa just hadn't found her way yet. How two such different women came from the same parents was a mystery.

Vanetta's grief had, at least, reduced to sniffles. Alyssa took Vanetta's hand in hers and said, "I'm really sorry, Van."

Eyes swollen and red, Vanetta nodded. "It's just awful. What happened? Was it a heart attack? I tried to get him to eat better, but he wouldn't listen."

Alyssa glanced at Jordan. No one had told her the full story yet. Everyone was talking about it in the house, but not in her hearing.

Matthew had been seventeen years older than Vanetta. Alyssa studied her cousin's eyes, searching for the truth. Vanetta really believed her husband had died of heart disease.

The door opened, and Lisa burst out like an avenging angel. "That lowdown son of a bitch."

"Lisa . . ." Imperceptibly, Alyssa shook her head.

Lisa glanced from her sister to Jordan to Alyssa.

"Oh. I thought you told her."

Vanetta sniffed and wiped her nose with Jordan's huge white handkerchief. "Told me what? What's wrong?"

Alyssa sighed.

"Told me what? What's going on?"

Lisa pointed to Alyssa. "You're the detective."

Vanetta straightened from Jordan's shoulder. "I want to know right now."

"Told you you couldn't trust men," Lisa said. "Lying cheats, every one of them."

"How dare you talk about Matthew that way?" Trembling with grief and rage, Vanetta pushed away from Jordan. "If you're going to talk like that, you just get out."

"I'm here for you, Van. I love you," Lisa said, holding out a hand.

Alyssa had to speak up before this got even more convoluted. "I'm sorry to have to tell you this, but Matthew and Vicky were found dead together."

"Dead together? Why?"

"Naked as jaybirds," Lisa said. "With the sun kissing his pale bare ass."

"Lisa, please let me do this," Alyssa warned.

Lisa rolled her eyes and sat on the other side of her sister.

Vanetta plunked both hands on her hips with the handkerchief fisted in one of them. "Somebody better help me understand this."

"I'm sorry," Alyssa said gently, "but Vicky Michaels and Matthew were found in a . . . compromising position."

"Are you telling me he had a heart attack while having sex with that woman?"

"I'm not saying anything. We won't know the cause of death until the autopsies are performed. We think they may have been murdered."

"Murdered? Who would want to murder them? She's almost divorced. And what the hell was she doing having sex with my husband?"

"We're investigating," Alyssa said gently. "Did you suspect Matthew might have been involved in any affairs?"

"No. I would have left him. And he knows that."

"Does the housekeeper know if he was home last night? We're trying to pinpoint the time of death."

She shook her head. "He said he had a late meeting at the club. His client's plane was arriving late, and the man was leaving early this morning. The last ferry to the island is at midnight, so Matthew said they would work late, maybe until two or three in the morning, and he was going to sleep at the club."

"Does he stay there often?" Alyssa asked.

"Sometimes. It's not unusual when he's working on business deals."

She'd ask Jordan whether Matthew actually checked into the club later.

"You think I killed him, don't you? I've seen enough detective stories to know you look at the spouses first."

"I'm just trying to pinpoint . . ."

"What would Grandma think of that? Blaming me for my own husband's death. Where's your loyalty?"

"I'm not blaming you for anything. But I have to investigate this case thoroughly," Alyssa pointed out gently. "I'm sure you'll want that."

Anger and despair sizzled between them.

"I want you to leave. That's what I want. Right now."

"I know you're upset, Van, but you can't blame Alyssa," Jordan said. "What happened isn't her fault. Eventually, she'll have to ask you these questions. She just wants to get them over with." Jordan stood beside Vanetta and rubbed her arm.

Vanetta crossed her arms. "A fine way to treat family."

Alyssa reached out to touch Vanetta, but her cousin drew back. "I'm sorry for everything, Vanetta. I'm glad you're here so family can take care of you."

Tears started rolling down Vanetta's cheeks. "Family like you? For your information, I spent the weekend in New York. I flew in yesterday and spent the night with my friend in Williamsburg. She has a meeting there tomorrow. I'll give you her phone number if you can't take my word for it."

"Thank you. I appreciate that." Vanetta might be family, but Alyssa had to check out everything.

Alyssa understood Van had been thrown a blow. She had to blame someone. Right now, that someone was her. She stood and looked at Jordan. "I'd like a word with you."

"Now you're going to blame Jordan, too? Is anybody safe from your suspicion?" Vanetta asked.

"Go on," Lisa said to Jordan. "I'll stay with her."

As soon as Alyssa made her way outside, Stanley Kingsley arrived. He wore an expensive black suit and a sad expression. "So sorry for your loss," he said in a quiet, deferential tone. "If there's anything I can do, please let me know."

"I would like to ask you a few questions in your office tomorrow," Alyssa said. "Since Vicky worked part-time for you."

"I'll be there. Call my secretary and set up a time."

Alyssa nodded.

"My wife is already here. I'm glad. I hope she's comforting Vanetta. Where are they?" he asked.

"On the deck," Alyssa told him.

"I'll just walk around the house then," he said and stepped over the pristine flower borders lining the path to the deck.

Jordan came up behind her. "He didn't stay at the club last night."

"You checked?"

"I've already spoken to my manager. We didn't have any late check-ins. And Matthew hadn't made arrangements to stay overnight. I would have been told." Jordan slid his hands deep into his pockets. "Except for the times I am away, Matthew is rarely at the club, Alyssa. He's a very silent partner."

"How would you know? You spent the weekend in the mountains."

"Wade keeps me informed."

"Were you aware of an affair with Vicky?"

"No. Like I told you last night, I'm not involved in his personal affairs. I know he's told Vanetta he stays there, but he doesn't."

"Do you know where he stays if he isn't home?"

"No, but I'll talk to my manager. He might know."

Alyssa nodded, jotted down notes. "Did you know he was on the island?"

"No." Jordan shook his head.

"Thanks for being with Van." Alyssa closed her book and stuck it in her purse.

"I wouldn't be anywhere else," he said. His gaze softened on her. "Are you okay? You've had a long day."

Alyssa nodded. "And it's not over yet."

He frowned. "You wouldn't tell me if you weren't."

She started to the car. "I have a job to do."

Jordan knew Alyssa had been hurt by Van's words. "It was the grief, you know. She doesn't blame you." He wanted to hold her in his arms, but she tilted that chin as if she were an island to herself. She was accustomed to standing on her own. She'd more than likely break his arm if he tried to hug her. He could use one himself, but everything between them was so new and unsettled.

"I know. If you find anything helpful from your employees, let me know," Alyssa said.

He nodded, then watched Alyssa leave. Tires squealed as she pulled out of the drive. Before he could get back into the house, two more cars arrived. Vanetta's grandparents. Mrs.

Claxton got out, fussing at her husband about something. Mr. Claxton ignored her as they walked to the house. Jordan spoke, then held the door for them.

Jordan was concerned at how beat Alyssa appeared. Obviously, she'd been going on overdrive since she returned from the mountains. He wanted to comfort her, but this wasn't the time. She was still wrapping her mind around the fact that they'd made love.

Damn, his gut tightened at the thought of that fantastic night. And to come back to this tragedy. The idea of Alyssa encountering the scene if she'd been home alone sent chills down Jordan's spine.

He went back inside. God, he still couldn't believe Matt was dead.

Soon, people would start arriving in droves to give their condolences. Then he'd leave.

Everyone finally left. Vanetta was tired of having to put up a front. Her parents were down the hall, and Lisa had zonked out in the bedroom next door.

Vanetta stared at the ceiling. Every time she closed her eyes, she imagined Matthew and Vicky coupled. She always knew Vicky was fast, but she'd never expected Vicky to go to bed with her husband.

Even now, everyone was snickering behind their hands about Matthew and Vicky together. She could hear it now: *Poor Vanetta. She may have landed herself a rich husband, but she couldn't please him, even as old as he was.* The idea made her feel sick and weak all over.

Maybe she *should* talk to Alyssa. No, she wasn't going to talk to anyone. She wasn't getting locked up for Matthew's death, damn him. Damn him!

* * *

It was late when Alyssa returned to the Eastons. She dialed Melinda's cell phone so she'd open the door for her. But Melinda was on the back deck with Reginald when she arrived.

Her night with Jordan came roaring back with a vengeance. For a while, she'd forgotten how she'd betrayed Reginald. She had to confront him, but not now. Not tonight. It was almost ten, and she was exhausted.

Alyssa wanted to release some emotions, but she didn't have the luxury of tears. Two of the people she cared about most had had their lives turned upside down. She needed answers.

Melinda was in the process of purchasing the island's newspaper. This was one story she wouldn't want to write.

People thought she and Melinda were men haters, but they weren't. When you'd been hurt enough times by life, you didn't wear your heart on your sleeve, and you made damn sure you swung first.

And there was Jordan. He really wasn't a bad guy, but he wasn't one to settle down. You couldn't get too close without him backing off. And Alyssa wasn't one to waste her time.

Alyssa liked puzzles. Had solved them, any kind, from the time she was a little girl. Her mother had often bought them to keep her occupied. But this was a puzzle she'd rather live without.

Everyone was still in shock. Alyssa spent a few minutes with Melinda's parents before she walked outside with Melinda. It had been an ordinary day—pleasant temperature, good hiking weather. But emotionally, they might as well be in the midst of a storm.

"It just doesn't seem real. I can't believe I'll never see my sister again."

Alyssa didn't know what to say. There was nothing she

could say to soothe her friend. But there were questions to ask. She wished she had the luxury of waiting until later.

"Do you feel like talking?" Alyssa asked.

"No, but ask anyway. I want the person caught."

"Was anything unusual going on in Vicky's life lately?"

Melinda shook her head. "Not that I know of. Going to bed with married men wasn't her thing. I know she was a little wild, especially after leaving Brit. I can't believe she did that . . . and with all her faults, I loved her."

People didn't always divulge their business to family members, but Alyssa said, "I know you did. Did she talk about her dates? Anything that seemed strange?"

"No other than fixing the hair and nails and doing the makeup for the bodies at the funeral home. She said it paid more. Besides, she used to work there with Brit before he sold his funeral home to Reginald and Stanley."

"She had lots of customers at the beauty parlor."

"She did. But she couldn't charge what they charged at Virginia Beach. I told her the overhead wasn't as expensive either, but Vicky always had these grand plans that never amounted to anything.

"She went to clubs in Norfolk sometimes, but I don't know which ones. I still can't believe it. This is going to kill Mama. I know your family must hate us."

"They don't hate you."

"I hate that people are saying mean things about my sister. Calling her all kinds of names."

She hugged Melinda. There just weren't sufficient words to express the depth of her grief. Alyssa was a professional, but she was also a friend.

Reginald hugged Melinda, too, and then walked with Alyssa to the car. A lone halogen light beamed from a tall pole in the yard, illuminating their path.

"Shall I stop by your place tonight?" Reginald asked when they stopped at her car.

Alyssa shook her head. "I'm beat."

"You still angry with me about the weekend?"

"No. I'm glad you stopped by to see Melinda."

"She's your friend." He massaged her shoulders the way he'd done a million times. It felt good, but the touch wasn't right. Jordan had spoiled even this simple pleasure, darn it. Reginald's hands slid down her arms, and she stepped out of his embrace to face him.

"We need to talk, but not now," Alyssa said.

Reginald nodded. Alyssa got into her car and left.

Patience Kingsley wore flattering off-white lounging pajamas, but she just didn't turn Stanley on the way she had in the old days. He still loved her, but the drinking had gone on much too long. It was time he did something about it.

"You're drunk."

"Honey, I'm not halfway there yet," she slurred.

He could smell the sweet, expensive perfume from across the room. She wore it to cover the smell of the stale alcohol, but the pungent smell of it was in her skin, her hair, her breath. It permeated every fiber of her being. Even when she wasn't drinking, she had the lingering odor typical of alcoholics.

"Why don't you get some help, honey?" Stanley said.

"For what? I'm perfectly fine. I only drink when I'm home. Alone."

"Which is most of the time." Stanley was a respected citizen in the community, and he expected his wife to conduct herself accordingly. She was educated. She could buy clothing from any damn store she wanted to. He made good money. He owned two funeral homes. One in Norfolk and a much smaller one on the island. It might be smaller, but it was still elaborate.

He could use a nightcap. Unloosening his tie, he headed for the bar and poured a shot of bourbon in a whiskey glass.

"I suppose you'll get that slut's body? I don't understand why you hired her."

"I didn't hire her. Your brother Reginald did. I let him do most of the work now. I'm more involved in other investments."

"Poor Vanetta is devastated. People are talking all over town."

"Vanetta will be fine."

"I suppose you talked her into a top-of-the-line casket."

"We haven't discussed that yet. But Matthew spent lavishly on Vanetta. Why should she choose anything less for his final resting place?"

"Maybe I should start working again. It will give me something to do."

"And put some employee out of a job? There aren't many jobs on the island, you know. And you don't have to work. Why don't you get more involved in church activities? Or help Naomi Claxton on her committees? She's on practically every committee in town. Now that's a woman who keeps busy. You can always find something to do."

"You don't want me around you," Patience voice slurred.

"Don't invent excuses as a reason to drink. You're lucky that your time is your own. I buy you everything you want. I work too damn hard to have to come home to this mess every night."

"That's not fair, Stanley."

Stanley sighed. It was no use arguing with her. "I'm going to bed." The average woman would be grateful for what he provided for her. Wouldn't nag him to death every evening.

"Our customers will miss Vicky," he said.

"Stanley, something strange happened yesterday."

Stanley stopped at the door. "What happened?"

"I found worms on me when I got up this morning."

"Worms?"

"And dirt."

Stanley sighed. "You fell in the garden again. You shouldn't drink out there. Lucky I came out to drag you into the house. Honey, the drinking is getting worse. You're making yourself sick. I don't like what's happening to you."

"But . . ."

"Please get some help."

"I don't understand . . . I couldn't . . ."

"I cleaned you up as best I could, but it was a long day and I hadn't realized you were that dirty. You must have been lying in the garden for a long time for worms to climb on you. Probably, the gardener sprayed the grass. You know how earthworms sometimes appear after his treatments."

She shuddered. Her hands shook as she carried the glass to her lips and swallowed hard.

"Honey, I only want the best for you. For us to get back to where we were. I'll promise to take you on the trip of your dreams if you get help."

She stared at her glass.

He approached her, his arms outstretched. "I'm lonely for you, honey. I miss you. I . . . I want my wife back," he said softly.

She gazed at the glass in her trembling hand and set it down on the coffee table, then rubbed her hands up and down her chilled arms. "Okay. I'll get help," she said, but she'd said that several times before.

Chapter 4

Shrouded in darkness, he observed Vanetta from his boat. His gaze followed her as she strolled her seaside deck alone and leaned against the railing in defeat. Lights were on in the kitchen, throwing a warm glow over her silhouette. With the backdrop of the huge house behind her, she reminded him of the tragic heroine of a play.

He'd seen her last night. Had it only been one night? Hmm. Seemed longer. She had been coming into the garage with the sole purpose of catching her man in the act. She'd almost caught him. He'd ducked for cover. He wished he could have seen the show. Would have been something. It was the first time he'd seen such intense spirit in her. She was the mild-mannered type while her sister, Lisa, was the slutty wildcat. Almost gave him a hard on, but she wasn't his Alyssa.

Oh, come on now. Don't look so sad. Ah, it will pass. You'll thank me one day. He was no good for you. And that Vicky had learned her lesson, hadn't she? Even if it was too late.

He shook his head. Vanetta was a beauty, to be sure. Matthew hadn't deserved her. All those Claxton women were beauties.

But Alyssa was the most beautiful one of all.

* * *

Alyssa knew she should go home, but she cruised by her grandparents' house instead. A light was on in the kitchen. She also remembered her total source of nutrition for the day had been a couple of stale crackers. Her stomach felt pressed against her back. Naomi always had food. It was late, but Alyssa needed the soothing sound of her grandmother's voice.

Alyssa pulled into her grandfather's driveway. As she walked to the house, she spotted her grandmother sitting on the front porch, fanning the mosquitoes away.

"Why aren't you in bed?" Alyssa asked, climbing the steps. Her hair up in pink sponge rollers, Naomi had tied a black hairnet on her head.

"Who can sleep?" Naomi rose from her rocker. "I'll fix you dinner. You look hungry."

Alyssa followed her into the white Cape Cod house that was always neat as a pin.

"How was your weekend?" Naomi asked.

"Relaxing."

Her grandmother opened the refrigerator door, and Alyssa stared as Naomi began to pull items out.

"Unbelievable. What did you do? Spend the day cooking?"

"From the moment I heard there were two dead bodies and you wouldn't release the names, I started calling all my children and grandchildren. And of course, I couldn't reach them all. I couldn't sit still. So I cooked. I've got everything in here," Naomi said without missing a beat. "Take your pick."

"Anything will do."

Naomi got a plate from the cabinet and started piling it with food, nuked it, and placed it before Alyssa.

She sat across from Alyssa munching on grapes.

"Reginald came by this weekend. Said you were angry with him."

"I just saw him at Melinda's."

Naomi shook her head. "That poor child and her family."

Alyssa laid the fork on her plate. How could she eat with her family and best friend suffering?

"Reginald's a nice young man," her grandmother said quickly, changing the topic. "Really made something of himself. Of course, Jordan's been sniffing around you, too. Heard he was back. Sometimes too many choices get you all confused and mixed up. Been stringing Reginald along." Obviously, she didn't want to talk about Matthew and Vicky.

"I'm not stringing him on, Grandma. We're friends. You know that. We used to play together when his parents lived next door to you."

"He's a man fully grown. And when he spends as much time with you as he does, he wants more than a handshake and a smile at the end of the day. I can already tell he's getting antsy. You're going to have to make up your mind sooner or later, and the way things are going, it's going to be sooner."

"What are you talking about?"

"I'm talking about him and Jordan, who's also been traipsing around the island waiting for you to notice him. But I already know you notice him. You're scared."

"Don't be ridiculous. I'm not afraid of anything."

"You're afraid to trust. You're afraid to trust in love."

"Well, you're a good advertisement for marriage. Look at you and Grandpa. If you can't make it work, what makes you think I can?" In the last year, her grandparents' marriage had been rocky. Her grandfather spent more time with his cronies across the street on Travis's front porch then he did with his wife.

"Hoyt will come around. Something's going on with him. I can't put a finger on it yet. You know men go through their changes, too. I know I did when the change of life came on me. And he stuck by me. One thing about it, I don't have to worry about him chasing women at his age."

"As long as they're breathing, they think they can chase women," Alyssa said to her grandmother's laugh. "He passed the change of life decades ago. Do you still love him?"

Naomi leaned back in her chair. "I wouldn't have stuck by him all these years if I didn't."

"I think with most people, especially those of your generation, it's a matter of settling. I don't want to settle."

"Maybe with Reginald, you'd be settling. But what about Jordan? You feel something for him, don't you? I can tell."

"He doesn't take relationships seriously. With Reginald, I don't have to worry about having my heart ripped apart. I don't love him. But you're right. I feel something for Jordan. But I'm not going to take a chance on a man whose work holds the only meaning in his life. At least he lets women know where they stand beforehand."

"You know, sometimes a man has to build his life before he starts looking for a serious relationship. He's done that. And maybe none of the women in his past meant anything to him. Nothing says you have to spend your life with the first person you date."

"I could easily fit into that category."

"Sometimes . . . sometimes, you've got to take a chance. Otherwise you're not living. You just exist. And life is for the living. Yes, you hurt sometimes, but you laugh a lot and you love a lot. Love's worth taking the risk." The chair squeaked as Naomi got up. "A man doesn't build a house next to a woman if he isn't serious."

"Did you hear any rumors about Matthew?"

"Not yet, but I'm sure people will be yakking about it

soon. What a blow. But Vanetta's strong. She'll get through this."

"What choice does she have?"

"The women in our family are resilient. Always have been. She'll bear up under the strain. Abiola did. So can we," Naomi said. "I told Vanetta not to tuck her head, not one inch. She did nothing wrong."

"You gave her a lecture today of all days, Grandma?"

"Sure I did. It was needed."

Alyssa shook her head in resignation. Naomi would always have the last word.

Naomi swatted at a gnat. "And start searching for the family's gold bowl."

Alyssa groaned. Her grandmother wouldn't forget the heirloom golden bowl Abiola, their first ancestor in America, had brought here in the early 1600s. Not for a second.

"We've torn up Aunt Anna's house and yard. It simply isn't there. I don't know where to look, Grandma."

"You're a detective, aren't you? Do some detecting."

"Maybe it will just show up one day."

"If you did your job . . ."

"I didn't come by here to be harassed by an old woman," Alyssa said, getting up to dump the scraps in the trash. She rinsed the plate and stuck it in the dishwasher. "I haven't gone to see my own mother yet."

"She's fine. I saw her in church yesterday morning. And if you call me old woman again, I'm going to box your ears."

"You have to catch me first. Where's your old man?"

"Don't ask me. Probably hanging out with your daddy and his brothers. Or his cronies. You know them. They're probably trying to solve the murders singlehandedly."

Now that her grandfather was retired, he and his cronies thought it was their responsibility to keep the island safe. They'd made pests of themselves to everyone from the city council to the police department. Only a few months ago, they tried to save one of their friends' grandsons by covering up a murder. And after the body was found, they confessed to a murder they didn't commit.

Alyssa rubbed her temples. She was getting a headache. "You tell Grandpa to stay out of police business. I don't want those men screwing up evidence or getting hurt if the murderer suspects they're onto him."

"Since when have I been able to tell that hardheaded man anything?"

Alyssa groaned. "Take care," she said. "Thanks for dinner." Then she left.

As Alyssa drove into her yard, she saw a car parked in front of her house. It was pretty dark. She should have gotten a yard light installed like her mother had told her a million times.

Alyssa unsnapped the safety on the gun in her shoulder holster. "Who's there?" Alyssa asked through the open window. With a murderer running loose, she wasn't taking any chances.

"Jordan." A tall, dark image stepped into the light and approached her car.

Alyssa sighed, slid her window up, snapped the safety on her revolver and opened her door to get out. He was the last person she wanted to see. She was a little self-conscious after last night. Gosh, was it just last night? Seemed like a week had passed. But the memory of being in his arms came rushing back. Her wanton behavior. She'd let loose in a way she hadn't in—jeez, since she didn't know when. What must he think of her? Sleeping with him like that, and they weren't even in a committed relationship.

"Not a good thing, your coming home late and alone," he said. "I never realized how isolated you were."

"I have neighbors."

He snorted. "Two miles down the road. A lot of help they'll be."

"Did you come here to lecture me?" It took her mind off the sex. That was good.

"No. I brought food." He held up a bag. "Your mother sent a plate. She's afraid you'll wilt away to a string bean. Her words, not mine."

Her mother? He'd told her mother he was coming here? Oh, crap. She was probably already picking out a china pattern.

"I just ate at Grandma's, but thanks." He followed her into her house. Good thing she'd cleaned before she'd gone on the trip, Alyssa thought. Other than dust, the place was in pretty good shape. It wasn't a fancy house. Nor was it large. Just a comfortable one-floor, three bedroom cottage on stilts.

In the kitchen, she got her first good look at Jordan. He looked terrible—haggard—as if he held the world on his shoulders.

"I'm sorry about Matthew," Alyssa said. "How are you holding up?"

He shrugged, leaned against the countertop, and sighed. "I just left Vanetta's. This is hard on her."

"I know. It's tough for you, too." She didn't want to empathize with him, but grief wrote a script on his face. This wasn't the cheerful Jordan from the weekend. The one who pestered the heck out of her. She couldn't kick a man when he was down.

But he didn't look down and out. He still looked damn good . . . and hot. It wouldn't take much for her to snuggle up with him. He was pure joy under the sheets. On the sheets. Heck, he was pure joy, period.

"Are you going to be able to sleep?" she asked.

"Probably not. But Curtis is headed to the B & B. We'll

talk half the night," he said, leveling that laser gaze on her. "I'm worried about you."

"No need to be."

"Alyssa . . ."

"Jordan, I know you're in pain, and I'm sorry, but we aren't a couple. Last night didn't change anything," she said gently. It was clear he wanted to be there for Vanetta. He needed someone, too, but she couldn't give him false hope. Jordan was a barracuda. Give him an inch, and he'd take the mile.

"Everything's changed."

Why hadn't she thought this through before she acted? He was like a bad penny that kept showing up.

"You're talking about sex. And you know you haven't made commitments to every woman you've had sex with." When he started to speak, she held up her hand. "The fact that you sneaked into my sleeping bag in the dead of night and I didn't throw you out gives you no rights."

"I went to your tent to talk. Not to make love, but it was what you wanted at the time. I wanted to make love with you, wanted it with a need you'd never understand, but I didn't go to your tent for that. And I didn't force you."

"I know you didn't." Alyssa sighed, swiped a hand over her forehead. "It's late. Neither of us is in a condition to make life-altering decisions. Especially not you."

"I didn't jump in the sack with just anybody, Alyssa."

"If you were serious, you would have courted me. You can't break the rules and expect me to play the game," Alyssa said. "It's too late for this argument. And I have to get some sleep. So do you."

"I've tried to date you. Since February."

The doorbell rang, and Alyssa jumped. Jordan cursed.

Who the heck would come to her house this time of night? Alyssa wondered. She left a frustrated Jordan and padded to her door. Her brother stood tall and impatient, his finger poised to ring again. Cleveland Jr., thirty-four years old and every bit as tall and as well built as Jordan, was standing on her porch with a duffle bag.

She opened the door. "What are you doing here?"

"Mama sent me. Those bodies you found down the road's got her worried," he said, pushing past her. "It was either me or Dad. You got problems with that, take it up with her. I need to crash."

Alyssa closed the door with a sigh.

Cleve stopped when he saw Jordan behind her. The men spoke, shook hands.

Cleve's business was in Norfolk, and sometimes, his visiting clients stayed at The Cove. Since he couldn't afford the membership fee, Alyssa wasn't going to even think about how that happened.

"I see you beat me here." Cleve said.

"Yeah," Jordan responded.

"Well, I'm going to crash in back," Cleve said and disappeared down the hall, giving Jordan and Alyssa privacy.

"Alyssa . . ." Jordan entreated.

"I betrayed my friend, and I'm having a hard time living with that. It's not your fault. It's mine. I should have sent you away, and I didn't."

"Maybe because you wanted me as much as I wanted you? If it wasn't right, you would have sent me packing."

Alyssa shook her head. "It doesn't matter."

"Yes—"

"It doesn't matter," she repeated firmly. "I want you to leave."

"Alyssa, this is only the beginning."

". . . now, please."

Jordan wanted to stay and plead his case, but one look at her face revealed now wasn't the time. She was exhausted and heartsick. This wasn't just about him. Their day would come.

He wanted to hug her, help ease the pain . . . help ease his own pain. But she saw him as her enemy. The best he could do was leave and regroup for another day.

"Good night, Alyssa."

She closed the door after him, and Jordan walked out into a beautiful, star-filled night. He heard the rush of waves against the shore. But as beautiful as the scenery was, the thought of Alyssa coming home alone every night gave him the creeps. She might be a detective, but out here, she was vulnerable.

Jordan headed for the B&B, the only lodging on the island. He'd already booked a room for the week. It was nearing midnight, and the last ferry back to the mainland would soon dock.

He drove through the quiet little town. The shops had closed up for the night. There wasn't even a MacDonald's out here. He passed the marina with the scores of boats bobbing in the water, passed the ferry dock, and drove on to the B&B just a couple of miles away.

It was a three-floor Victorian situated down a quiet gravel lane. A light fog had settled in and the building looked foreboding in the distance.

Nothing in life had come easy to Jordan. But he went after every goal with single-minded determination. When he had fallen for Alyssa, he'd never imagined getting her would be as hard as the most trying business negotiation.

And he couldn't believe Matthew was gone. They had grown up in the same community in Norfolk, although Matthew was years older than Jordan and Curtis. Matthew took over management of his father's corner store after his tour in Vietnam. Curtis and Jordan went there every day for soda and candy or whatever their parents had sent them to purchase.

Jordan and Curtis had been best friends for forever. They had both wanted to attend college, but they didn't know how they were going to because they were both too poor. Matthew was the first person to tell them about scholarships and saving everything they earned for the future. He even sent to colleges for brochures. After his tour in the Army, he knew more about the world, so he encouraged them to think bigger than their small community. To think about what they wanted for their futures. He had been a good introduction to the world outside of their neighborhood.

When they were broke, Matthew would let them sweep the floor or stock the shelves to make a little money. And he'd let them man the cash register when he wanted to make out with a pretty sister in the back room. He had always been a lady's man. For some reason, women loved him, but he was never serious about any of them.

He'd met Vanetta when she student-taught in a neighborhood school. It surprised the heck out of Jordan and Curtis when she started dating him. It surprised her even more when he treated her differently. There were never any quick passes in the back room. And when he proposed to her and she actually accepted, it floored them. He was years older than she was. What did a classy lady like her see in a man like Matthew? But he was one smooth-talking brother.

However, from the expression on Curtis's face when Matthew gave them the news, Jordan knew that Curtis was also in love with Vanetta.

Curtis had even warned Matthew that if he treated Vanetta like he treated his other women, he'd knock his lights out. Matthew had laughed and patted Curtis on the back.

Jesus. Did Curtis know about Matthew's affairs? No. If he'd known, he would have confronted him. Heck, Curtis worked himself half to death. He never had the time for local gossip. Heck, they all worked too hard.

Jordan only dated one woman at a time, and he always made it clear he wasn't ready to settle down. For the first time, he knew how Curtis must have felt having the woman he loved within his reach, but she might as well be on the other side of the globe.

The sound of an electric drill awakened Alyssa from a sound sleep the next morning. The piercing sound was her wake-up call nearly every morning. Jordan's house might be across the sound, but it was still much too close.

Naomi's words had haunted her last night. Alyssa had tossed and turned far into the night. *A man doesn't build a house near a woman if he isn't serious.* Of course, she'd thought long and hard about that. She didn't want a daily dose of Jordan's tall form across the water from her own sanctuary. At least, it used to be a sanctuary, she thought as with eyes half-closed, she made her way down the hallway to the kitchen and started the coffeemaker before padding into the bathroom for her shower. After, she quickly dressed.

The construction crew had started building his house while Jordan was in California.

For a while after she'd rebuffed his advances, she hadn't heard from him. Then suddenly, he was building a house across from her. She couldn't look out her front door without seeing the back of his house. Maybe she'd block the view with a few well-placed trees. But she'd still know he was there.

She'd bought her place in an isolated spot because she didn't want neighbors. This little inlet jutted out and was reachable by land, but it required her to drive far out of the way. From Jordan's property, a motor boat only took a couple of minutes and it saved her twenty on her drive to work.

The owner had promised her he wouldn't sell to anyone

Candice Poarch

else without giving her the opportunity to purchase the property first. But he'd sold to Jordan without saying a word to her. The traitor.

Cleve was still sleeping soundly when she left. She was on her way to the beauty shop when Harper called her.

"I want you in the office now," he said.

"I was on my way to interview the ladies in the beauty shop," she said.

"In my office. Now," he said without giving her a chance to argue.

Sighing, Alyssa turned around and drove to the office. Last night, she had gotten the key to Vicky's house from Melinda. She and John had gone through it, but the only thing of note they found was a piece of paper with "The Den" written on it. *What in the world was The Den?* Alyssa wondered. She'd called Melinda to see if she knew. She hadn't. Alyssa had a million questions with no answers.

It took ten minutes to get to the office.

Harper was one of the few men she actually had to look up to. Most were either her own height or shorter. Gave her an edge when one wanted to get sassy with her, being able to look down at him.

"You know, if you weren't the only detective in the county you wouldn't be working this case," he said. "You're related to the victim's wife and best friends with the victim's sister, for crissakes."

"But I am the only detective. I can do my job."

"Before you go, give me an update."

"I can do my job, Harper."

"I need objectivity here. I told you you'd run into this situation when you were promoted. It's a small town."

"This situation would present itself with any officer who grew up on the island," she said and took out her notebook to update him on everything she and John had done, making sure not to miss anything. "As soon as we go by Vanetta's, we'll take a swing by the beauty parlor."

"I'll visit the beauty parlor. You can take your time at Vanetta's."

For the first time, Alyssa chuckled. "You're going by the beauty parlor and expecting to get answers?"

He ignored her, and she shook her head and left.

Harper had to think this through carefully. Alyssa was a great detective. Had natural instincts.

The beauty parlor was two miles from downtown. A pretty sign reading "Barbara's Hair Salon" blinked in the window. And when Harper entered, the noise dimmed to silence. A couple of heads were tucked under dryers. Three were at the shampoo bowls, their hands flying to their heads as if they could instantly pretty up their dos. As if their hair wasn't already slicked back with soap, or conditioner, or whatever, leaving the bare face for the world to see.

Harper felt distinctly uncomfortable. Maybe he should have sent Alyssa or come another time. He wouldn't put it past her to be laughing in her coffee cup at his plight. The whole town was going to be abuzz about the sheriff making a trip to the beauty parlor. One of the customers had already pulled out her cell phone as if she was waiting for him to leave so she could make her call. He was so thrown that he completely forgot how enamored he was of the saucy Barbara until she acknowledged him.

"How may I help you, Sheriff?" Barbara Turner was substantially built, but a beauty of a woman. Her short black hair was in disarray, but it couldn't detract from the beauty of her round, rich deep brown face.

"Afternoon, Miss Turner. I'd like to speak to you privately."

She glanced around. "If you could give me a moment to finish washing the perm out, I'll be right with you."

Harper's family had moved to the island his junior year

of high school, and he still felt like an outsider. He often wondered how he got voted in as Sheriff when his rivals were islanders of several generations residence.

Harper nodded and stood near the door, wishing he could escape, while she worked with the woman's head. The hand sprayer was swishing across the woman's head in fast motion. Barbara patted the head with a towel, put a plastic cap on the woman's head, and led her to a hood dryer, setting the air before she tucked the woman's wet head under it.

One of the women waiting asked, "Do you have any idea who murdered those people yet? I'm going to miss Vicky's manicures. That woman was an artist."

"We're investigating," he said.

"We haven't had anything this bad in a very long time," another woman said.

Harper nodded. "We have a very capable police force."

The woman's hand tightened around the phone.

"Do you think this is a serial killing? Should I get myself a gun? You know, with that mess that went on last spring and now this."

"We don't have any evidence at this time indicating a serial killing." The last thing he wanted was islanders running out to purchase guns and shooting when they heard a bump in the night. "Just use everyday precautions and common sense."

During the spring, a robbery ring had moved to town to steal the Claxton's heirloom golden bowl, bullion, and coins. And they had been under the misguided belief there were precious jewels hidden somewhere as well. At the time, the islanders were unaware there was any bullion or coins left. Those, they thought, had been used centuries ago to purchase the initial plot of land and to keep them solvent during hard times. But coins and bullion were found along with one of the golden bowls—not the original bowl that belonged to Naomi Claxton's ancestor—but one that had been traded for supplies so that a battered white woman named Mary and a couple of slaves from Virginia Beach could escape to Philly through the Underground Railroad in the 1800s. Oddly enough, one of her descendents from Philly visited the island in the late 1970s, looking for genealogy information and had married Naomi Claxton's daughter. Naomi's granddaughter had moved back to the island to run the B&B Naomi's sister had built with her husband. They never had children.

Harper focused on Barbara. She was a fantastic cook and unkind people remarked on her weight. He'd had the good fortune to eat some of her fried chicken and banana pudding at a church birthday bash during the summer. Lord, that woman could cook. He'd wanted to go back for seconds, but didn't want to look like a pig.

Finally, Barbara wiped off her hands again and approached him. She might be heavy, he thought for the umpteenth time, but she sure was a pretty woman.

"I tell you, Sheriff, I don't know who could have done such an awful thing. I just won't believe Vicky was carrying on with that man. True, she was a little wild, but she had a heart of gold. She never hurt a soul. It's going to be hard coming in here every day and not seeing her. She was the life of the salon."

She wore black slacks and a green top long enough to cover her hips. "Her mama asked me to do up her hair. Any idea when Kingsley will get the body?"

"After the autopsy. I'm sure he'll let you know."

She nodded. "We can talk outside or in the supply room."

"The supply room will work." Every eye followed them as they walked toward the back of the shop. He closed the door firmly behind them.

Supplies were stacked neatly on shelves. An old full-size fridge was tucked into a corner with a small table and a couple chairs next to it. A couple of cabinets and a coffee pot finished the furnishings.

"Do you know if Vicky was dating anyone in particular or had plans for the weekend?"

"I know she was excited about something, but I don't know what. She wouldn't talk about it, but she had that hopeful light in her eyes."

"Did you know where she spent the weekend?"

"Only that she was off the island. Norfolk or Virginia Beach would be my guess."

"Was there anything unusual going on in her life lately? Maybe someone or something she feared."

Barbara frowned. "Not that I know of. She had nerves of steel. Took a lot to frighten her."

"Did she talk jokingly about any of her dates?"

"Now and then. She always did that. Nothing specific comes to mind."

"If you remember anything, give me a call."

"I thought Alyssa was investigating," Barbara said.

"We have a small force. Everyone has to pitch in," Harper said.

"Well, I hope you find that person soon. I know I won't sleep well until you do."

"We're on it," the sheriff said. "But feel free to call anytime you're worried."

Chapter 5

While Harper was at the hairdresser's, Alyssa drove to the funeral home. She called to let them know she was on her way. She wasn't waiting around for an appointment.

It was a sunny, warm day, and Alyssa rolled her window down to catch the fresh breeze. She stopped at John's house. He came running out with his jacket over his arm. He wasn't dressed in his police uniform today. Alyssa smothered a laugh. Did he think he was a detective already?

"Where's your uniform?" she asked as he climbed into the car.

"Well, I thought since I was working with you today, I didn't need it."

"You can still wear your uniform." Alyssa pulled onto the road. The funeral home was just a short drive away.

"Did you get any sleep last night?" John asked.

"Barely any."

"Me, either. Murders like that rarely, if ever, happen here."

"We don't have a fence around the island," Alyssa said.

Kingsley and Jones Funeral Home occupied a stately brick building with white wood trim. Stanley and Reginald had done extensive renovations after purchasing it from Brit. Alyssa drove into the freshly paved parking area where a line of six cars was parked.

Shana Jones, Kingsley's secretary and Reginald's cousin, met them in the reception area. They must have a little bell or something else on the door to warn them when someone entered the building because she never had to wait even though there wasn't a reception desk in that area.

"Mr. Kingsley told me you were calling for an appointment. Luckily, he has time this morning. Follow me," Shana said, turning on spiked heels, her skirt swishing back and forth as she marched down the carpeted hallway. She wore an elaborate hairpiece that reached halfway down her back. Her natural hair looked better, Alyssa thought. She'd never understood the fixation on fake hair.

"I have a few questions for you," Alyssa said.

"We can talk in my office," Shana said as she led the way through a series of hallways, past a chapel and viewing rooms, and into a lavish office with rich mahogany furniture. Shana pointed to a rose, burgundy, and white-striped chair. "Have a seat."

Alyssa sat and pulled out her notebook. John sat in the opposite chair. "You and Vicky were friends?" she asked.

"Not bosom buddies, but we went out sometimes after she started working here."

"Where did she usually socialize off the island?"

"Some of the clubs." Shana named a couple. "She didn't tell me all her business."

"Do you know where she was this weekend?"

Shana glanced down, an indication she might know more than she was telling. "No. I wasn't with her this weekend."

"I didn't ask if you were with her. Where did she go?"

"Off the island, but I don't know where."

"Shana, we have a double murder," John said in an agreeable tone. "If you know anything, you need to tell us."

"But I don't know," she said. "I don't know who would want to kill her."

"What about some of the people she socialized with?" Alyssa asked.

"Just her usual crowd from the island. We always went in a group. The same old group you see around here."

"Was she with that group this weekend?" Alyssa asked.

"No. I was with them, but she wasn't."

"We'll still question them. In the meantime, if you remember anything about this weekend, please call me."

"I will." Shana stood and led them to Kingsley's equally well-appointed office.

He stood and buttoned his jacket when they entered. A handsome man in his fifties, he wore a black Brooks Brothers suit. He came around the desk to shake their hands. "What unfortunate circumstances," he said a somber tone. "I'll be happy to help you any way I can."

Naomi had called Alyssa earlier to tell her Vanetta had scheduled a meeting with Kingsley today. He'd pulled out his best suit, obviously trying to outdo Vanetta in the fashion department.

Alyssa was ashamed of herself. He was a nice man, and he had always been kind to Aunt Anna and her grandparents.

"How often did Vicky work with you?"

"Quite often. But she worked more with Reginald than me. He's in charge of the day-to-day activities. I'm here to cover sometimes, but he's the funeral director, and I let him handle most of the work."

Alyssa knew that. But business was brisk in Norfolk, and Reginald handled all of the work there. He only made sporadic trips to the island.

"Who hired her?"

"She was asked to work here after she did the nails of one of her deceased clients. She used to work for Brit, you know. She's a licensed beautician, and we decided to keep her on. Families are always pleased with her work."

"Did she discuss her personal life?"

"No. I don't see her that often. I rarely handle the embalming, although I'm qualified."

Everyone knew that. But he did keep his hand in enough not to lose his skills, he often said. And he kept a hawk's eye on the business. Nothing happened here that he didn't know about. *Especially* if it involved money.

Alyssa gave him her usual spiel and a business card before they left.

"You know most of the islanders entertain off the island. It's odd no one knows what Vicky was up to," John said.

"Or aren't telling."

Curtis was already in the dining room brooding into his untouched coffee when Jordan came down to breakfast. And a good thing, too, since the dining room was packed. It was the only place in town to get a decent breakfast, and the buzz of the conversations centered on the deaths. Newspapers were open at each table.

"Jordan, good to see you."

"Good morning, Mrs. Long." Gabrielle's mother was managing the B&B while Gabrielle was on her honeymoon with Cornell Price.

"I can seat you in the other room. We have far more customers than anticipated."

"I'll join Curtis at his table," he said.

She thrust a laminated menu in his hand. "Someone will be right over to take your order."

"Thank you." Jordan wove his way through the tables.

Curtis glanced up when Jordan pulled out a chair and sat.

"Did you get any sleep?" Jordan asked, signaling a waitress to fill his coffee cup.

"Not much," Curtis said, placing his paper on the table. It was a special edition with the story of the deaths on the front page. "I can't believe Matthew's gone. He's been a part of our lives forever."

"I'm going to miss him. Without him, I wouldn't be here."

"Yes, you would. You were always ambitious. All our business ventures were your ideas. He made it possible for our dreams to happen earlier than we'd anticipated," Curtis said. "It's Vanetta I'm worried about. She has to work through her grief and anger."

That was an understatement.

"Are you going to continue with the expansion?" Curtis asked.

"That's the plan. I'm not going to be able to babysit the Novaks the way I've been."

"Wade should be able to run things here."

Jordan shrugged. "For the most part."

"Sure puts a crimp in your plans for Alyssa. How was the weekend?"

"She's a hard woman to tie down."

"If she's the one, don't give up, man."

"Take your own advice."

Curtis leaned back in his seat. "My situation is different."

"For what it's worth, I don't think Matt loved Vanetta. She's classy."

"She's not a snob," Curtis defended.

"No, she isn't, but she represented a different kind of woman from the ones Matt usually dated."

"Well, I'm from that same world. And after this mess, she isn't going to trust either of us."

"You're not Matt. She'll see the difference."

Curtis sighed. "Did you tell your mother?"

"She's coming into town tomorrow. Although Jordan purchased a house in South Carolina near his aunt, his mother still owned his childhood home in Norfolk.

"I'm surprised. She never liked Matt."

"I know. She felt he was competing with my father, for some reason." Jordan had never understood his mother's antipathy to Matthew.

"Are you ready to order?" the waitress asked, her pen at the ready.

Jordan glanced at the card and made a selection, although he didn't have much of an appetite.

Alyssa and John separated to do interviews before she reached Vanetta's house. There were plenty of people around, but Alyssa and Vanetta managed to find a quiet place to talk.

"I'm sorry, Alyssa. I didn't mean to take my feelings out on you," Vanetta said.

"I understand. I'm sorry I can't be here more for you."

"I'm tripping over family as it is."

They both chuckled.

"I wish this was just a social visit, Van, but it's not."

"I know. What do you want to know?"

"Did you know about Matt's affairs?"

"He spent a lot of time away from home. He always claimed business kept him overnight in Virginia Beach."

"You were never suspicious enough to hire a PI to tail him? You could afford to."

"Silly, isn't it? No, I never hired one. It wasn't until recently that things began to go sour. What marriage doesn't go through its share of ups and downs? If you're asking, I didn't kill him. I could have just left him and taken half of his assets. I didn't sign a prenup and we've been married enough years for me to get half the assets. Remember, he was poor when we married."

With Matthew dead, she got everything, Alyssa thought, not just a fraction. Though it wasn't her cousin's nature to think of money first. Now her sister Lisa was a totally different story.

"Besides, I have an alibi. My friend is still in Williamsburg. I have a card for the hotel. You can call there if you can't trust me." She took a pen and wrote something and handed the card to Alyssa. "That's her name and room number."

"I need to go through Matthew's things. I have a warrant."

Vanetta held her hands up. "Be my guest."

Alyssa made it back to the station around eight. Harper was still there. "They're doing the autopsies in the morning," she said.

"We'll go together then."

"Did you find out anything at the hair salon?" Alyssa asked.

"No."

"You're an enigma, Harper. And you're a man. The women at Barbara's place will be more willing to talk to me. You were in a beauty parlor, for heaven's sake. Where women are at their worst—hair all messed up. Don't forget you're still single, and *someone* might want you for a husband."

His eyes focused on hers with disgust. "We aren't picking out my future bride."

But he couldn't help thinking of Barbara. He was fifty, much too old for his tongue to get all tied up around a woman. He'd been married once, while he lived in Baltimore, but only briefly. His wife had hated being married to a policeman. The worry. The danger. Unkind people would say that by now, he was too set in his ways to commit to a lasting relationship. He couldn't adapt to a woman's ways. He dated frequently, although not with the islanders. It was still a closed community.

Perhaps if he dated an islander, things would change. He'd feel connected. His father was career Navy, and with the constant moves, he never really felt he'd had a home base until they had moved to the island.

He kept his distance, in part to maintain his authority. People just didn't know how to take him.

The next morning, Alyssa and Harper rode to Virginia Beach to observe the autopsy.

The medical examiner was a tall, thin black woman.

"The man was given the drug Rohypnol," she said.

"The roofies killed him?" Alyssa asked.

"No. The drug incapacitated him. He was murdered by a single stab wound to the chest. There were no defensive wounds," she continued.

"He was totally helpless," Alyssa said.

"Never knew what hit him," the examiner continued.

"So the murderer might be someone he knew and trusted," Harper offered.

"The woman was murdered by asphyxiation due to strangulation. One more thing. There was evidence of sexual intercourse after her death, not before."

"So we're dealing with necrophilia?"

"It's possible. She put up quite a fight. She had bruises in several places, but there was no DNA under her nails. And he used a condom."

"We'll do a database search for necrophiliacs in the area."

"There was also evidence of dragging. The bodies were

definitely moved after death. The man would have bled a lot," the medical examiner continued.

Jordan spent a couple of hours at Vanetta's, then left for his office. He was only putting in half a day, and he found himself thinking about Alyssa. He was fixated on her, for some reason. He'd tried so many tactics to get her attention, but none of them had worked. He sighed in total disgust.

Sitting at his desk, he tapped the top of his pen against the surface, then swiveled his chair toward the huge window in back of him and took stock of all he'd accomplished. It was a peaceful scene. An eighteen-hole golf course, the ocean behind it. A garden worthy of entering in a show. He couldn't see the swimming pool from here. A business center to take care of all his guests' needs. A five-star dining room. Everything the traveling businessman or businesswoman would need.

Even now, a few guests were on the course. But most of them were conducting business. More amiable business took place away from the office environment.

Jordan had lived like a pauper after he graduated from Harvard Business School in order to maximize his investment in the business. And once Curtis began practicing, he worked too hard to enjoy the money he earned.

Matthew, Curtis, and he had conquered it all, starting from nothing and working their way up until they could afford to build this place. Matthew had been the lesser investor.

Wade peeked in. "The Novaks have been trying to reach you. Mr. Novak's on the phone."

"Put him through." Jordan pressed the button on his phone. "Tom, what can I do for you?"

Jordan listened to the man's ideas for the project.

"Thomas, my best friend died yesterday. I'll get back with you in a couple of weeks."

Thomas extended his condolences and rang off.

As much as Jordan wanted to build sites in California and New Orleans, he did not want the aggravation this group of investors was producing. Maybe he should think of alternatives.

They disconnected, and Jordan thought of Alyssa again. She was very close to her family. Maybe the way to her heart was through them. He should get to know her parents. He already knew her grandparents and had met her parents. But he needed to build those relationships.

He waited until evening to drive to Vanetta's house. More family would be there. Even the very difficult Alyssa would put in an appearance.

Vanetta's sister, Lisa, had had a harrowing year. First, she nearly lost her job at the B&B. Gabrielle, her own cousin, fired her after she'd worked for Aunt Anna since she graduated from high school. But Aunt Anna was dead, and there was nobody to protect her. Gabrielle had so much going on, trying to find the golden bowl, then with thieves trying to steal it. Then Grandma's best friend and neighbor died, and it was discovered she'd chopped up her husband and stored him in the freezer. Gabrielle was the one Grandma called when shit went down. Good thing, too, because it gave Lisa the chance to walk back into her job.

Since then, she'd toed the line. Hadn't had an unscheduled day off in months. She'd hated Gabrielle back then and had thought she was holding that bowl for herself. But then Lisa had gotten kidnapped by the thieves, and Gabrielle and so many of the islanders had searched high and low for the bowl. They had really come through for her.

Surprising, because she didn't think Gabrielle would so much as pour a glass of water to douse a flame if her butt was on fire. Goes to show you never knew about folks. But it was hard to let go of the old Lisa. She enjoyed a good time, only she couldn't afford it.

Lisa just had to get a break from all this grief. She'd spent an hour at the bar—not many places to hang out on the island unless you wanted to take a walk along the shore, and she wasn't too much for walking. She was on her feet enough, cleaning rooms at the B&B every day. Except she hadn't been to work since Matthew died.

Lisa always wondered why her sister had married that old man. He was loaded. Guess that was reason enough. Except Vanetta wasn't after money the way some women were. Good things just had a way of falling into her lap.

Lisa sighed, swallowed the last of her drink, and left for her sister's house. There would be a crowd gathered by the time she got back.

The thing that disturbed Lisa the most was that her sister lived up to her goody-goody name as much as Lisa lived up to her title of black sheep. When shit stirred, it was usually her slinging it. She hated that her sister was hurt this way, but Lisa couldn't help but feel relief that it wasn't her this time. Maybe that was selfish. But so what? She wasn't applying for sainthood.

She couldn't remember the number of times her mom and dad had shaken their heads in despair and asked why she couldn't be more like Vanetta. Her dad had even mumbled that maybe they'd taken the wrong child home from the hospital.

But Grandma had stood up for her. Told her dad that he had been every bit as confused as Lisa was before he'd settled down. Lisa hadn't heard a word out of him since. Thank God for grandmothers. They didn't take any stuff off nobody. There was a bit of hope for her, too. If her dad had settled down, maybe she could straighten up and be a respectable person one day.

Lisa shook her head. She just couldn't see herself settled down like her sister. It was just too damn boring. What was the sense of living if you couldn't have some fun? And what good did it do her sister when your old man was out there sleeping with other women? She also couldn't believe Vicky would do something so lowdown and dirty. She liked a good time, but she didn't usually court married men. She must have been as confused as Lisa.

Confused. Was she confused? Lisa didn't think so. She knew her likes and dislikes. It was just too bad she couldn't find a good guy.

Her sister had had it made. Maybe her husband was old. But he'd encouraged Vanetta to quit her job right after they married. A big, beautiful house. A closet and master bath larger than Lisa's apartment. Huge bedroom. Enough clothes for ten women. And she didn't have to lift a finger—not even to clean. She had a staff. Her sister was one lucky woman. Luck had always followed her, Lisa thought. Until now.

People were arriving in droves when Lisa made it back. So much for her rest.

An hour later, the doorbell rang for the millionth time, and Lisa went to open it. The help had gone upstairs for something.

"Hello . . . Lisa, I believe," Jordan said. He'd been sniffing after Alyssa. Good luck to him.

"Come on in. There are a million people here." All her cousins were getting themselves rich men. No rich men were sniffing after her. The story of her life.

"Don't worry about me. I know my way around," Jordan said.

Lisa left, and Jordan took stock of the great room. He saw Alyssa's mother and grandmother on opposite sides of the room, but not her father. Through a window, he saw men milling out back. The men had obviously found an escape.

Vanetta was surrounded by a group of women, so Jordan made his way to Miranda Claxton, Alyssa's mother.

He leaned over her and extended a hand. "Good evening, Mrs. Claxton. I met you briefly before. I'm Jordan Ellis, Alyssa's friend and Matthew's friend and associate." Jordan knew that wasn't a positive for his case. What woman wanted a cheater for a son-in-law?

"It's a pleasure to meet you," she said, gripping his hand with a firm hold. She studied him closely while Jordan pulled up a chair beside her and sat.

Miranda Claxton was short compared to the rest of her family. No more than five-three or five-four even though she had a couple of sons around Jordan's height. But she was lovely and petite. Made a man want to protect her. Of course, looks could be deceiving. He'd better be careful. This woman had raised three boys and a daughter. She was married to a huge man. And Alyssa had to get her attitude from someone.

"It's kind of you to visit Vanetta. She said you'll help her get Matthew's business affairs in order."

"Vanetta is a wonderful woman. We've worked on some charity events together. I'll help her in any way I can."

"And how do you know my daughter, Mr. Ellis?"

He smiled. "Jordan, please."

She regally nodded her head just a fraction.

"We're . . . friends," Jordan said, ensuring her mother understood the romantic connection.

"I see," she said, not seeing at all. "I wonder why you haven't visited the family before now."

"I will as soon as Alyssa invites me."

"You don't have to wait for an invitation from my daughter. Please come to Sunday dinner, Jordan."

"Thank you for inviting me, Mrs. Claxton."

Someone came to speak to her, and Jordan relinquished his seat. He spent a few minutes with Alyssa's grandmother before he made his way outside to speak to her father, uncles, and grandfather.

Might as well be a small village. He understood the connection between a woman and her relatives. He'd learned years ago, at Matthew and Vanetta's wedding, what a *huge* family this was. And every last one of them played some significant role in Alyssa's life.

Courting was no more than a business in some respects. You had to play the rules of the game if you expected to win.

A couple of hours passed before he could safely leave. He was quite pleased with himself. Alyssa didn't understand the lengths Jordan would go to once he made a decision.

She didn't make an appearance before he left, and maybe that was a good thing.

Chapter 6

It was almost dark, and Alyssa hadn't seen Melinda or called her today.

"Can you get away?" Alyssa asked her. She knew her friend needed a shoulder. She was trying to put on a front for her parents, which was really tough when you were staggering through your own grief.

"Yes."

"Get your bike."

"It's at my house. I drove Mom, Dad, and Grandma around today. They released . . ."

"What are you waiting for. Go home and get your bike. Do you need a ride?"

"Let me tell Mom I'm leaving, and I'll meet you at my house in twenty minutes." Melinda seemed eager to get away.

Alyssa drank half a bottle of water before she suited up. Then she climbed on her bike. It seemed like years since she'd last taken it out.

She hated wearing all the cumbersome gear, but if she didn't wear her gear, the news would get back to Harper and he'd drill her once again about being a role model. How so many riders would be saved if they wore the proper equipment. Jeans and sneakers were no protection against road burn and broken ankles if they crashed. So she wore the damn gear—everywhere she went. Even in ninety-some degree temperatures. On the bike with the wind whipping against her, it was okay. But once she got off, she had to peel off some of the gear or faint from the heat. The price she paid for being a cop.

In ten minutes, she was at Melinda's. All suited up, Melinda was outside waiting for her. Alyssa had made it clear that if she had to wear the gear, Melinda had to wear it, too.

With a rush of noise and speed, they headed through town to the ferry. The force of the cool air against her felt good, Alyssa thought. She knew Melinda enjoyed it, too. It was apparent in her expression, what little she could see of it with the helmet hiding half her face.

Although a CB was attached to their helmets and they were tuned into the same frequency so they could talk to each other, they elected not to. Just the peace of the adventure was enough.

Side by side, they rode past the Dismal Swamp toward North Carolina. They made it to the border as dusk settled in before they turned around to head for home.

"Let's go to my place," Alyssa said over her CB.

"Okay."

They arrived home well after dark, parked behind Alyssa's cottage, and walked down to the beach.

"I'm going to make a fire," Alyssa said. The temperature had dipped. It wasn't bad when they rode bikes while geared up in leather, but when they took off their gear cool air raised goose bumps on their arms. Alyssa gave Melinda a blanket to wrap around her and found one for herself. Melinda sat on an old log while Alyssa gathered driftwood for a fire.

Nothing compared to a blaze on the beach on a star-filled night, listening to and watching the waves crash against the shore.

Alyssa sat on an adjacent log and tugged the blanket around herself.

"We've done this a million times, haven't we?" Melinda said.

"Yeah." Alyssa arranged the logs with paper in a fire pit. Then she lit the paper with a lighter. The wind quickly blew the smoldering paper out, but not before the driftwood caught fire.

"You're crazy, you know that? You've brought us out here in the dead of winter to roast hot dogs and marshmallows. The wind was whistling around us," Melinda said, remembering another time.

Alyssa chuckled. "Guess I should have been a bear or something."

"You were always different," Melinda said. "Always fighting. Always getting us into trouble. Always getting Reginald into trouble."

"It was worth it."

"I didn't think so when Mrs. Naomi got so mad she took a switch to us."

"Always a downside."

"And poor Reginald always followed, even when you were wrong."

Jesus. What was she going to do about Reginald? Alyssa thought. They couldn't go forward. There was no question. She had to tell him soon.

"I think I started hanging out with you because I wanted to be that bad girl who wasn't afraid of anything. Who didn't need anyone. You could always stand on your own. I think that's what Reginald likes about you, too."

"Not always." Alyssa didn't know where this was going.

"And we knew that bad attitude was a cover for the hurt.

You were tall, and boys were intimidated. You pretended you didn't need them—didn't need anyone."

This was going to a place Alyssa didn't want to visit.

"But we weren't alone. We were friends," Melinda said. "We had each other. We had families. You had brothers and"—she swallowed audibly—"and I had Vicky." Her voice choked on Vicky's name.

Alyssa was at a loss, but couldn't stop the direction this was going.

"Damn it." Melinda hit the log ineffectively. "We were supposed to die of old age after our teeth fell out and . . . our hair turned gray and thin."

Alyssa moved to Melinda and held her in her arms. And there they sat until Melinda had purged her tears and grief—for now. It was going to take years for her to get over this.

Finally, Melinda pulled away, wiping her eyes and nose with tissues Alyssa dug up from her pocket.

"You're a fool, Alyssa."

"What did I do?" Alyssa asked. Melinda never followed a conversation. Always jumped from one topic to another. Alyssa should be used to that by now.

"Love is precious. Here today, gone tomorrow. You know you have it as bad for Jordan as he has it for you. Stop playing so damn hard to get. That house on the other side of yours says he's more than a man playing games. And I know he spent the night in your tent."

"You were dreaming."

"It was a dream all right."

"You are one nosey woman. The reason I moved my tent to an isolated area was so nosey folks wouldn't be wagging their tongues about me."

"Nighttime has eyes. People notice things. For chrissakes, he didn't take his eyes off you the entire trip. I knew he was going to try something before the weekend was over. I was curious about your reaction."

"He barely spoke to me."

"Didn't have to. You knew why he was there."

Alyssa sighed, preferring to broach this topic more than a maudlin one. "Melinda, I've been down that road so many times. Some giant of a man who wants to see how it is with a tall woman, only to settle with a dainty one like my mother. My dad's six-five. My mother is five-four. That should tell you something."

"Coward. Maybe this time you'll get it right."

Silence.

"I'm counting on you to find whoever did this to Vicky. And just give me five minutes alone with him."

"I'll find him. And if I didn't represent the law, I'd take my own five minutes with him."

It was a good thing Alyssa and Melinda were on the ocean side of the island and not the little inlet. He couldn't watch them from the inlet. Not enough water between him and the shore and he'd be too obvious. Alyssa usually stoked a great fire on that side for a reason he didn't understand. Maybe she didn't like watching that big house going up across from her.

He was out in his boat, letting it bob in the water. He took a long cool drink from his bottle of water, then continued to scan them with his binoculars.

They weren't doing very much, but he liked to keep an eye on Alyssa.

He stroked himself. What he'd do to get her in his bed. She might be tall, and he liked that, but she was built like a man's dream. Alyssa and Vicky were both sassy women, and so was Melinda, but Alyssa was worse. She was powerful. She was the law.

He took out the rumpled remains of his newspaper and read the article again.

He missed Vicky already. What was he going to do now that she would no longer be available?

He had to see her one last time—alone. She sat in that funeral home with no one around. No reason why he couldn't go there and get a look. He smiled. Maybe even touch her. See how she felt.

He set his binoculars down and started the boat's motor. A brisk breeze whipped against him as he headed for shore.

It took him forty-five minutes to dock the boat and drive to the funeral home. There were no cars in the yard and no other buildings in the vicinity. He parked in back. A thick cover of woods hid his car.

The lock on the door was flimsy. He knew because he'd done this before.

He took out a penlight and found his way into the room where Vicky was. She wasn't even in a casket yet.

He had all the time in the world to say his good-byes, he thought as he ran a hand across her cold skin.

The hours with Alyssa's family went a long way toward settling Jordan's dilemma regarding her, but grief for his friend still lingered. He went to the only bar in town for a drink, and to think. Wanting to be alone, he settled in a corner booth. For a while, the one next to him was vacant and blessedly silent.

But it wasn't long before a couple slid into it. Jordan sighed as the waitress came over, and they ordered drinks. He'd thought the place would be slow on a weeknight.

"Did you know Vicky was carrying on with that man?" a woman's voice Jordan didn't recognize said.

"How would I know?" an impatient male voice responded. "I don't keep up with her schedule."

"Unless you're gossiping with your boys, you rarely do. I knew she liked to sleep around but never with Matthew. He seemed so straight. I've never seen him with other women, even at clubs in Norfolk. And he's from there."

"I guess," the guy said.

"Who else do you think she slept with?"

"I wouldn't know."

"And poor Vanetta," the woman said. "You think she found out about it and killed them?"

"Where did that come from? I don't want to talk about them."

"I know I'd be pissed off if I caught you with another woman."

"Why're you putting me in the middle of this mess?"

"I saw her car," the woman said adamantly.

"She was in New York. On one of those spending trips."

"I know what I saw, and I saw her car here that night. When I went down to the burger place for a sandwich. You wouldn't go for me, remember? I'm still pissed off about that."

"It was late. I was knocked out. Besides, you didn't see anything," the guy said. "It could've been another car. Let's talk about something else."

"Fine. But I know what I saw."

While Jordan pondered the woman's assumptions, the waitress appeared with their drinks. Did Vanetta really return that night? Or was the woman just a talker?

Jordan shook his head. Vanetta couldn't kill a fly. She'd never kill Matthew. Leave him, maybe, but not kill him. She was too delicate. Too sweet.

But when a man pushed a woman too far, no telling what she could do. Even the sweet ones like Mrs. Naomi's old neighbor. After the woman killed her husband, she'd carried on as if the man was out of town on one of his jobs. And she was certainly a sweet and meek woman.

Oh, Lord. He better keep this bit of news to himself. But it wouldn't do any good. Word got around on the island.

It was late when Alyssa rode with Melinda to her parents' home.

Mrs. Easton ran out of the door as if her coattail was on fire, wagging her finger. "What are you doing on that bike, Melinda? I want you to sell it. No more riding that dangerous thing."

"I was careful, Mama."

"Alyssa, don't come around here with that bike anymore encouraging Melinda. I can't afford to lose her, too. No more. I never liked those things, but I put up with it. It's time you put it up for good. I want you to sell it. I'll even pay for an ad in the paper, or you can put it up on the bulletin board in the grocery store."

"Mama, I'm not selling my bike." That tired look had gathered on Melinda's face again. For a short space of time, she'd looked her old self again.

"I can include an ad for you, too, Alyssa," Mrs. Easton continued.

Alyssa understood her fear. With one daughter gone, she wanted the other one to be extra careful. In time, the worry and grief would settle.

"No, thank you, Mrs. Easton. We were very careful."

"Don't take Melinda riding with you anymore, you hear?"

"Come on, Mama. Let's go inside. It's late."

Melinda threw a sad smile at Alyssa before she ushered her mother inside.

After leaving the Easton's, Alyssa headed to the bar. Shana was there. She and Vicky had become good friends when Vicky started working at the funeral home a year and a half ago.

Alyssa had wanted to visit Vanetta, too, but she wasn't going to make it tonight.

Shana was sitting at the end of the bar, drinking alone.

"Hi Shana." Alyssa eased onto a seat beside her. "Coke, please," she said to the bartender.

From the looks of her, Shana was halfway to drunk, if she wasn't there already.

"Why don't you get her a cup of coffee?" Alyssa said to the bartender.

"Coming up. I wasn't going to let her drive like this. But she's had a hard blow. Thought she might need help unwinding."

Alyssa nodded. The bartender had a thing for Shana, but she was the only one who didn't know. Alyssa was surprised no one had told her yet. Or maybe they had.

"I hope that's for you, 'cause I'm not drinking any damn coffee," Shana slurred, taking a tight grip on her drink.

"I'm sorry about Vicky," Alyssa said.

"Everybody's sorry." Shana wrapped both hands tightly around her glass as if to keep Alyssa from taking it from her.

The bartender handed Alyssa the Coke and set a cup of hot, black coffee in front of Shana.

"Everybody thinks Vicky was bad 'cause they found her with that man. But she wasn't. Vicky had a heart. She was my friend." Hands shaking, Shana gulped another swallow as if it could take the grief away.

Alyssa let Shana talk. Sometimes, it helped to get some of the bottled up grief and anger out. And she might let useful information slip. Shana continued to talk while Alyssa tried to get her to drink some coffee.

When Shana had unwound somewhat, Alyssa asked questions.

"How long has Vicky been seeing Matthew?"

"I didn't know she was seeing him."

"Was she seeing anyone else?" It could have been a crime of passion.

Shana shrugged. "I don't know. She said she and Brit were hooking up again, but she was real secretive."

Going to bed with a married man was reason enough. In a town like Paradise, you didn't broadcast it. Someone would find out. Evidently, someone had. But the killer liked to bed dead women. Or maybe he killed her in the act and didn't know she was dead during his sexual encounter. She'd researched deaths from the last few years to see if there was a pattern. A woman who was the victim of post-mortem sex had died two years ago in Norfolk. The perpetrator had never been found.

Alyssa asked Shana a few more questions before getting someone to take her home. It was after ten, and she was getting ready to leave the bar when she spotted Jordan in a corner nursing a drink. He was watching her.

She started over to his booth, then changed her mind. She didn't feel like dealing with him tonight.

Alyssa went outside and donned her gear before she climbed on her bike. Before she started it, Jordan was beside her.

"Still pissed off with me?"

"I'm not annoyed with you, but I have a couple of questions."

"Okay."

"Did Matthew have business enemies?"

"If it was business related, the murderer would have come after me. I think this was personal." He stood so close she could feel the heat from his body.

"Unless the goal was to make it look personal. What about other girlfriends?"

Jordan shook his head. "I wasn't even aware he was seeing Vicky."

Alyssa stepped back, and her legs pressed against the bike. "You know where to find me if you come across anything useful."

"Yes, I do," Jordan said before deftly pulling her to him. She felt his gaze traveling across her features, and her body reacted a second before his lips captured hers in a kiss so sweet and unexpected that pleasure rushed through her before she had time to consider.

He was a man of many skills, Alyssa thought, as he slid his arms around her to hold her in a gentle hug. Much too soon, his lips left hers. She felt the absence of them immediately. He nibbled on her ear, then kissed her again before moving back, putting distance between them.

"Good night, Alyssa." He turned, headed to his truck.

Alyssa started her bike and took off. She was confused about her feelings for Jordan. She didn't want to like him. He was making it hard, but she still had unfinished business with Reginald. And she wasn't dealing with one until she'd settled the other. But, Lord, he made it tough.

Both funerals were on Saturday. Alyssa wished she could attend both of them, but they were held at the same time so she went to Matthew's. He was family, after all, and his couldn't be missed. Harper attended Vicky's.

While standing at the graveyard, Alyssa wondered if Matthew's murderer was in their midst.

She noticed Jordan was there. And so was Dr. Curtis Durant.

Concerned islanders sought Alyssa out for news of progress on the investigation. When the path cleared, she saw Shana's car pull up, along with several others. She hadn't been at the funeral. More than likely, she'd attended Vicky's funeral. As it was a small island and many people knew each other, many who had attended Matthew's funeral were absent from the graveyard. They probably had gone to Vicky's grave site to pay respect to both families. What a mess.

Shana talked to the family members before she approached Alyssa. Her eyes were red, and tissues had wiped off some of her makeup.

"Alyssa, do you have a minute?"

"Sure," Alyssa said. Shana looked nervous, twisting the strap of her purse in her hand. The tissue was shredding in her fingers.

"I didn't think about this the other night and I don't know if it'll help, but Vicky started going to swinging clubs a few weeks ago."

"Where?"

"Somewhere in Norfolk."

"Do you have an address?"

"No." Shana reared back as if Alyssa had struck her. "Not me."

"The murderer is still out there. If he was one of the people at the club, then everyone there is in danger. Think about that, Shana."

Shana nodded. "I'll see what I can find out."

"Thank you."

Shana left to speak to some of the family members again.

Swinging was the hot thing again, but not everyone necessarily wanted to reveal to the world they were participating, especially in this area. Shana could very well have attended some swinging sessions, only she didn't want to reveal that.

Those clubs were tricky. They could be anything from an informal gathering in a home to some formal arrangement masquerading as a legitimate club with private rooms. Norfolk was out of her jurisdiction, although she knew detectives in the Norfolk area. And to date, they hadn't found the murder scene.

Alyssa was just about to leave when Jordan approached her. She sighed heavily. He'd been by Vanetta's side most of the day. Vanetta was the kind of woman men liked to protect. She was a good woman, too. Kind and considerate. Much kinder than Alyssa was. She could see why men gravitated to her.

For a second, the green-eyed monster got the better of Alyssa. Now that Vanetta was free, was Jordan attracted to her?

That man. She was at a grave site, for heaven's sake. Why was she getting all hot and bothered?

Jordan brought an older woman over to her. "Alyssa, I'd like you to meet my mother, Rachel Ellis."

Alyssa extended a hand. Mrs. Ellis had a head full of the most beautiful salt and pepper hair. No hair color for her. In her mid-fifties, she was no more than five-eight and her face was also quite beautiful. "How was your trip from South Carolina, Mrs. Ellis?"

"It was good. Jordan hired a car to bring me."

"Will you be in the area long?"

"A couple of weeks at least. We'll see." She glanced at Jordan. "I think Curtis was motioning for you. I can take care of myself."

Jordan hesitated before leaving the women. They watched until he was far enough away that he couldn't overhear their conversation.

"My son must be quite taken with you."

"We aren't dating."

"Giving him a hard time, are you?"

"It's . . ." Alyssa started, not wanting to make a bad impression—mothers were protective of their sons.

"You don't have to explain. I have to be honest. I don't like the women Jordan has been dating. There was nothing there. No love, I mean. They were after money. He was after flash. Neither is worth a hill of beans. But you're different. So give him hell." She hugged Alyssa. "It's a pleasure meeting you, Alyssa. Have Jordan bring you by sometime." Then she walked off to join her son.

Alyssa didn't know what to make of Mrs. Ellis. But she liked her.

Thick woods surrounded the graveyard and kept the heat at bay. As Alyssa walked into a clearing, the sun shone brightly on her. It had drizzled a little in the morning. Old folks used to say it was a sign that you were going to heaven. Everybody sinned, but Alyssa wondered if it was any indication of Matthew's destination or if he'd had a chance to say a quick prayer of regret before the death blow.

The family had turned out in huge numbers. The twins, Lance and Chance Claxton, had come home from college. Gabrielle and Cornell Price had cut their honeymoon short. Gabrielle's father had flown in from Philly. She guessed her aunt would be going back with him. She'd worked at the B&B while Gabrielle was on her honeymoon.

Harper attended Vicky's funeral. Barbara looked some kind of good in that black dress. He sidled up to her.

"Good turnout today."

"Yes," Barbara said around a sigh. "I wanted to attend both, but I had to choose."

"That's the dilemma for most people."

"I was thinking about skipping the graveyard and driving to Cornell's place afterward," Barbara said.

"Want to go with me?" When she didn't respond, he quickly added, "No sense in both of us driving. Parking is going to be tight. I have to go anyway."

"Well . . ."

"We can talk a little about Vicky. See if anything jars your memory. We're still gathering information."

"I don't know if I can be much help," she said, uncertain.

"You'd be surprised at what we can decipher from the simplest bit of information."

She nodded. "I'd like to help any way I can."

"You want to drive your car home first? I'll bring you back when you're ready to leave."

She frowned and answered slowly. "If you're sure. Cornell's place isn't that far."

"Where're you parked?" Harper didn't want to give her too much time to talk herself out of it.

"It's right over there." She pointed to a place on the opposite side of the parking lot.

"Shouldn't take more than a few minutes to get to your house." He glanced at his watch. "If we leave now, we'll be one of the first ones to get there."

She was still a little hesitant when he turned. He'd walk her to her car, except she'd think of some excuse on the way. Best not to give her the chance.

At the car, Harper shucked his jacket and laid it in the back seat. He'd need it again once they got to the restaurant.

Maybe he should come right out and ask her on a date, except she hadn't dated much since she moved to the island. And he knew men had asked her out, and she'd turned them down flat.

She parked under her carport, and Harper pulled into the driveway behind her. He could see her glancing in the rearview mirror as if she wished he'd changed his mind before she opened the door and climbed out. Quickly, she walked back to his car. Harper had the door open. She frowned as she settled herself in the passenger seat.

Harper put the car in reverse and quickly backed out. "Comfortable?"

"The air conditioning feels good. Mine stopped, and it's hot out there."

"Is it the coolant?"

"Probably. I'm dropping it by the garage Monday, my day off."

"Do you have the usual hairdresser days off?"

"Sunday and Monday."

"And when do you take vacations?"

She paused. Finally, she said. "I can't remember. I thought we were going to talk about Vicky."

"We are." Harper drove slowly to the restaurant. They were the first to arrive.

"Want to get out and walk around?" Harper asked, glancing over at Barbara.

"Yes. I've been cooped up all day."

"Just slide your purse under the seat."

"Let me get some change first for a bottle of water."

"I have water in a cooler in my trunk."

After retrieving two bottles of water, Harper joined Barbara as they walked down to the water's edge.

She'd changed into flats, but she kept taking them off to dump the sand out.

"Why don't you just pull the shoes off? I'll carry them," Harper finally said.

You'd have thought he'd asked her to grow two heads. "I'll just leave them here. We have to come back this way."

"Good idea," he said. She looked quite pretty in her black V-neck dress. Her clothes were always flattering on her figure.

He took a long swallow of water. "So what do women talk about in the beauty shop?"

"Everything from gossip to what's going on in their lives."

"What did Vicky talk about?"

"Her divorce. How she liked the extra money she made at the funeral home. They paid her well."

"You did a good job on her hair."

Barbara nodded. "I don't usually dress hair for the departed, but she was a friend."

"She talk about her social life?"

"She talked about parties she went to in Norfolk. She never mentioned any place in particular."

After this case was over, Harper would ask Barbara out on a date. She still seemed skittish, so he'd give her a little time to get used to him.

They walked a while on the beach before they returned to the restaurant. Cornell had a couple of refrigerated trucks that drove to Virginia Beach, Norfolk, and the surrounding area to stock refrigerators. Many retirees lived in the area and hated cooking every day. Eating out got old fast. The business had grown faster than even Cornell had expected.

Cornell's great uncle, Lucky Price, had left him the restaurant. But Cornell didn't want to run a restaurant, so he'd built a personal chef's business. The islanders had no place to eat on the weekends except for The Greasy Spoon, so Cornell had agreed to open the restaurant on Friday nights. He planned to do this only during the summer, but time would tell.

Barbara and Harper did more socializing than eating. They were getting ready to leave when Harper said, "I didn't eat very much. Would you like to have dinner with me?"

"With all that food, it doesn't make sense to buy supper. Just wait a minute."

"Barbara . . ." Harper sighed. Barbara had already skipped out of sight. Harper made conversation with the Claxton twins about school. Five minutes later, Barbara came back with two plates filled to the brim.

"Hi, boys," Barbara said. "When are you going back to school?"

"Tomorrow."

"How do you like being away from home?"

"Love it."

"Well, you all have a safe trip back."

Harper and Barbara left. She'd neatly cut his little plans to the quick. He didn't want a plate. He wanted to take her to the mainland to dinner.

But Harper wouldn't push it yet, or the lady would shove him out of her life as quickly as she'd done all the other men who'd knocked on her door. He turned on the music and made small talk.

Harper carried one of the plates. "This is way too much food for me."

"One plate is for me."

"Maybe we could . . ."

"I'll stick it in the fridge and eat later. I don't have much of an appetite right now."

Okay. So much for her inviting him in. He'd take it slow. He wanted her to be comfortable with him. In no time, he'd be as familiar as a comfortable old shoe.

Chapter 7

On Sunday, Alyssa drove to her parents' house. She should be working on the case, but she needed time to mull it over in her mind. Besides, she had to eat.

There would be so many people there, including her grandparents, she'd be lucky to find a parking space. Her mother was a great cook, but her aunts, cousins, and brothers were also bringing dishes. Although Alyssa could cook—her mother had made sure of that—she never spent too much time in the kitchen, and nobody expected her to bring anything. She'd told her mother she'd set the table and help her with the last minute chores. And of course, there was always the cleanup afterward. Stacking the dishwasher and washing pots and pans would certainly make up for not cooking.

Vanetta's parents wouldn't be there. Vanetta wasn't up for a gathering, and her parents were staying with her, helping her sort through things.

The house came into view. It was a four-bedroom colonial perched high up on stilts. One of the things she had in common with her parents was the love of the ocean in back of the house.

Just by the cars, Alyssa knew who was already there.

But one motorcycle looked like . . . it couldn't be. He wouldn't have the nerve. She parked her bike near Jordan's and hopped off, then stored the helmet and jacket before she marched up to the house. She entered through the side door leading into the kitchen.

Even before Alyssa saw her mother, she saw Jordan sitting at the bar cutting up cucumbers as if it was a chore he did on a regular basis.

"You finally made it," Miranda said. "Look who's here. I invited your friend over."

Alyssa grunted and glared at him. As many times as she'd asked him to wait, he had the nerve to show up at her house. She needed time to end things with Reginald and to think about her move from there. He was a persistent son of a gun.

Her mother smiled as if he was the answer to her prayers. Alyssa expected her to start humming merrily any minute.

"How is that investigation going, dear?" Miranda asked in the strained silence.

"Slowly."

"How is Melinda?"

"Not well."

"If this hasn't turned the island upside down, I don't know what has."

"You can say that again."

"Sit down."

"I'll help you." Alyssa escaped to wash her hands. In the backyard, it sounded like the real party was going on. She dried her hands and returned to the kitchen where Jordan was now slicing tomatoes.

After dinner, Jordan followed Alyssa outside. "Why won't you give me a chance?" he began.

"What's wrong with you? I'm tired of you showing up."

He leaned against the railing. "Saying you have no time for me is like saying you have no time for life."

Alyssa chuckled. "A little melodramatic, aren't you?"

"Have you ever met anyone who says I have to do this or that? I don't have time for entertainment or to do things with the children. Before you know it, the kids are grown, and there's no one left to nurture. You see, life goes on. There's always going to be a case. Maybe not as involved as this one. But something will always get in the way. Eventually, the kids grow up, and you'll grow old thinking of the things you wished you'd taken the time to do."

"And what makes you so knowledgeable?"

"I've been thinking of Matt, and my life, too. The way I've put things on hold, waiting for this deal to go through or another deal. I'm thirty-five. Before you know it, I could be fifty like Matt and still not have a family, or wife, or children."

"Jorda—"

"Maybe I've put my life on hold for the last few years just like you. There was always a project that needed my undivided attention. But the projects, while important, don't contain the most important elements of my life."

"You're getting way too heavy for me."

"Alyssa, I want you. And I'm not giving up for a project, as important as it is. Or anything else."

"You come with quite a reputation."

"I've never deceived a woman. Every one of them knew up front where I was coming from. It was her decision whether she was willing to accept the terms."

"You're an intelligent man. You know women go into relationships thinking they can change a man."

"Is that my fault?"

"No. And it's my fault if I connect with you, knowing your background, and things stay the same. And the thing that really pisses me off is how you think you can use chicanery to trap me. That's how you see women. And it's the same for most powerful men. Women are theirs for the taking."

"You're wrong."

"I don't see anything that proves otherwise so far."

"All I'm asking for is a chance."

"I can't make any commitments until I've settled unfinished business. That's the best I can do." Alyssa hopped on her bike, started it, and roared down the road, leaving Jordan staring after her.

Jordan ran his hand across his forehead in frustration. In all his life, he'd never wanted a woman as much as he wanted Alyssa. And one had never thwarted him as much as she had.

Jordan went back inside. Practically everyone had gone. Her mother was on the deck relaxing.

"Alyssa's gone?" she asked.

"Yes," Jordan said.

"Take a walk with me?" Miranda Claxton was still a beautiful woman. Probably in her late fifties. Her short hair feathered around her face. She was slim and obviously kept in shape.

"I'll be happy to."

Silently, they walked toward the shore. She wore sneakers, as did Jordan. He paced his steps with hers so she wouldn't have to jog to keep up with him. He felt as if he were walking in slow motion. With Alyssa's long legs, she'd easily keep pace with him.

"I take it she's giving you a hard time," her mother finally said.

"That's an understatement," Jordan said, wondering how much of the mother's attitude had rubbed off on the daughter.

Miranda paused for a moment and watched Jordan closely. "What are your intentions with my daughter?"

"I care deeply for Alyssa." There was nothing like being under a protective mother's scrutiny.

They continued to walk. "She's had many disappointments, but of course, I'm not going to discuss them with you. And let's not forget that Matthew was your friend, and he's put this family in quite a bind."

"I wouldn't expect you to break a confidence. Yes, Matthew was my friend, and I'll miss him. He taught me a lot. I wouldn't be where I am today without him. My father died my senior year in high school, and Matt became sort of a surrogate father for my friend Curtis and me.

She nodded.

"My relationship with my father was a good one. He was a great man, a solid man with high morals. I'll never forget the lessons he taught me." Jordan realized he'd never talked to anyone about his relationship with Matthew. "Matthew was different. He'd served in the army. He knew a world beyond our small community, a world I wanted to reach for. There was this hunger in me, actually in both Curtis and me, and Matthew fed it. I don't think I would have reached this success without him. My parents wanted me to attend college, but to become a teacher or work in some local business. But that wouldn't have satisfied me." Jordan stopped suddenly, realizing he'd said more than he'd intended. "Sorry. I must be boring you."

"I'm enjoying this conversation. Please continue."

"I majored in business finance and management. Continued on for my MBA at Harvard. Curtis became a surgeon. The three of us went into business together. And the rest, as they say, is history."

"I'm truly sorry for your loss. It has to be difficult for you to listen to our family bash the man who played such an important role in your life."

"Thank you."

"It's up to you to get to know Alyssa and to let her know

you," she said. "If you're truly interested. Of course, my daughter has a stubborn streak. She won't let anybody rule her. So if that's what you're looking for, you're in for disappointment."

"I want a partner, not a lapdog."

Miranda chuckled. "She certainly isn't that. I like you, Jordan."

"And I like you, Mrs. Claxton." Jordan felt a breath of hope in his chest. He'd have to regroup again. Of course, that was nothing new with Alyssa. But at least her mother had given him hope.

You couldn't trust women. Gone was the time women were loyal. Then, even if you only made an appearance once a week or so, a man could trust that she'd wait patiently for him to reappear. No more. Couldn't take a damn business trip without them cheating while you're gone. They'd start drumming up plans as soon as the words left your mouth, and those plans were solidified long before you left town. They planned for the occurrence. Waited with baited breath until the moment you left so they could break free.

It was late Sunday night when he saw April Wesley walking home from the bus stop. He drove up beside her and lowered the window.

"Ma'am, may I give you a ride?"

"No thanks." She didn't break her stride, just kept on trucking using long, quick steps. She was almost into a jog. Didn't even look at him as her hand tightened around her purse straps hugging it close to her as if to keep him from snatching it. It wasn't the purse he was after.

"Hey, April. You going to ignore me?"

Finally, she glanced in his direction without slowing her steps. "Oh," she laughed, the breath rushing out of her. She carried her hand to her chest as if she had been given a reprieve. Slowing her steps, she changed directions and approached the car. "It's you. What are you doing here this time of night?"

"I came to see you. Lucky I dropped by. Get in," he said, releasing the lock. "You shouldn't have to walk home alone late like this. It isn't safe."

"I know." She got in the car and shut the door behind her.

He drove down the ill-kept road toward her house. "You should have caught a cab."

"By the time it got here, I could have been home and in bed."

He was silent as he navigated the few blocks to her house.

The streets were dark in this part of town. Now and then, a yard light glowed a dim shaft of light out front. It *really* wasn't safe for a woman alone in isolated areas.

He drove up her gravel path and parked in front of her old clapboard house. Time and weather had beaten the paint raw on the small two-bedroom home. She was renting in fairly safe area. But what area was really safe anymore? Matthew and Vicky were in the best part of town, and they hadn't been safe.

She sighed, but she didn't reach for the door handle once he stopped.

"Tired?" he asked.

"Not really. Just need to relax. I'm full of energy. Too stirred up to settle down."

"I could do that for you," he said, only half joking.

"I bet you could."

"I can make life easier for you, too," he said. "I want to."

"No, you can't."

"I'm a man. I have certain needs. You're a single woman. As far as I know, you aren't dating. I could be wrong. Are you dating?"

She shook her head.

"I could help you there." He reached over and caressed the side of her face with the back of his fingers. "When's the last time you've been with a man?" he asked.

April always tried to do the right thing. Live a clean Christian life. She had gone to bed with him one time at a low point when need clawed in her belly, her whole system. She was depressed when it happened. She'd told him then it couldn't happen again. He'd stayed away for months. And now he was back, and she should send him away again. Why was he back? she wondered.

But she was so tired of being alone. Tired of struggling all the time. She wanted to come home to warm arms. Just fall asleep in a man's embrace instead of hugging a pillow. He was rich enough. And the one time they had gone to bed, if she could get past the weird part, he took care of her needs. Best of all, they fell asleep together. She lay comfortably in the warmth of his arms. She didn't know when he'd eased out of bed to go home.

She wasn't tired tonight, but she was stressed and worried. There was never enough money to stretch from one month to the next. She was renting this place with the option to buy. It wasn't much, but she could fix it up to be a nice house. Her brother had told her it had good bones and he'd help her. She stifled a sigh. It wasn't easy for a single woman, especially when relatives always needed something.

The money she'd saved up to buy a used car went for her niece's summer program. She was proud of her niece. Smart as a whip, she had been accepted in a special academic program, but they had to pay a portion of the fees. Both of the girls were accepted in programs. She'd promised her brother she'd pay for one, and he'd paid for the other. She didn't have any children, so the kids kind of belonged to her, too.

She was still walking. But those girls were worth it.

She was single and lonely, and she just wanted to be with someone. Lying in a man's arms for a little while made the need seem less sharp. She gazed at him. He was a handsome man. Strong lines. A little older than she liked, perhaps, but at least he wasn't ready for assisted living yet.

It was dark. The moon hid behind thick clouds. She was trying to cut back on the bills so she left the outside lights off. Winter was coming, and Lord knew, the utility bills were going to jump sky high, cutting into the down payment for her car once again.

If they dated, she could afford to leave the light on. She could drive instead of taking the bus late at night when it was most dangerous. Walking frightened her. But what could she do? The taxi money went into savings. She rubbed a hand across her brow. She felt as if she was giving in to Satan's temptations. But she was going to do it.

"All right," she finally said.

He tripped the door lock, releasing her from the close confines of the car. She climbed out, and they went into her small place. Leaving her purse and jacket in the hall closet, they walked down the hallway together. In the bathroom, she ran cold water into the tub. As the water ran, he slowly peeled off her clothes. She shivered as the cool night air touched her skin. He had peculiar tastes. It could be worse. At least he didn't bring out the whips and chains. Now that, she wouldn't tolerate.

Still, she hated getting into cold water. But after that one awful part, it would be good. He was a gentle and thorough lover. Much more gentle than most men, who only thought of their own satisfaction. He made sure she was completely satisfied.

If only she didn't have to . . .

* * *

Two days later, Alyssa was weary when she parked her car near Jordan's house. The investigation wasn't going as well as she'd hoped. She'd left her car in his yard the other day and had taken the boat. Someone had mentioned to him she'd parked there before he bought the property, and he'd told her to continue to use it at her convenience. She didn't want him getting ideas, although it saved time.

Her boat bobbed at the pier. She threw a frustrated glance toward Jordan's house. He was in the yard. What was he doing here?

Several men were struggling with something huge, and he watched them. He wore a sleeveless T-shirt, and muscled arms crossed his chest. She couldn't deny there was some magnetism there.

She shut the car door, and he peered back at her.

"Hey. Come check this out," he said cheerfully.

Curious, Alyssa approached him. "What's that?"

"The opening to the secret door in the children's room."

Her chest tightened. "You have children?" He was trying to court her, and he already had a family and didn't mention them?

"No. But I'll have them one day."

Relief she wasn't ready to acknowledge unfurled in her chest. "Oh."

"Had you going there, didn't I?" he teased.

"It's none of my business."

"When a man takes a woman to bed, she has a right to expect certain things," he said, but before she could respond, he continued. "The secret door is already in place in the master suite."

"Is this a playhouse or what?"

"The kids will think so because it will definitely be fun."

Alyssa had never pictured him as a father.

"I had some good times with my old man. I plan to be the same kind of father," he said. His eyes clouded.

"I have great memories. My mom was more serious. She's a good woman. Dad was more laid back, but he instilled the work ethic in me. Man never missed a day of work although we were never well off. Couldn't tell it, though. Everyone around me was in the same boat."

She wanted to reach out and stroke him, but she didn't.

With a lot of grunting, the men disappeared into the house. Alyssa started to head to the dock when Jordan spoke. "Want to take a look at my secret room?"

She should get in that boat and go home. "Sure," she said, intrigued. She'd heard about these secret rooms. Seen commercials on a show on the HGTV channel. But she was cautious. Jordan was determined to pursue her.

But he wasn't making advances now. He was treating her like a neighbor. Had he finally gotten the message?

He let her precede him into the house.

"What a huge foyer! My living room is smaller than this. I didn't think they made them so large anymore." It was like a receiving room in period homes.

"The wife might want to put something there," he said, pointing to a place perfect for a mirror and chair. "Who knows? This way. The master suite is on this floor. At least, one of them is."

"You have more than one?"

"One is upstairs. Women don't like to be too far from the babies. But when we get older, she might not want to climb stairs. Although we will have an elevator."

"You thought of everything," Alyssa murmured as she looked around.

"I'm sure she'll want to make changes."

This was another trick. But Alyssa couldn't help but be intrigued. He was tenacious. There were so many women about that men usually didn't waste a lot of time on one difficult woman. What did he see in her anyway?

When Alyssa was younger and daydreaming about

having children, she'd thought of marrying a shorter man, one around five-six or five-seven in hopes her children would be shorter. But her mother was short, and that hadn't helped her. Her youngest brother had ended up at five-ten while she sprouted to six feet. And Jordan was at least six-five. A curse for any girls he might have.

They arrived at a small library. Rich wooden bookcases ready to be filled with books lined one wall. All classics. Nothing fun to read like mysteries or romances.

Jordan did something, and suddenly, one group of shelves moved to reveal a room behind it. Jordan grabbed her hand and pulled her through the opening. Alyssa noticed he'd showered. He smelled fresh and clean while she wore the day's grunge.

The master bedroom was almost the size of her entire house. Maybe she was exaggerating, but it was huge.

"A bar is going over there," he said. "And through here are the closets."

Alyssa peered into the bedroom-sized closet.

"And here's the bath," Jordan continued.

This was what Alyssa called living large.

"I'm hungry," Jordan suddenly said. "Have you had dinner yet?"

Alyssa shook her head.

"I have a little something in the car. Enough to share, in fact."

"You're all prepared, aren't you?"

He shrugged. He was still holding her hand, she noticed as they left the room. He pushed something, and the door closed.

As they walked, he said. "I hope you like chicken salad. My mother made it."

"I'm sure I'll love it," she said.

By the time they finished their dinner, night was closing in.

"Will you be okay?"

"I do this all the time," she said.

"I enjoyed dinner. Take care."

Alyssa left, but she was in a quandary. She liked this Jordan. This more easygoing man who was building his house for a wife and children.

The fun gadgets were for him. She tried to picture him as an easygoing father with children wrestling with him on the floor. With that huge bedroom, she could picture them on the floor on Saturdays and Sunday mornings before everyone got ready for church.

"Get your head straight, Alyssa," she warned herself. When her boat made it to the other side of the water, she glanced back. Jordan's truck was pulling away.

Jordan drove to Vanetta's house. The horde of cars usually present was no longer there. But there was a little sports car parked in the yard. When Jordan rang the doorbell, Lisa answered.

"Is Vanetta in?" he asked.

"Van!" Lisa cried out. "You've got company." Then she glanced at Jordan. "Go on into the family room. She'll be right down."

Jordan didn't know how to approach Vanetta with this. He still wouldn't believe she killed Matthew. He rubbed his hands together, regarded the flat-screen TV over the fireplace. Vanetta had never watched very much TV. Matthew was never home enough to watch it. But it was there and silent. Lisa had disappeared, but she suddenly popped in.

"Can I get you something to drink?" she asked.

"No thanks."

"Holler if you need anything. I think the whole B & B was filled today. And I got in to work late. I'm as tired as

I can be," she said. "Mind if I get out of these clothes? Vanetta will be right down."

"I'm okay," Jordan assured her.

He wasn't alone long. A minute after Lisa left, Vanetta appeared. She wore neat brown slacks and a beige silk top. Jordan stood as she entered.

"Jordan, it's good to see you, but I know you're tired of making these trips to the island. I'm fine. I don't want to be a burden."

"You're not a burden," he said as he kissed her on the cheek. He was reminded of her gentle nature. "Want to take a walk with me?"

"Sure," she said slowly, a question on her face. "Give me a moment to change my shoes."

"I'll wait." Jordan didn't want her sister overhearing their conversation. He kept telling himself that Vanetta couldn't have killed Matthew. No way. But she needed to know the gossip and to have the opportunity to explain herself.

"I'm ready," Vanetta said.

They walked outside to the gardens of the estate. Darkness was closing in fast. There was a rose arbor and Jordan headed there. And there was a light nearby that turned on as they neared the area.

"I gather something serious is on your mind."

Jordan nodded. "I was at the bar the other night, and I overheard a conversation."

Vanetta hissed. "Another tale about the wife with the cheating husband, I'm sure."

"No. That you were here the night of the murders. Were you here, Vanetta?"

She was silent as they neared the arbor.

"You're really asking me if I killed Matthew."

Jordan's first impression was that no, Vanetta couldn't have killed Matthew. But who knew what a person would do when the hurt dug too deep. "This is an island," he said. "Gossip spreads."

"I didn't kill my husband. He was one of your best friends."

"He was more than a friend."

She nodded. "I know."

"Did you know about his affair with Vicky?"

"No. I wouldn't have guessed her. She was a family friend. I suspected he was having an affair with someone, and I was desperate to find out who with." She ran her tongue over her lips. "It's true. I came to the island. I had bought this sexy outfit, you see, to try to put some life back into my marriage. I didn't understand why my husband no longer wanted to have sex with me. So I went to your club to find him. He wasn't there, and Wade wouldn't tell me where he was. End of story. It was too late for the ferry. I decided to drive back to Williamsburg to spend the night with my friend. We had planned to see Busch Gardens the next day. Why should I change my plans because he was a lying cheat? You can ask Wade. He sent me away."

The anger was hot and lethal beneath her words. One day, the rage would push to the surface. He reached for her hand, knowing there was nothing he could do but be there. Damn it, Matthew was his hero, but acid burned through this woman's soul.

"I'm so sorry, Vanetta." Inadequate words, but they had to be said.

"I know."

He cleared his throat. "People talk. Alyssa is going to find out."

Her eyes pierced him like lasers. "Are you going to tell her?"

He shook his head. "I'll leave that in your hands. She's your cousin."

"And you're dying to get in her bed."

Again, Jordan thought.

Chapter 8

Soon after Alyssa made it home, Reginald stopped by.

"Hey, lady," Reginald said. "It's been a while."

"Just seems that way."

"Well, I'm here to take you away from all the drudg-ery. How would you like to go to town tomorrow night? Get dinner or something? A little music. Some dancing." He danced a little step.

For a second, a picture of Jordan playing on the floor with a couple of kids flashed into Alyssa's mind. "Wish I could, but I have to work this case."

"How's it coming?"

Alyssa sighed. "Puzzling as heck."

"I wish I could take some of the strain off you."

Alyssa chuckled. "I'm used to standing on my own two feet."

"I know. But wouldn't it be better to have someone to love? Someone to share your life with?"

How unfair.

"Are you saying you love me?" Alyssa asked.

"You're growing on me. I can love you."

"I think you're confusing love with friendship. We've

always been good friends, haven't we? But that isn't the same as love."

He flicked her hair behind her ear and kissed her forehead. It was a brotherly kiss. "I'm ready for something deeper, Alyssa. You're a beautiful woman."

As much as she fought Jordan, the chemistry was there. It wasn't for Reginald. Unfortunately. Reginald was a good man. She shook her head, wishing she could give her friend what he wanted. "I can't give you what you need. I wish I could. I tried to make myself believe we could make it as a couple. But we could never make intimacy work. It's not fair to you. I'm tying you up. Keeping you from finding someone you can really love."

"That someone could be you."

"No, it can't. If I was the one, you wouldn't use terms like *could* love or that I'm growing on you." She touched his arm. "We're good friends, and I hope we'll remain good friends."

His shoulders slumped. "I'm still available if you need me."

She hadn't realized until now how unfair she had been. Or how much she'd depended on him when she needed a male escort. "If you settled with me, you'd be cheating yourself, Reg. You deserve better than a woman who thinks you're her best friend. You need someone who loves you deeply and passionately."

"Is that even possible?"

"I don't know. I won't short change either of us." Call her stupid, but she was a romantic at heart. Besides, her grandparents were going through their share of problems even with love. Her granddad was suddenly cool and distant, centered on his friends rather than on his wife these days. It hadn't always been that way. He'd changed recently. And they loved each other. What would happen if they hadn't?

Reginald closed the distance between them, held her face in his hands, and kissed her on each cheek before he left.

Alyssa's world had shifted, and she wondered if she'd ever land safely again. She rose each morning to a stunning sunrise. She jogged the familiar beach in her backyard. The most spectacular sight of all was watching the stormy ocean from her sunroom or the waves crash against the shore. The lightning crackling in the air. So beautiful, but routine. Although it was utter turmoil, still it was peaceful in its complexity. But right now, the turbulence of change put her on edge.

When Jordan had gone by Alyssa's house earlier, she was not home. She'd had more than enough time to deal with Reginald. He wanted to see her, but she didn't respond when he called her cell phone.

He wanted to spend the night on the island, but he had a meeting in his Virginia Beach office first thing in the morning. Some of the investors were getting antsy now that Matthew was dead. They wondered how his passing would affect their business. Little did they know that Matthew was not a player—at least not with business decisions. He'd always been a player of another kind.

Around lunchtime, Jordan was meeting with Curtis to discuss Vanetta.

Jordan boarded the ferry back to Virginia Beach and stayed at his place, all the while thinking of Alyssa.

The next morning, he was in the office early. Wade was there as well. Recommended by Matthew, Wade was from the old neighborhood. He was in his forties and had served fifteen years in the military. After a medical discharge from the Navy, he began working with them. Jordan understood Wade's loyalty was solidly in Matthew's corner.

He approached Wade as soon as he entered the club. "Walk with me to my office," Jordan said. Wade needed to understand this was Jordan's show now.

"Curtis called," Wade said. "He might be a little late for your meeting. He has a long surgery scheduled."

Jordan nodded and set his briefcase by his desk. "Close the door behind you, please. And have a seat," he said. "I had an interesting conversation with Vanetta. Why didn't you tell me she came here looking for Matt the night he died?"

Wade nodded, shifted his stance. "I didn't think it was important. She left right after I told her I didn't know where he was. She demanded to check the books to see who was in the rooms."

A determined wife who thought her husband was cheating would go to any lengths to find him. She wouldn't throw up her hands and say, *Gave it my best shot. Now I'll go to the amusement park in Williamsburg.*

"Did you tell Matthew that Vanetta was in town and looking for him?"

"I couldn't reach him. He wasn't answering his phone."

Jordan wondered if Matthew was already dead by that time. Or if Wade was lying.

"I went home shortly after Vanetta left," Wade said.

"Where did Matthew stay when he wasn't on the island?" If anyone knew, Wade would.

"I don't know. He didn't tell me everything about his life."

Jordan wondered if Matthew was paying for a condo or apartment for his trysts. And he wondered about Wade's secrets. What was he hiding? Jordan had to keep a closer eye on Wade. The manager left five minutes before Jordan's meeting started.

* * *

Vanetta's phone rang just before she left home.

"He's asking questions," Wade said as soon as she picked up the phone.

"Who?"

"Jordan, that's who."

"So what? Let him ask."

"Look, he's dating Alyssa. Sooner or later, he's going to tell her about you."

"But you're my alibi."

"I didn't kill them. You . . ."

"Keeping secrets should be easy for you," Vanetta retorted in a disgusted voice. "You've had years of experience keeping Matthew's."

"But—"

"Let's get one thing straight. I'm not going to jail for the rest of my life for Matthew's death. A weak woman like me couldn't have moved those bodies. Don't call me again. No telling when Alyssa will start monitoring my calls. I don't have time to talk to you now. I have a hair appointment."

Vanetta hung up and started toward the garage. Before she could close the door behind her, the phone started ringing again. She ignored it, backed her car out of the garage and drove downtown.

Vanetta had tried to sneak into Barbara's hair salon before the crowd. By the number of cars parked in the yard, she'd failed miserably. She parked and walked briskly to the door. If her hair didn't need doing so badly, she wouldn't have come. She should have paid extra to have Barbara come to her house, but she tried not to act like a diva. The bell tinkled as she opened the door. Hushed voices immediately silenced. Quiet screamed in the shop. Barbara recently moved to the island from New York. With her new styles and cuts, her shop quickly grew in popularity.

"Hi, Vanetta," Barbara said. "Have a seat. I'll be right with you."

"Good morning," Vanetta said to everyone in general. But it wasn't a good morning. She went to the magazine rack and picked up an *Ebony* before sitting in a cushioned seat. Conversation still hadn't resumed. She must have been the sole topic of interest when she walked in. Big surprise. She flipped the magazine open.

"Sorry about your husband," the woman across from her said. She'd stopped leafing through *Essence* and placed it on her lap.

"Thank you," Vanetta responded and focused on an article, hoping the woman had the good sense to take the message. Seconds later, she heard paper rattle and assumed the woman had resumed perusing her magazine. Vanetta hoped her own magazine wasn't upside down. That's all she needed to fuel the wagging tongues. *She was sitting in the beauty parlor reading the paper upside down. You know she wasn't reading it.* People liked to say bad things about you. Made their own miserable lives seem better. A quick glance told her the magazine was indeed right-side up.

Normally, Vanetta wasn't catty, but lately, she'd undergone a personality change. Once again, she thought she should have asked Barbara to come to her house.

Vanetta sat straighter in her chair. No. She wasn't going to hide away like some skittish rabbit because her husband couldn't keep his pants zipped. He had been damn lucky to get her in the first place. His fooling around had nothing to do with her and everything to do with his own character flaws, and she wasn't going to carry his disgrace on her shoulders. Damn it, it was time for her to reassess her life. Start a new chapter.

Only, it wasn't his disgrace. He was dead. He knew nothing of the feelings of betrayal, the whispers, the inadequacy she felt. She felt her shoulders droop and deliberately straightened up. Inside, she might feel defeated, but outside, she was going to portray the conqueror.

She was letting too many projects go by the wayside while waiting to get herself together. She should dive into Matthew's business matters, but that involved Matthew and she wanted a project that didn't have his stamp on it.

Her grandmother had agreed to work with her on an art show for the artist colony at the end of the island. All kinds of great sculpture, painting, jewelry, and ceramics were waiting to be discovered. That's what she'd do. She'd start working on that project again. Naomi would help her make this happen. She'd soon be too busy to think about Matthew.

"Vanetta?" When she heard Barbara call her name, she snapped out of her woolgathering. She looked at the woman. "I'm ready," Barbara said.

Vanetta rose from her seat and placed the magazine back in the holder. With her head tilted high, she glided gracefully to the chair.

Alyssa went by Barbara's place. Harper was a great investigator, but he had tried to interview women in a beauty parlor. They were more interested in getting in his pants than in revealing information. And when their hair was hanging over a washbowl, their goal was to get him out of there as quickly as possible, not on concentrating on thinking about what they'd seen or heard on the day of the murder.

She opened the door.

"I wouldn't be surprised if she didn't kill him herself." Racine Hammerfield's catty voice carried across the room loud and clear. "She was . . ." She closed up when she spotted Alyssa.

Alyssa glanced at the woman and walked toward her. "You have something you want to share with me?" Alyssa asked. "You have proof that someone killed Vicky and Matthew? Because if you do, I want to hear about it."

"Your cousin just left," one of the customers said, but Alyssa kept her focus on Racine. Alyssa had a million cousins on the island.

"Which one?" she asked.

"Vanetta."

"Guess she has to get her hair done sometime." Alyssa gazed at Racine again. "Be careful of slander," she said and, after one last glare, approached Barbara.

"Speaking of hair, yours need trimming," Barbara said, reaching out to finger through Alyssa's curls. She was clearly trying to change the subject. "Why don't you set up an appointment?"

"Soon," Alyssa said, still smarting over Racine's words. "I could use a visit, too. But right now, I'd like a word with you."

"Give me a couple of minutes. In the meantime, you can think about a time for an appointment."

Alyssa crossed her arms and stood by the storage room door. The storage room was Barbara's private conversation area. For a moment, Alyssa gazed at her old-time Achilles heel. Racine was a bitch without equal. And during junior high, Alyssa had had a growth spurt that sent her soaring even taller.

All she heard then was, "Gosh, Alyssa, you're taller than *all* the guys."

When Alyssa had tried out for the cheerleading squad, Racine had said, "Honey, you're better suited for basketball. Why don't you just try out for that? You'll be sure to make every basket since you'll be at least a head taller than all the other female players." To which Alyssa had responded, "Worry about your own self making the squad, and let me worry about me."

The first thing that came out of people's mouths was to ask if she played basketball. As if that was the only sport for a tall woman. Alyssa had no interest in basketball. And only one of her brothers had played, even though the coaches had pushed hard to get all of them on the team. Their parents had never pressured them to play the sport expected of them.

Of course, Alyssa hadn't made the cheerleading squad. Racine had not only made it, but she was also the captain.

To this day, Alyssa couldn't stand cheerleading.

Now Racine was newly divorced with a five-year-old daughter who showed signs of being just as obnoxious as her mother.

"I'm getting my hair done for a date with Jordan this weekend," Racine said.

Alyssa uncrossed her arms. "Jordan who?" she asked.

"Jordan Ellis. Who else?" She used that same high school know-it-all tone.

"That's going to be difficult," Alyssa said. "Because he's going to be with me, and I don't go for threesomes."

"What do you mean?"

"Exactly what I said."

"But you're dating Reginald." Racine's voice had lost its aggressive pitch.

"Racine, I didn't know my love life was that interesting to you," Alyssa responded. "Just don't count on going out with Jordan. This weekend or any other."

That son of a bitch. He couldn't give her a few days to straighten out her life without making plans with another woman? Alyssa was raking him over the coals in her mind until she caught herself. She had to consider the source. Half of what Racine said was a lie, but still. . . . Alyssa crossed her arms again and focused on Barbara, who was shaking her head.

Alyssa wiped Racine from her mind like a pesky insect and focused on the conversation that had been going on when she walked in. Did the islanders think Vanetta had killed Matthew and Vicky? If so, why? If she wasn't on the island or in the area, how could they possibly think she could have killed them? Vanetta was a small woman. How did they think she could lift two bodies and not leave signs of dragging them?

Alyssa made a mental note to ask Barbara.

Jordan and Curtis were supposed to start going over some of Matthew's business papers. Eventually, Vanetta would need to make decisions about some of the holdings she'd just inherited. Right now, she needed to know exactly what she owned. Jordan was hoping Matthew's affairs would reveal some of his secrets.

Jordan didn't expect Curtis to do much. Curtis jokingly claimed that one day he'd marry a wife to handle his business matters. Jordan suspected Curtis was half-serious. Most guys got over their high school love before they finished the first semester of their freshman year at college, but not Curtis.

There would always be a soft spot in Curtis's heart for Vanetta, although she was four years older than he.

When Jordan got to his office, Curtis was sitting on the sofa eating a sandwich, sipping coffee, and reading *The New York Times*.

Jordan shut the door behind him and let out a long sigh. "Did you convince the investors everything would continue as usual?"

"Only one had doubts. He's been a thorn in my side from the beginning."

"You'll handle him."

"Thanks for your vote of confidence."

Jordan settled behind his desk and ordered lunch to be brought to his office. He had a lot of work to cover that afternoon, especially if he planned to make it to the island.

"What was so important you couldn't tell me over the phone?" Curtis asked.

"Vanetta was here the night Matt was murdered."

Silence greeted him. Then, "Here as in on the island or here in Virginia Beach?"

"Both." Jordan repeated the tale.

Curtis scrubbed a hand over his face. "You think she found him?"

"I don't know," Jordan said.

"Do you think Wade knows more than he revealed to you?"

"Wade was loyal to Matt. I think he knows more than he's telling me."

"I'll talk to Vanetta," Curtis said. "Not that I can help her."

"Well, she's carrying a lot of pain, and I don't think she's talking to anyone," Jordan said.

"I loved Matt like a father. Besides yours, he was the only father figure I had. But I could punch his lights out for what he did to Vanetta."

Jordan sighed. "I know how you feel."

Jordan's phone buzzed, and he pressed the button. "I thought I told you to hold all calls."

"It's Ms. Claxton," the operator announced.

"Which Claxton?" Jordan asked, frowning.

"Alyssa Claxton, sir."

"Thank you." Jordan depressed the button on his phone. "Alyssa."

"What the hell kind of game are you playing?"

"Excuse me?" What the heck was she talking about?

"Racine Hammerfield. Are you following me now?"

Jordan shook his head. "Who is she?"

"Don't play dumb."

"I don't have a clue. Does she have something to do with Matt's murder?"

"You really don't know Racine?" a doubting voice asked.

"No."

"She was the one displaying her boobs and butt to you on the mountain trip."

"I've never spoken to that woman."

Silence. Jordan was wondering if Alyssa had hung up when finally she said, "Okay . . . okay. Are you coming to the island for the weekend?" she asked in lieu of an answer.

"Should I?" She wasn't the only one who could play hard to get. Jordan picked up his pen and wrote this Racine's name on a pad.

"What time will you arrive?" Alyssa asked.

Jordan glanced at his watch, liking the fact that Alyssa was jealous for no reason. The bug was definitely there. "I'll try to make the seven o'clock ferry."

She hung up.

Jordan sighed. Was it too much for the woman to come right out and ask him to drop by her place? Didn't even give him a chance to ask if she wanted him to take her to dinner. But this was progress. He was finally getting the message that she'd ended things with Reginald.

Curtis was looking at him strangely.

Jordan shook his head. "It was the witch."

"Oh, she's the witch now."

"She's softening some."

Curtis chuckled. "For a while there, I thought you'd lost your magic touch."

Jordan chuckled. "Yeah, me too. She's something else." He glanced at the pad. "Do you know anything about a Racine Hammerfield?"

"Oh, gad."

"Who is she?"

"A man eater. Skinny cheerleader type. I went to dinner last Friday night at Cornell's place. She just plunked herself down at my table and started to tell me the story of her life. When she started on her college years, I asked for a doggie bag."

"I wonder how her name got mixed up with mine? She must have said something to upset Alyssa."

"I heard she and Alyssa were rivals."

"Oh." But Jordan didn't see any humor in that. He knew Alyssa must have had a complex about her height in her younger years, no matter how self-assured she seemed now.

"I'm going to the island early after I drop by to see my mother. I'll see you later."

"I hope not." Curtis stood. "If I do, you have a serious problem, friend."

Jordan sighed and clapped Curtis on the shoulder. Neither of them had had much luck with women lately. But maybe their luck was about to change.

After Vanetta left the hair salon, she visited with friends at the artist colony. They were glad to see her. And it was refreshing to be with people who weren't burdened with Matthew's death. After spending an hour there, she went to her grandmother's house. Naomi was sitting on the porch shelling peas. Vanetta pulled up a chair beside her and dipped her hand into the bowl for a pea. Such a simple task. Women had shared it for generations. It required little thought and left plenty of time for conversation. Made the job less of a drudgery. Vanetta remembered summers of sitting on the front porch with Naomi, completing this mundane chore. She shelled several peas in silence.

"Lisa's coming over soon," Naomi said. "I told her I'd made some macaroni and cheese and fried chicken."

"Is she getting off early today?"

"She went in early and got her work done. Your hair looks nice. Went to the beauty parlor?"

"Just came from there."

"Barbara does a nice job. I should go there and get my hair trimmed."

Vanetta didn't want to talk about hair.

"Can I get you a glass of lemonade?" Naomi asked.

Vanetta shook her head. She couldn't swallow a thing past her clogged throat.

"Grandma, it's time we start on the art project again," Vanetta said. "We've put it off long enough."

Naomi's knowledgeable eyes met Vanetta's. "Keeping busy won't make you forget."

"I don't want to talk about it." Vanetta busily shelled more peas as if her sanity depended on shelling as many as she could as quickly as she could.

"You don't have to talk until you're ready." Naomi fell silent, but she wasn't known for long stretches of silence. She always had something to say. Vanetta questioned her own motive for going there in the first place.

"I know you're hurting. It's hard to grieve when there's so much anger stirring around in you. You feel like a blender, all those emotions whirling up together."

Vanetta was too full of those whirling emotions to speak. Grandma didn't know the half of it. She didn't know Vanetta had peered at Matthew and Vicky's lifeless bodies before Alyssa had found them. She didn't know Vanetta had seen the blood covering the chair. She didn't know she'd seen the intimate setting and clothes Vicky had worn. And she didn't know Matthew was waiting for his whore.

"Peace isn't going to come right away," Naomi was

saying. "But one day you're going to remember a time when he was a better man."

A better man. Was anything about her marriage real? Had it all been an illusion?

Lisa peeled into the yard as if someone was chasing her. She pulled to an abrupt stop and got out with the car still rocking.

"I hope that chicken's ready," she said. "I'm starved."

"It's on the stove. Help yourself."

"I didn't know you were stopping by," she said to Vanetta. She'd changed into jeans and a short-sleeve sweater. She climbed the porch and went into the house, the screen door slamming after her. Five minutes later, she came back with a plate of food and sat in Grandpa's rocker.

"Lord, Grandma, this chicken is something else. Mama doesn't cook anymore."

"All you children are grown. You should cook for her."

"You still cook," Lisa said.

"I went through a period when I didn't cook much. It was when the grandchildren started coming around that I started again."

"I'm grateful you did."

"Vanetta and I are going to start on the project at the artist colony again," Naomi said.

Lisa stopped eating. She looked first at Vanetta as if thinking she needed to be locked up for her own good, then she glanced at Naomi. Grandma continued to shell peas as if she didn't have a care.

"But you have a million things to do," Lisa reminded her, as if she needed a reminder.

"I know," Vanetta said.

"And I thought you were going to stay with Mama for a while."

"I don't think so. There's too much to do at the house."

"It's not like you have to do it all this minute," Lisa said and tore the wing pieces apart. "You've got all those companies to sort through. It'll take time."

"Jordan's helping me with it. Besides, it's common knowledge that you shouldn't make major changes for at least for a year."

Lisa sighed, took a sip of her lemonade. People were going around saying Vanetta was on the island when Matthew and Vicky were killed. They all thought she'd killed them. She wondered if Vanetta had heard. How in the heck was she going to bring up the subject to her perfect sister?

Maybe she wasn't so perfect after all, Lisa thought and then felt guilty for thinking bad thoughts about her sister when she was hurting.

Chapter 9

Jordan left the office early to run by his mother's house. She was leaving for South Carolina in a few days, and he was spending the weekend on the island.

Aromas of cooking hit him as soon as he got out of the car. His mother was expecting him.

"Something smells good," he called out.

"Come on back. I cooked enough for you."

"Sorry I can't stay long enough to eat. I was supposed to get off earlier."

"Going to see Alyssa?"

"Yeah." He grabbed his mother, lifted her up off the floor, and whirled her around.

She squealed and laughed at once. "Put me down, boy. What happened?" she asked, catching her breath. "Got a new business deal?"

"Nothing like that. I'm scheming, I'm planning things, I'm trying everything to get this woman to take me seriously, and suddenly, she's thinking I'm seeing someone else, and everything finally falls into place." He chuckled. "Does your son have skills or not?"

"And you've hit pay dirt, have you?" She turned her

back to him and stirred something on the stove. "And that's great in your book."

"What is it now?" he asked, catching the note of censure in her voice. "I thought you'd be happy for me. I thought you liked Alyssa."

"I do. But here you have a woman who has some feelings for you, who has every right to be cautious about taking a chance with you because of your history, and it's all a game. You've closed another deal. So what? You've closed plenty in the past. What is she going to be? Another of your bimbos who waits on you hand and foot? Who hovers by the phone waiting for a phone call when you don't give crap about her?"

"I'm not like that."

Raising an eyebrow, she faced him with the wooden spoon in her hand. "You're not? Do you really think I don't know what's running through your mind?"

It took everything in Jordan not to give an eye roll, knowing very well if he did, that spoon would come sailing at his head. "It's time you worried about yourself. I'm more than capable to taking care of me."

"What can you offer Alyssa?" his mother asked.

Jordan frowned. "Everything I have."

She laid the cup towel on the countertop. "And what's that?"

"I'm building a home. Stability." Damn it. Why was she going on this way?

His mother nodded. "It's a fine house, all right," she said as if he was building an outhouse instead of a luxury beach estate.

"Enough money to satisfy her wildest dreams," Jordan continued. He'd worked damn hard all his life, and he was proud of his success. Yes, he could afford the bling, and he wasn't hiding it.

"Maybe she doesn't have as much money as you have,

but she has money of her own, enough to keep her comfortable. Her house isn't as large as yours, but it's a home in a nice area. Something she can be proud of." She shook her head, sent him a sad smile. He felt ten again. "She won't marry you for your home or your money, son. A woman like Alyssa needs more than what your money can buy. So I ask you again, what do you have to offer her?"

"According to you, I don't have very much to offer her, do I?" he said, barely concealing his anger. How could she whittle his accomplishments down to insignificance? "Except me."

"Your love comes with a high price if I go by what you've offered women in the past."

Where did she get off with the L word? He'd never said he loved Alyssa, never even thought about it.

"In some ways, you haven't turned into the man your father and I taught you to be. And that disappoints me."

Jordan was stunned. "I thought you were proud of my accomplishments."

"I am, but your moral values have gotten skewed along the way. Women are just another commodity to be bought and sold for a price. I've seen the women you've dated. They cater to your whims as if they don't have minds of their own."

"Well, you don't have to worry about that with Alyssa," he snapped.

"Thank God for that."

"Should I thank you? I didn't know you had such low opinions of me. That I was such a disappointment."

"You're not a disappointment." She sighed. "You're missing the point, knucklehead. I don't want you to end up with a woman who's all about the money, all about the bling, as your generation says. I want you settled with a *good* woman. Someone who will make a great mother. Who will be there for the good times and bad because in life, no matter how much money you have, there are going to be some storms," she said. "Son, women have been too easy for you. Go back to your roots. Remember what your dad and I taught you about respect, about love. Your dad never treated me the way you've treated your women. You can't put a price on love."

"That bad, huh?" Her criticism annoyed the heck out of him. Women catered to him. They thought he was the greatest thing coming, and his own dear mother, the one he'd spent a fortune on, raked him over the coals as if he was some pauper barely eking out a living. As if he didn't bust his butt to make a success out of his life.

"I'm afraid if you continue down the path you're going," she continued through his rage, "you're going to suffer for it. You'll lose Alyssa. And you'll end up just like Matthew. I know what he offered you—the life he lived seemed glamorous. But everything that shines isn't gold. Look where he ended up. What kind of legacy is that to leave a loving wife? You think about that. Your dad and I didn't always see eye to eye, but we respected each other. We were close as close could get. There wasn't anything I couldn't trust him with. Do you think Matthew had that with Vanetta? Do you think she could trust him with her most tender, most intimate secrets and desires? Do you think he had the presence of mind to value them if she did?"

Jesus. His mother had said a mouthful. He knew Matthew had some flaws. And he knew he wanted something different.

"Is that why you never remarried?" he asked around his clogged throat.

"I never placed myself on a pedestal to save myself for your dad. I just haven't found anyone who I can trust the way I trusted him. And I'm not settling for second best. Marriage is just too hard to put up with foolishness." She turned back to the stove. "If Alyssa is just another successful business deal, leave her alone now, before it's too late and you hurt her."

"I'm not giving her up."

"What's the difference between now and a few months later when she starts making demands you aren't willing to agree to? You'll just cut and run as you always do."

"Those women knew the score."

"I raised a moron." She glanced toward the ceiling. "Lord, where did I go wrong?"

Nobody raised his frustration level the way his mother did. "You just don't understand today's world."

"You said the same thing at fifteen. I've lived longer than you have, son. I understand more than you think I do. Like I said, leave Alyssa alone."

Like hell he would.

"Since you can't stay, I'll fix a couple of plates for you and put them in a cooler. You can eat them later."

"I feel like I'm missing something, John," Alyssa said later on. She was running in circles and getting nowhere.

"Like what?"

"You ever get the feeling everyone's holding something back from you?"

"Like conversations coming to an abrupt halt when you walk in?"

"Right. What does everyone know that they aren't telling us?" Alyssa didn't mention that she felt as if someone was watching her. He'd think she was paranoid as well as overly suspicious. "I'm going over all my notes this weekend. See you later."

Alyssa stopped at The Greasy Spoon in town to grab a sandwich. Stanley was coming out of the hardware store with old Mr. Jimmy Jones, Patience and Reginald's uncle. He was a retired ferry captain, who only worked part-time now. With his wind-beaten and sunburned face, he was as weathered as driftwood. He often worked the holidays when the regular captain scheduled time off or was on vacation.

"Hey, Alyssa," Stanley called out.

Alyssa's mouth was full, so she waved.

"How is Vanetta?" Jimmy asked. "Takes a while to recover."

Alyssa swallowed quickly. "She's taking it a day at a time. Her parents are trying to get her to move in with them for a while. We'll see how that works."

"Change of scenery will be good for her," Jimmy said, nodding his gray head.

"Sure is a shame about Matthew," Stanley said. "The families were always very pleased with Vicky's work. Everyone misses her."

"That Vicky was something else," Jimmy said fondly. "Always doing something. A whirlwind of a woman. Always had something nice to say to me when she saw me, too. You know a lot of young ones are too busy for old folks these days. But not Vicky. I'm gonna miss that gal. I dropped by to see her mama the other day." He shook his gray head. "She's still taking it hard, bless her soul. Melinda's keeping a close eye on her, though. I'm glad of that. That poor girl has it hard."

"Guess you haven't had much time to spend with Melinda since everything happened," Stanley said to Alyssa in his quiet voice.

"I take some time for her," Alyssa said. "But it's not enough. Never enough."

"Must be keeping you busy, between her and Vanetta. Family entanglements can be something."

"Vanetta's a good woman," Jimmy said. "She told me the Sunday before you found the bodies that she'd help me research some places to send Patience. Her drinking's getting worse and worse. So bad she's passing out now. Having blackouts. It's just got to stop. Before long, her liver's just gonna give out. And she's a young gal. Reg has talked to her. Doesn't do a lick of good. Stanley has been like a rock." He clapped Stanley on the back. The man almost toppled over. "I'm grateful for what you've done for her."

"I hope she listens to you," Stanley said. "I took her to an AA meeting, but she wouldn't talk or go back. You've got to want to get help. And she just isn't at that point yet. She's been drinking since the last miscarriage when the doctor told her she couldn't have children. I told her we could adopt. There are plenty of children who need homes, but she said she'll think about it."

"She can't adopt in the condition she's in," Jimmy said. "She's liable to pass out with the baby in her arms."

The men rambled on about Patience, but one of Jimmy's statements had caught Alyssa's attention. "Jimmy, did you say you talked to Vanetta on Sunday, the day before I found Matthew?" she asked, feeling a catch in her throat.

He nodded. "It was late. She rode the last ferry," Jimmy said. "It was slow that night. A lot of people out of town for the holidays. Busy the next day, though, with everybody coming back. Such a nice day, too. Who could guess what it would turn out to be?"

Vanetta had told Alyssa that she spent the night in Williamsburg with her friend and didn't return until late Monday. She'd gone to Vanetta's *after* visiting the Eastons with the bad news because Vanetta hadn't returned to town yet. But according to Jimmy, she was on the island the night before. Why would she lie?

Did she know the scene of the crime? Dear Lord, she didn't even want to consider that Vanetta had killed her husband, but as an officer of the law, she had to. Why the secrets?

* * *

Alyssa was deep in thought as she left downtown and headed to her aunt's house. Vanetta was in the kitchen with her mother, peeling apples for her aunt's prized apple jelly.

"I'll save a jar for you, Alyssa."

"Thanks, Aunt Dorothy." She gazed at Vanetta, who looked slightly nervous. "Can I have a word with you, Van?"

They walked outside, and Alyssa closed the door behind them. Vanetta's mother was nosy, so she wouldn't put it past her to listen in.

"You want to tell me again where you were Sunday night?"

She scrubbed a hand over her face. "I didn't find him, Alyssa. Yes, I looked for him. I tried to call him, and he wouldn't answer. I found a nearly empty Viagra bottle when I returned home. He must have gotten careless and left it out. And yes, I looked high and low for him, but I didn't find him. I know he wasn't at the club. I checked every place I could think of." She emitted a dry chuckle. "The truth was I didn't know him anymore. I didn't know where he spent his time."

"What were you going to do once you found him?"

"I just wanted to catch him in the act. I was going to demand a divorce."

"Where did you look?"

Vanetta sighed and sat down on one of her mother's lounge chairs.

"The Cove. A few clubs in Norfolk he used to take me to when we dated. A few new clubs I'd heard about. I didn't see his car anywhere."

"Why did you stay in Williamsburg?"

"It was too late to return home unless I got somebody with a boat to bring me back. And my friend wanted me to spend the night in Williamsburg. I just didn't want to be alone. And with him chasing skirts, I saw no reason for me to stick around. I needed some time to think."

Alyssa sighed. "You had motive and opportunity."

"But I didn't do it. How was I supposed to lift Matthew, as heavy as he is? It would take someone a lot stronger than me."

"Who says you had to do it alone, or that you even did it? You could have hired someone. At least, that's what a Commonwealth's Attorney would say."

Vanetta lifted her chin in a stubborn angle. "Are you arresting me?"

"No. But I do have to tell you not to leave town."

"Where am I going?"

"Are you telling me everything? I need to know the scene of the crime, Vanetta. It'll go easier on you if you come clean now."

But Vanetta closed her mouth.

Angrily, Alyssa went through the house, but Vanetta stayed on the deck. Her aunt's lips were pinched—obviously she'd eavesdropped. Guess Alyssa wasn't getting any jam.

"How could you accuse Van of killing that vile man? She's your kin. Where's your loyalty?"

"I have to investigate everyone, Aunt Dorothy," Alyssa bit out. "I can't treat this case differently than any other just because Vanetta's kin. Why don't you tell her to tell the truth?"

When Alyssa got into her car, she wanted to hit something. The phones would start up soon, and tongues would be wagging. A couple of uncles would come by her place. And she'd be persona non grata. That didn't worry her. What worried her was whether Vanetta was holding on to more secrets. Whether Vanetta knew the scene of the crime and was holding out. She was right that Matthew was too heavy for her to lift. Was there another player in this drama?

Harper had called her earlier for an update on the case. She would have to go in. She'd have to report this new information.

Half and hour later, John and Harper left, and Alyssa stopped by her mom's to take food home for dinner.

Alyssa's mom had called earlier to tell her she'd fixed her favorites for dinner. She was immediately weary. Sometimes her mother fixed a favorite dinner to soften her up for something. Alyssa had skipped lunch, and she was hungry. And it was her favorite. She was on the run. She'd stop by long enough to pick up her plate.

"I thought the food was ready," Alyssa said.

"Does that mean you expected to grab a plate and disappear?"

"I'm still on the clock."

"You have to sleep and eat, too. Sit while I fix your plate. Bet you haven't had a moment to rest all day."

Alyssa sat, but her mother was taking her own good time taking out the plastic containers. She stirred something on the stove.

"Fifty percent of black women your age will never marry," she began, and Alyssa checked herself to keep from sighing. You didn't sigh at Miranda Claxton. "Did you know that, Alyssa?"

"I've heard. How many times have you told me?"

"The news got back to me that you and dear Reginald broke up. You've been friends since when?"

"We're still friends, Mama. We don't work as a couple." Alyssa knew her mother spoke the truth, but friendship wasn't the simmering in the stomach kind of thrill she got with Jordan. She recognized it as lust, but there was something to be said for intense desire. She couldn't marry one man and think of being in bed with another. Of course, she didn't know what kind of lover Reginald was since they'd never shared intimacy. That alone was telling.

"Reginald works long hours so he won't mind if you aren't home to fix meals. He likes to grill, too. So he won't be one of those husbands who would worry you about cooking."

"I know he's a really nice guy. And I hope he finds someone to love him the way he should be loved. I'm not the one. And I'm not so desperate that I'm settling. If it isn't right, I'll live alone. I can live with myself."

"Pride is okay now. You're young, and your life is ahead of you. But at fifty, you might sing a different tone."

Alyssa couldn't contain a sigh.

"Do you have special feelings for Jordan? Is he the reason you suddenly know it won't work with Reginald?"

"I don't know Jordan that well." No sense in throwing her the bone that she was seeing Jordan this weekend. Her mother would gnaw on it like steak.

"He isn't confused about the way he feels for you. He's the one building that big, beautiful castle not far from your place, isn't he?"

Her mother would have made a great detective. She probably knew Jordan's life history by now. "I'm sure he'll give you a tour if you ask."

"Has he given you a tour?"

Alyssa should have kept her mouth shut.

"Are you serious about him?"

"Mama, I don't know the guy that well."

"Alyssa, Alyssa, Alyssa." Her mother's sigh was long and drawn out.

"Tell you what, I have a million things to do. I'll fix my own plate."

"Sit!" her mother barked, and Alyssa eased back into

the chair. "You aren't getting any younger. Now either of those men would make good husbands. Friendship and things in common is three-fourths of the battle.

"If I can't get the food I came for, I'm leaving."

"Be patient." Finally, Miranda began to pull containers from the cabinet. "And make sure you return them."

"I thought you bought the cheap stuff now. Not like the expensive Tupperware. Isn't that what the commercial says?"

With containers of food in hand, Alyssa headed home. Once there, she went to the bedroom to pull off her clothes. In the bathroom, she used scented soap and made quick work of her shower. She'd invited the man, but she hadn't given a thought to what she would wear. As she dried off, she considered what in her closet was appropriate. She discarded several outfits and finally thought of the long thin dress with short sleeves. While it didn't show much cleavage, it was enough to tease. The evenings were cool now. Maybe she shouldn't wear such a thin dress, Alyssa thought as she smoothed the sides and considered herself in the mirror.

He'd keep her warm, she decided as she spritzed on perfume and just a touch of makeup. The most she could do with her hair was to comb it out. Finally, she donned earrings and a gold necklace to complete the outfit.

Then she went to her office and pulled out her notes on the case. When the phone rang, she realized she'd been studying them for an hour. It was Naomi.

"What's up, Grandma?" Alyssa asked.

"What's happening with the heirloom golden bowl?" she asked.

The bowl hadn't crossed Alyssa's mind. "Nothing."

"You're the detective. You should have found out something by now."

"I'm sure it'll turn up on its own. It's probably stashed

in somebody's attic or basement." She wouldn't mention it had probably been sold.

"I think somebody's stolen it."

"You have no proof of that."

"Those thieves who were here aren't the only ones after that bowl. It could be one of the islanders. There are some jealous people in this world."

"Grandma, don't get paranoid. Before long, you'll be accusing every islander who isn't a family member."

"I want the bowl," her grandmother said stubbornly.

"Okay. Okay. As soon as this investigation is over, I'll get to it."

"I had a hard time sleeping last night. I'm worried about Vanetta," Naomi said. "And I'm gravely disappointed in Matthew. I never thought he was the best suitor for Vanetta, but I didn't think he'd cheat right under our noses. And with an island girl, no less. Some people have no couth. No sense of decency at all."

"Yes, well, there's no accounting for taste."

"I know Melinda is your friend. But Vicky should have known better. She came from a good family, too. How could she do such a thing?"

"Well, it's put a strain on family relations."

"How is Melinda holding up?"

"She's still in shock," Alyssa said.

"If only young people would think before they do stupid things."

"Matthew wasn't a young man, Grandma."

"We know what he was thinking with. Shame on him. My granddaughter is a beautiful woman any sane man would be proud to have on his arm."

"Grandma, she's not an expensive jacket or an ornament."

Naomi ignored her comment. "So what do you have on the murders so far?"

Alyssa groaned. "I can't discuss it, not even with my dear old grandma."

Naomi harrumphed. "Are you at least eating?"

"Mama made my favorite."

"I'm frying fish. I'll save enough for you."

"Thanks, Grandma. How are you and Grandpa doing?"

"I don't know. He's still hanging with his cronies. He's probably trying to solve the case," she said. "I'm thinking about taking a vacation as soon as this thing with Vanetta dies down. I need to get away. If it's not one thing, it's another. Something's always going on."

"It'll be good for you and Grandpa to get away. Get that old romance stirring again."

"Don't be foolish, girl."

Naomi might put on airs, but Alyssa knew the average woman, regardless the age, wanted a little romance in her life. They needed to get Hoyt away from his cronies so he could concentrate on his wife, for a change.

A nice little vacation would be just the ticket. Maybe the grands could get together and send them somewhere. Their grandmother's birthday was coming up. They needed to figure out a place to send them. It was time to hold a family meeting with the grandchildren . . . as if she had the time. Alyssa began to think of who she could rope into doing the legwork. The grandchildren were listed on her computer in an address folder. She'd just shoot something over the Internet.

After she hung the phone up, Alyssa logged onto her computer and sent the message announcing a meeting at her place Saturday, then turned off the computer. She'd read through the protest messages tonight for arranging a meeting without much warning. Whatever meeting date she set wouldn't coincide with someone's schedule even if she gave them a month's notice.

* * *

Jordan ran five miles on the treadmill. He pumped iron for a half hour, and his frustration still hadn't abated. He was sweating and breathing hard by the time he finished.

He didn't treat women like day-old trash.

He'd gone back to the office after he left his mother's house, changed into workout clothes, and headed straight to the club's exercise room. He wiped the sweat with a fluffy white towel and headed to his private shower.

Half an hour later, Jordan glanced up at the knock on his office door. "Come in."

"Package for you," a bellman said.

"Right on time," Jordan said, spotting the white floral box. "Just set it on the table."

"You're going to make some woman happy."

Jordan gritted a smile while he dug his wallet out of his pocket for a tip. "Let's hope."

"Thank you, sir. Have a nice weekend."

Jordan nodded. "The same to you."

It was time for him to leave. His weekend bag was already packed. He grabbed the roses and bag and left for the island. Although it was close to seven, he should make it to the ferry in time. He couldn't believe he'd let her lead him around since February. And now, he was finally getting a night with her. He'd checked the B&B to make sure they had rooms for the weekend, just in case. He wouldn't put it past Alyssa to send him packing at the strike of midnight. He was seriously losing his touch.

He wouldn't focus on his mother's diatribe.

The ferry moved ponderously to the island. It was a cool afternoon, but pleasant. He could understand why the islanders protected their territory so fiercely. He could feel the stress from the day draining from his shoulders. It had the effect the gym had failed to produce. It was worth the hassle of getting to and from work when you had a place like this to come home to on the weekends.

He just wished Alyssa could finish up with that case so she could concentrate on them.

The ferry docked, and Jordan went to his car, starting the motor just in time for a place in the line to drive off. In fifteen minutes, he was pulling into Alyssa's yard. He grabbed the box of flowers on the seat beside him and exited the car.

Alyssa's car was parked in the yard. It was so isolated out here, he thought as he went to the door. Which was okay if she lived with someone, but she was alone and as brave as all get out. Too brave, he thought. The fact that the bodies had been found near her home still gave him nightmares.

He rang the doorbell. She answered it quickly. And she looked heavenly.

"Hi," she said, leading him toward the back of the house. "You can just . . . Oops . . ."

He hauled her into his arms and kissed her. It was the sweetest nectar. And she responded as if she was as hungry for him as he was for her.

She eased away from him, her hand pressing on his chest. "Just give me a few minutes."

She grasped his hand. "Come to the sunroom and enjoy the sunset. I mixed peach margaritas."

He started to say something trite like he'd prefer to sip on her, then let it go. He'd forgotten to hand her the flowers. Before she disappeared through the door, he placed them in her arms.

"Thank you." She opened the box. "Oh, my gosh. These are absolutely lovely."

"I'm glad they please you."

"I'll"—she cleared her throat—"I'll place them in a vase. Enjoy your drink." She pointed to the table. "And there's the remote if you want to watch the tube." But he didn't reach for it.

As Alyssa searched under the kitchen cabinet for a vase, she pressed a hand to her heart. His kiss had knocked her for a loop. Finding a vase, she filled it with water and quickly cut the ends off the roses. One by one, she placed the perfect blossoms in the water. Not one was blemished, and all the thorns had been removed.

What was she getting herself into? she thought as she held the last rose in her hand and took a brief sniff. The end was capped with a tiny water tube. She took it to the bathroom, swept her hair to the side, cut the rose, and tucked it behind her ear. Her stomach was only jumping a little when she joined Jordan in the sunroom.

"Ah, just in tim . . ." He caught his breath. Alyssa's heart thumped.

She cleared her throat. "In time for what?"

"What? Oh, the sunset." He stood, reached out his hand. "Let's go out on the deck. I think it's still warm. If not, I'll keep you warm."

"I'm sure you will."

On the deck, they stood at the railing with their drinks and watched the magnificent sunset. Boats bobbed in the water. But when Alyssa glanced at Jordan, he was gazing at her.

"You look absolutely beautiful," he said in a husky voice.

"You'll miss the sunset."

"No, I won't." He took the drink from her hand.

"Dinner is ready. Are you hungry?"

He pulled her closer to him and kissed her. "I'm hungry for you."

Chapter 10

It was Friday, and he settled in his usual observation area. He liked that term. Observation Point. He chuckled as he got his binoculars ready to view his lovely Alyssa. Often, she'd come outside to jog, walk the beach, or just chill out on the deck. What would it be this time? Of course, with the extra work of trying to solve the case, she spent less time relaxing these days. He had himself to blame for that, but things would eventually go back to normal.

He could feel the desire bubbling through him in anticipation of her arrival.

He took a beer out of his cooler, popped the top, and sipped. Ah, what more could a man want? A cold beer and a beautiful woman, he thought as he crossed his ankles on the rail of the boat.

He'd heard she dumped Reginald. There was nothing there anyway. It just took her too long to see the light. He had been getting worried about Reginald for a while, but he'd relied on Alyssa to do the right thing. He could always rely on her.

Impatient, he tapped his fingers on the chair. She usually watched the sunset while most women would be getting dolled up to go out for the night. Not his Alyssa. She was a homebody. Women these days were so busy they didn't have time to take care of home or their men. But not Alyssa. He was so proud of her he could burst his shirt.

She might dress in a severe suit for a uniform during the day, but at night, she was all sweet and feminine. Don't get him wrong. She was a tough woman, but he liked the softer side of her, too.

He glanced at his watch. It was right about the time she usually came outside. Impatience stirred in him. He focused the binoculars to get a clearer view. He'd never revered anyone as much as Alyssa. He didn't know how long worshiping her from afar would satisfy him. Sweat gathered on his forehead, and his pants grew uncomfortably tight at his body's reaction to her.

The door opened. He smiled, then frowned. His feet dropped to the deck.

What the hell?

Alyssa came through the door, and a man came out immediately behind her. He was holding her damn hand. What the hell was wrong with them? Alyssa was *his* woman. She'd just gotten rid of that good-for-nothing Reginald. She'd taken up with another man already? Freaking whore.

Anger seethed through him as he watched them act like star-struck lovers. She was dressed like a whore, too, and on a cool evening. And she was acting like one, his arms tight around her. They were kissing. And he knew she was kissing his money, not him. Women were such whores. He whipped the binoculars away, dropped them on the seat.

He would teach her a lesson, and soon. She'd learn not to spoil his Friday nights. He wasn't staying around to watch this shit.

He stomped to the wheel, started up his engine, and sped off.

* * *

Alyssa heard the motor roar up and disturb the silence as a boat left its place in the ocean several hundred yards away. She frowned. Swiftly, it moved across the waves.

"What's wrong?" Jordan asked.

Alyssa shook her head. "Nothing. Let's eat."

"I forgot to tell you my mother sent dinner."

"I'll have to thank her. We won't have to go out for food then because my mom sent food, too."

"What do you want to do after dinner? Go to a club on the mainland? Take in a movie?"

"A quiet evening at home."

"Works for me."

Her mother had outdone herself with the fried fish, potato salad, and greens. His mom had sent shrimp, macaroni and cheese, and green beans. A battle of the cooks, Alyssa thought.

"I don't want you to think I can't cook," she said as they settled at the table.

"I'll get to sample your culinary skills sometime, won't I?"

"When do I get to sample yours?" Alyssa asked.

"I'll gladly prepare a meal for you at your own peril."

Alyssa laughed. "You can make a multimillion dollar deal but can't fry an egg?"

"I can fry an egg. My mama made sure I knew the basics in case I married a woman who couldn't."

"How long will she be here?"

"Not long. But let's not talk about mothers," he said before his vision clouded.

"What's wrong?" Alyssa asked.

"I'm thinking about Matthew. I keep asking myself, why now? He seemed pretty happy and content with Vanetta. So why did he screw up now when he was getting up in the years and was married to a young and beautiful wife?"

"Let me tell you, the wrong kind of woman can turn a man's head, especially if he's open to having it turned," Alyssa said. "I don't know why Vicky was having an affair with him, especially if according to her husband, she was considering repairing their relationship."

"When I think of that man, I feel sorry for him. I don't know if he killed Matt, but he looks like a man who's gone through hell and lost." Jordan scrubbed a hand across his face. "None of it makes sense. Maybe it was a last hurrah for both of them. But let's not spend this one night discussing your case. Don't you need time away from it?"

"You're right, I do," Alyssa said. She needed a break so that she could think clearly.

Jordan stood. "I'll help with the dishes."

They worked companionably getting the few dishes they used washed and put away. Then they went back to the sunroom to watch TV. But mostly, they talked about their past.

"Do you want to tell me about Racine?" Jordan asked finally.

Alyssa stiffened, her calm immediately fleeing. "Not really."

"Well, maybe I need to send her roses if she was responsible for you calling me."

"Only if you're ready to die."

Jordan chuckled. Alyssa elbowed him.

"Ouch. You're a vicious woman." He held her close. "It's that serious, huh? Why don't you tell me about her?"

Alyssa groaned. "You're not going to be satisfied until I do, are you?"

"Nope." But she noticed he tightened his arm around her shoulder. And for some reason, she felt comforted.

"She was my . . . rival is a tame word for it. Thorn in the backside fits her more accurately."

"One of those, huh?"

"I was tall. Taller than all the girls and most of the boys. And the hussy never let me forget it."

He stroked her tense arm. "You strike me as being comfortable in your own skin."

"I am for the most part. But what teenager wants to be taller than her dates? And the look football players gave dainty little Racine used to burn me up inside."

"Did you ever consider there was something about you that made her feel inadequate, lacking? I don't remember this Racine because my eyes were only on you, but most kids who feel a need to torment another to the degree she tormented you are insecure and want you to feel the same insecurity."

"I learned all that. Believe me, my mother gave me a steady dose of being proud of who I am. So I grew to accept me. But there are still times . . ."

"Well, I like you exactly the way you are." He nipped her earlobe. "If I didn't, I wouldn't have spent the last seven and a half months running you down."

"You're exaggerating. It hasn't been that long."

"It has. Just because I was away doesn't count. You were still on my mind. You were still my goal."

"And now that you think you have me, what do you plan to do with me?"

"Woman, that's a loaded question." Jordan could take a hint when he heard one. She didn't have to inquire twice. Because suddenly her head was tilted and in the flickering light of the TV, her luminous eyes were seeking his. He could not resist a kiss. First, he teased her with soft, brushing strokes across her lips that only served to tantalize him. It felt as if a lifetime had passed since they were last together.

The first time they had been so eager to get at each other, they'd wasted no time. And although this time, Jordan was equally as needy, he wanted to pleasure her in ways she'd only dreamed of. He only hoped he could hold off long enough.

His hands stroked her first through the thin fabric of the dress that had been tempting him from the moment he saw her in it. There were so many complex layers to her, and he wanted to get to know every one. She ranged from ultra feminine to extremely efficient.

He kissed her cheek a moment before brushing his lips against her ear. Alyssa moaned as unexpected pleasure rushed through her. Inhaling her sweet perfume, he kissed her collarbone, her neck, then strung kisses downward, nudging the wispy fabric aside.

Her hands were doing amazing things to his body. "Baby, you keep touching me like that, and I'm not going to last long."

"Who's asking you to?"

As he nearly came apart, he remembered some quote about the best laid plans. But he grabbed her up in his arms and went in the only direction the bedrooms could be.

"Point out the right one," he said, and she did. He only used a second to glance at the feminine room. She was definitely a nester. He liked that. So many contrasts in this amazing woman. He laid her on the bed and nudged the dress aside.

Her hands tugged at his clothing. He wanted to take it slow. Had every intention to. But before he knew it, he was kissing her frantically, and then he was peeling on the condom and he was in her.

"Sweet Jesus," he said. For a moment, he just lay there, enjoying the feel of her. And then he was moving. Stroking his hard length to her very core. With her long legs wrapped around him, he nearly lost control, but he held on until she sang out in fulfillment. He was only seconds behind her.

* * *

Around midnight, he waited by the bus stop for April, but she never came. He waited for the next bus, but she wasn't on that, either. Finally, he drove to her house. The house was dark, but he got out and rang the doorbell. No one answered.

Whore. Where was she this time of night? Angrily, he stomped to his car. He drove to Church Street to search for the woman he used when he was desperate.

He wasn't desperate, he reminded himself. No, he wasn't desperate at all. Two women had betrayed him. They would both pay. But for now, he needed relief.

It took him an hour, but he finally hunted her down.

"Hey, sweetness," he called out.

With an extra swing in her hips, she came to the car and leaned in the open window. She wore bright red lipstick and a badly fitting wig that hung to the middle of her back.

"Haven't seen you in a while," she said.

He shrugged. She looked haggard, but she never gave him sass.

"Busy?" he asked.

"Never too busy for you."

"Why don't you spend the night with me?"

He pushed open the door, and she climbed in.

He had a boat waiting for him. He parked down a long, wooded dirt path.

"Honey, why don't you leave the shoes in the car? You can't wear them on the boat. Hand the shoes to me."

"Whatever you say, sweetie." She pulled her spike heels off and handed them over. While she stood in her bare feet, he tossed the shoes in the trunk.

"You be careful with them. They're expensive."

"I'm sure they are," he said.

Losing no time, they climbed aboard his boat. He led her to a seat, and soon, they were jetting across the water.

"It's cold out here," she called out. "Got a jacket?"

"We'll be there soon," he hollered back. "You'll be okay." She was rubbing her hands up and down her arms to keep the chill away, but she wore a skimpy little outfit. All the rubbing in the world wasn't going to help her. And that was exactly the way he wanted it.

They made it to the boathouse a few minutes later.

"You sure that thing isn't going to cave in on us?"

"It's sturdy," he assured her.

"Doesn't look it."

"You know what I like most about you?" he asked.

"Naw, what?"

"Your silence."

"Whatever you want, sugar."

She was silent as he activated the door opener and slid the boat into place as smooth as could be.

She was silent as they walked through the woods to an ancient barn.

After he paid her, she remained silent as he undressed her and positioned her on the table. And she was still silent as he rubbed his hands lightly over her skin before he positioned her body exactly the way he wanted her.

The silence was just the way he liked it. He liked women who were malleable. She didn't resist when he spread her legs apart. Merely waited for him to do as he chose. That's what he liked best about her. For a price, his wish was her command.

He unzipped his trousers and freed himself. After smoothing on a condom, he entered her slowly, gaining every ounce of pleasure from her.

It was an out-of-body experience until he thought of Alyssa with Jordan, then he leaned heavily on her. His hands went to her throat as if it was Alyssa's.

She screamed out and hit at him. "What are you doing?"

"Shut up," he bit between gritted teeth. He easily captured her flailing hands, secured them with the rope that was always nearby, and tied them above her head on a chain.

"Please, no!" she cried out.

His mind had escaped to another place. "Didn't I tell you to shut up!" His fingers tightened around her neck. Her body twitched as his fingers compressed until she lay slack.

Now she knew his power. Alyssa would soon know that power. He pumped himself into her over and over until he came to such tumultuous satisfaction it sucked the breath out of him. He fell on her, and there he lay until he gained enough strength to move. And then he made love to her again. And again.

In the blessed silence.

When he was finished, he cleaned himself and her. He positioned her as she should be. Her eyes watched him as he zipped his pants, but she didn't move and she didn't talk. Then he left her and closed the door behind him as he made his way to his boat.

She was second best, but she'd have to do. Vicky was gone. How he missed Vicky . . . if only she hadn't betrayed him. Alyssa had betrayed him, and the slut in Smithfield had betrayed him, as well.

A man couldn't trust a woman. How many times had he heard his old man say that while he beat the crap out of his mother?

But he'd thought that Alyssa was different. He thought she was perfect. She'd turned out to be just like the others.

It was time he taught her a lesson.

Alyssa and Jordan made love again that night before Jordan went outside to retrieve his bag. He stood there a moment, appreciating the differences between where he lived in the city and the country. He'd grown up in the city, had lived in the city his entire life. But being out here where the night was nearly pitch black was different as night and day. He stayed so long that Alyssa came looking for him with her revolver in her hand.

"When you didn't come back, I thought something had happened," she said.

"Just enjoying the evening," he said and retrieved his bag from his car. She must be more disturbed by the latest crimes than she let on. Slowly, they walked back inside together.

Jordan didn't make a big deal out of the gun, but it weighed heavily on his mind for a long time.

Alyssa didn't have a TV in her bedroom, so they talked until they got too sleepy to keep their eyes open. She fell asleep in his arms.

When Jordan awakened the next morning, he smelled bacon.

"Bacon?" His feet hung over the foot of the bed. It took a minute before he realized he wasn't in his own specially made bed. He'd had it outfitted to his tall proportions.

He took the time to peruse the room. It was a nice size, about eighteen by fifteen. There was a window seat beneath the window. Probably for reading. A dresser with a sculpture in the center, more than likely bought from the artist colony. On the side table, there was a lamp and two books on one and a lamp and a sculpture on the other. Last night, he'd moved a few pillows to the bench at the foot of the bed. There wasn't an excess of anything.

Jordan showered and dressed, then made his way to the kitchen. Alyssa wore jogging pants and a sweater.

"I was just coming to get you," she said.

Jordan wrapped his arms around her from behind and kissed her on the neck. "Good morning."

She laughed. "Oh, it is."

With one more kiss, he said. "What can I do to help?"

"You can get the juice out the fridge."

"What are your plans for the day?" he asked.

"I have to go into the office for a couple of hours. After that, I'll be free. What about you?"

"I'm free all day. Don't you even get a day off?"

"Most of the time, but not now. I'll take half of Sunday off, but I have a meeting this morning."

"We could meet for lunch."

"Sounds good, but maybe we should go to Grandma's."

"Should I pull out the suit?"

"Definitely not." Alyssa set the platter on the table, and they sat to eat.

At the station, Harper wore his jogging suit. John and Alyssa both wore jeans, and Alyssa sported a powder-blue sweater. This wasn't a regular work day, but time to be updated on the case.

"Talk to me," Harper said, glancing at the clock.

"We have some new information. Vanetta was on the island the night Vicky and Matthew were murdered."

"Bring her in for questioning."

"I've already questioned her." Alyssa went into detail about their conversation. "We have the same problem with her that we have with Brit. There's no evidence anywhere in her house. We went through it to gather information about Matthew and found nothing."

"Set up surveillance on her in addition to the surveillance on Brit."

"That's stretching our small department pretty thin," she said.

"I'll approve more overtime."

"Like we haven't been working overtime."

"You're the detective," Harper said. He usually said it just to annoy her because she'd wanted the job so badly. "I want Vanetta in here today," Harper finished.

"All right." So much for her day with Jordan. Alyssa left for her office and called him, then her cousin. Deep in her heart, she didn't believe Vanetta had killed those two people. It was physically impossible for her to do so alone.

"Vanetta, we need to talk to you . . . you might want to ask your lawyer to come in with you."

"Am I being charged with murder?" she asked.

Alyssa didn't know what to say.

Jordan, Curtis, and Vanetta's high-powered attorney walked into the station with Vanetta. Alyssa shouldn't have been surprised to see Matthew's partners.

All three men wore expensive suits. Vanetta seemed delicate, in need of all the males there to protect her, while Alyssa was the capable detective who could stand on her own.

Jordan and Curtis stayed in the reception area while the lawyer, Vanetta, Alyssa, and Harper went into his office for the interview.

They were there for an hour, but they didn't get any more information out of her.

Later that afternoon Jordan raked his gaze over the paper he was analyzing for the third time. Why were company funds being used for a building he had no knowledge of? All decisions went through him. Maybe Curtis knew something. Matthew might have discussed a buy with Curtis. Jordan dropped the pages on the desk and dialed Curtis's number.

"I'm going through Matthew's papers, and I found something on a building on Coast Street," he said. "It's all houses over there. Did Matthew mention any major purchases while I was out of town?"

"Matthew didn't discuss any business concerns with me. You and he kept tabs on that."

"Why would he buy a house?"

"How would I know? Maybe he planned to fix it up and flip it. Who knows."

Jordan wondered who had a key to the property and whether Matthew had listed it with an agent. Of course, it could have been a place he used for his trysts.

Jordan hated to bother Vanetta. She had enough on her mind, but he called her anyway.

"Just a quick question. Do you know about a house in Virginia Beach Matthew purchased in the company's name?"

"No. Where is it?"

He read off the address.

"I didn't get involved in any of his business interests," Vanetta said, knowing very well where the house was and wondering how quickly they would discover she'd been there that fateful night.

"I'll see if I can find a key and take a look. In the meantime, if you find a key, let me know."

"Sure."

Vanetta grabbed her purse from the bedroom her mother had transformed into a beautiful guest suite. Her mother had been hovering around her since she had been called to the station. It was driving her insane. "Mom, I have to run home. I'll be a while, so don't hold supper for me."

"Where are you going?"

"Jordan wants me to check out some things for him."

"Can't he take care of the business? You have enough on your mind."

"He can't do everything, Mama. Besides, I need to do something, or I'll just go crazy." Vanetta headed to the door. "I have to help him."

Vanetta got into her car. Driving down her parent's short lane, she tried to clear her head. When Matthew had started dating her, she'd thought it was a match made in heaven. He was so kind and worldly, while her entire life had centered on the island. She'd lived a rather tame existence. It wasn't until she went to college that she learned the world was a complex place. She never went without in her entire life. They weren't rich, but they'd always had food and shelter.

Of course, they read about poor areas, and her family donated money to charities. In college, some kids from humble backgrounds were on scholarships, but it was during her student teaching that she learned mothers actually spent the money for food and bills on drugs. And that dealers were threatening the kids, forcing them to sell drugs to pay back their parents' debt.

Watching it on the news wasn't like seeing it up close and personal.

Matthew's family had owned a little mom and pop store, and he had spent lots of time with his grandparents. He was very mannerly and kind, she thought. She'd been married to him for years before she realized that there were layers beneath that smile and smooth demeanor. And years longer before she realized he was cheating on her, although he always denied it.

I work hard, Vanetta. When would I have time for another woman? Where would I get the energy?

There was no medical purpose for Viagra except sex. She should have burned that house to the ground that night. Everything had been so hazy. She hoped she hadn't left fingerprints behind. Over the last few days, rage had poured over her like a driving rain. She'd had to smile at the knowing faces of people who'd found out her husband died in another woman's arms. And she had to accept condolences while they were snickering up their sleeves and talking about her behind her back.

She wasn't like her sister, Lisa. Lisa gave as good as she

got. Sure she landed in trouble, but she wasn't afraid to live. And she was more likely to stick it to a man before he stuck it to her.

Vanetta drove into the yard of her imposing home. She felt as if her husband had locked her away in this mausoleum while he lived his real life without her. She'd dutifully waited for him while he charmed the ladies, the SOB. But who hated him enough to kill him? Besides her, that was. And her anger hadn't gotten the best of her until she'd found that pill bottle.

How many times had he told her she was crazy for thinking he was having an affair? He'd made her doubt her own reasoning. If Alyssa had seen her that Sunday night, she'd arrest her for sure. Because she'd been angry enough to stab his mangy butt a thousand times.

Vanetta left the car and went inside. Matthew always kept an extra set of keys in his desk. She went straight there and grabbed the key ring.

The room still smelled of his cigars.

Then she drove to the ferry. She had the address scribbled on a piece of paper, but she remembered how to get there. When the ferry was almost to the dock, her cell phone began to ring. She looked at the number. It was Jordan. With all the seagulls squawking and the rumbling of the ferry's motor, if she answered it, he'd know she was on the ferry, so she let it ring.

Jordan hung up the phone and flipped through his file until he saw the number for Vanetta's mother.

"Mrs. Claxton, may I speak to Vanetta, please?"

"She went to her house to get something for you," she said. "She told me not to expect her anytime soon. Is everything all right?"

"Of course. I'll call her there." But when Jordan called

her house, she wasn't there. He tried her cell phone, but there was no reply. Why didn't she answer her cell phone? Unless she was going to the address to check it out.

He copied the address on a piece of paper and headed to the property. Vanetta was holding a lot inside. She refused to talk about Matthew's affair, and the hurt emotions were building up. And that wasn't good. That the affair was with a close family friend only made the pain deeper. She was like a volcano on the verge of erupting.

Maybe she was meeting Curtis. Curtis loved her, although she didn't know that. Jordan dialed Curtis again, and after finding out the two weren't meeting, he told him of his suspicion. Curtis asked for the address of the house. He was heading over there, too. Like Jordan, he believed Matthew had used the house for his trysts.

Chapter 11

"If you're going to sit here and brood over Alyssa, you can just go home," Melinda told Reginald. It was unusual for him to visit so often, but Melinda was delighted. Maybe he was beginning to see the light, at least a glimmer.

Reginald stared at her. "Have a little sympathy for a man, will you? I don't know how I slept last night after Alyssa broke my heart. But I slept like I was in a coma. Can I get a little sympathy here?"

"Sympathy, my foot. She didn't break your heart."

"How do you know?" he said, his eyes narrowing. "Spent half your life hating me."

"If I hated you so much, why are you here?" she asked.

"Because I don't hate you. And I want to be here."

Melinda's gaze met his directly. He was so confused, and it just pissed her off how obtuse men were. "I don't hate you, Reginald. I think you're a moron, sometimes. But I don't hate you."

"Oh, thanks for the vote of confidence."

Melinda blew out a quick breath of impatience. "Don't you know by now you and Alyssa don't match?"

"We've been great frien—"

"Oh, God. Spare me. If you say that one more time, I'll

choke you. I'll tell you the same thing I told Alyssa. Friendship doesn't necessarily make a good mate. Yes, you are her friend, but you don't love her any more than she loves you."

He came out of his seat so fast Melinda tried to step back, but as she was already leaning against the deck railing, there was nowhere to go.

He stood over her, tall and overbearing, nearly pressing his chest into hers, the deck pressing solidly into her behind. No more than an inch of space separated them. Melinda caught her breath. She'd never seen this unleashed fury in him before.

"You talked Alyssa out of dating me?"

"It didn't take much. And you'll soon get over your so-called heartache," Melinda said sarcastically.

"How dare you," he said, boiling over with outrage. "It was none of your damn business."

Melinda grabbed him by the neck and reeled him in. She crushed her mouth to his. At first, he was stiff, his hands collapsed on the railing, but then his mouth softened, his hard body leaned into hers, and a mere crushing of lips turned into a duel of tongues and whispers of breath. He stroked her gently, passionately. Sharp desire stole her breath as it spiraled through her.

His strong arms came around her, pressing her body close to him. Her breasts pressed into his chest as her hands caressed his back. Oh, God, she'd wanted this so long. Her love blossomed and exploded out of control.

Melinda felt his erection rise against her abdomen, solid and urgent, and she ground her hips against him, lowering her hands to hold on to his hips. She sighed against his lips.

His reply, a deep guttural moan, brought her back to reality. How in the heck had her hands gotten there? She released him like he was a hot poker and pressed a hand against his chest until he moved back.

His breath was as ragged as hers. The desire in his eyes surely matched her own.

"If you loved Alyssa," she said shakily, "why were you kissing me like that?" She glanced down at his bold erection, then her gaze traveled up to his eyes. "This was just a test, so don't get any ideas. Why don't you go home and think about it?"

Keeping firm control over her erratic emotions, Melinda strolled unflappably inside the house, leaving him on the deck. She could feel his gaze drilling a hole in her back, and it took everything in her to keep from collapsing.

Her intentions were to ruffle his feathers, to knock some sense into him, to get *him* to open his eyes for once in his blind life so he could see past his ridiculous fixation on Alyssa.

But the joke was on her. Not only had she ruffled his feathers—and by his intense erection, she knew she had—but she'd also managed to unsettle her own.

The chemistry was there—she'd known that for a long time—only she hadn't expected it to be so strong, so violently potent. Desire screamed through her. Closing her eyes, she pressed her hand against her thundering heart. When she opened them, her mother's horrified gaze pierced hers from less than a yard away.

"Why in the world were you necking with Alyssa's boyfriend?" she asked. "How can you betray your best friend? Haven't we had enough of that in this family? People are already talking about us. I thought better of you."

Melinda groaned. "He's not Alyssa's boyfriend," she said. "If he was, I wouldn't have kissed him." She veered around her mother and made a hasty retreat upstairs.

Jordan drove up the long tree-lined drive to Matthew's hidden house, a three-floor Colonial tucked away in an isolated neighborhood. There was a small well-kept lawn in front, but most of the area close to the house was a paved parking lot of the type sported by upscale funeral homes. After parking in the space closest to the house, he went to the door and rang the doorbell. He wasn't surprised when no one responded.

He left the door to walk around the house. It was a huge estate with at least two acres of land and huge trees sprouting up everywhere and more space for parking in back of the house—all told, enough for thirty or forty cars.

The blinds on all the windows were drawn. Why would a parking area that immense be necessary for what was clearly a single-family home?

Jordan was still pondering this when he retraced his steps to the front and saw Curtis's Benz make its way toward him. He parked a yard from Jordan and got out of his car, eyes as mystified as Jordan's as he took in the estate.

"What did you do?" Jordan asked. "Rush right over?"

"I was finished with my rounds and the emergency surgery. I headed out after your call. No sense in hanging around the hospital." He nodded to the house. "So this is the place Matthew bought through the company."

"Looks like it," Jordan said just before Vanetta's car came charging up the driveway and screeched to a halt beside Curtis's. Curtis made it to her car door by the time she'd put the car in park.

With a frown, Vanetta was out the car and headed to the door. "So this is where he holed up with his women," she said, taking determined steps.

"Hold up, Vanetta."

She had the keys in her hand ready to open the door.

"You found keys to this house?" Curtis asked the obvious question.

"Matthew always kept an extra set of everything in his office. I think one of these might fit."

Jordan reached for the keys. "Let me try them."

She snatched her hand back. "Do I look helpless to you? I'm perfectly capable of opening a door," she said and started to the door again.

"You can't go in there," Jordan said gently. "You might walk in on the scene of the crime and disturb evidence."

She leveled him with a heated stare. "I don't care."

Curtis gently tugged on her elbow, wrapping an arm around her shoulder when she tried to resist. "We have to tell Alyssa about the place," he said quietly. "If it is the scene, then there's evidence you don't want to disturb."

"I don't need you telling me what to do. I'm a single woman perfectly capable of running my own life." Her voice cracked on the last word.

Vanetta was coming unglued, and she didn't want to go stark, raving mad in front of these people. Half the people in town thought she was crazy anyway.

She felt as if some alien thing was taking possession of her body, her mind. A fine trembling started in the pit of her stomach and spread through her. She tried to control it, but it was controlling her.

She damn well knew Matthew hadn't been making out outside on the path to Alyssa's place. It was all clean sheets and lavish, comfortable surroundings for him.

At least that was the way he was with her. What did she know about his secret cravings? There were men who led normal, sedate sex lives with their wives, but who had mistresses on the side for their more fantasy-oriented needs and desires. In many cases, they were pretty mundane desires, but for some unknown reason, they couldn't see themselves fulfilling their needs with their wives.

This house was exactly the type of place he would choose for his trysts.

She felt Curtis tugging her against his chest, mumbling soothing phrases. She didn't realize she was crying until the cool wind touched the tears on her cheeks and created cold streaks down her face.

She balled up her fists. "Damn him. Damn him." She released the tears she'd bottled up for two weeks like corked champagne. She purged betrayal, humiliation, and loss. Because, like it or not, she'd loved him once. She wouldn't venture to put an emotion to what she felt right now, but when you lived with a man for as long as she'd been married to Matthew, you felt something.

"Let's go to The Cove," Curtis said once Vanetta had calmed.

"I don't want to be any place he was."

"He never stayed at the club," Jordan said.

"More lies."

"Just leave your car here," Jordan said. "I'll have some-one retrieve it for you."

"Please," Curtis said.

"If it's that important to you, I'll drive and meet you there."

But before they left, Jordan tried the keys to see if one fit the lock. He took the house key off and slid the set of keys in his pocket. Vanetta seemed to have forgotten she'd handed them over as Curtis escorted her to her car.

Alyssa stood in her back yard near the water's edge at-tempting to clear her head. Her family should be arriving any moment now for their meeting concerning their grand-parents. She'd showered and helped Cornell set out the trays of food he'd brought over for her, bless him. It was great having a personal chef in the family.

But she needed a moment for herself. She'd had pre-cious few lately.

She lifted her face to the cool breeze. It had been a hell of a day with Vanetta's interview and family calls afterward. With a mountain of paperwork to complete, she'd spent the afternoon sitting at her office computer.

She loved the beach so much. She often wondered why she hadn't been born a dolphin or a whale where she could spend her life frolicking in the water. She chuckled. Would Fate have paired her with a Jordan-type mate?

The faint thud of a car door slamming five minutes later broke her momentary beach fantasy.

Reluctantly, Alyssa headed back to the house. She'd left the door open. Maybe that was foolish considering the murders, but with her car parked in the yard, her cousins would know where to find her.

Before she could make it to the house, a few more doors slammed. Regina, Lisa, Gabrielle, and a few more cousins were eating snacks in the kitchen when Alyssa got there, and a couple of male cousins had their heads in the fridge, searching for beer.

"Just help yourselves," Alyssa said mockingly.

"We are."

"Are you really going to arrest Vanetta?" Lisa asked. "Mama sent me over here to get the lowdown."

"Have I said anything about arresting anyone?" Alyssa said. "And I don't discuss my cases with you."

"Mama thinks you think Vanetta killed Matthew. How can you even conceive of the notion?" Lisa said.

Alyssa ignored the question and prepared herself a plate. This would be supper for her.

"Why don't you ever have beer?" Cleve asked.

"Are you and Sam getting married anytime soon?" someone asked Regina.

"I want to finish school first," Regina said, "but we're doing just fine, thank you very much."

Regina and Sam had started a hot romance last spring when Alyssa had left town for a course in Arizona. It had only gotten hotter as time progressed. Sam owned the island's only garden shop, and Regina was working on her master's in nursing. Two more dissimilar people Alyssa had not had the fortune of meeting. Sam's quiet nature and Regina's bold in-your-face personality were like mixing oil with vinegar. All she could say was that love sometimes found its way in the most unlikely of circumstances.

The cousins stood around talking, waiting for a few more to arrive before they started the meeting.

"I initiated this meeting for two reasons. First, Grandma and Grandpa need a vacation off on their own."

"A cruise would be perfect," Lisa said. "I could use one myself."

"They won't leave with this hanging over Vanetta's head," Regina said.

"By the time we make the arrangements, this should be over," Alyssa assured them.

"It is a good idea," Gabrielle said. "They barely have any time together anymore."

"What's the second topic?" Cleve asked.

"The bowl. Grandma's on the warpath again. I'd like you to make a list of people who visited Aunt Anna the last couple of years. Try to find out when they last saw the bowl."

"Everybody visited," Gabrielle said. "That's not going to help you narrow the list of suspects."

"Just send me a list of names. Then I'll investigate. We can ask them if they saw the bowl and where. Someone may know more than we realize."

"Back to the grands," Regina said. "Where do you want to send them?"

"I was thinking about D.C. They don't like to fly any-more, and it's close enough for Grandpa to drive. He doesn't like to be without his wheels. I considered a bus trip with other retirees, but they'd be with other people, and I want them isolated so they'll have time to talk and bond again," Alyssa said. "But I like Lisa's idea of the cruise, too, if they can take one from Virginia Beach."

"In that case, they won't have to fly," Lisa said.

"Since you women have that under control, just tell me what I have to pay," Cleve said as if the decision was a foregone conclusion.

"We'll check out the cost and send you an e-mail," Alyssa said.

"That's okay with me," her brother said. As long as he didn't have to plan, he was fine.

Alyssa shook her head. Typical male.

When Vanetta made it back to The Cove, a doorman took her keys and whisked her car away. Curtis came to a stop behind her and handed his keys to another doorman.

Uncertain as to whether she wanted to spend the night here, she entered the building slowly, walking beside Curtis while she thought. Wade was talking to a client in the lobby, but she didn't acknowledge him.

"Why don't we get a room for some privacy?" Curtis asked, his hand resting in the small of her back. "You don't have to spend the night. We'll just talk. I don't think you've talked much about what happened."

"No one understands," Vanetta said. He didn't know the half of it. "People tell you to forget it, not to worry about it. But I worry, and I can't forget."

"And I know because of my friendship with Matt, you think I'm the last person you think you can trust. You see me as the enemy, but I'm not, Vanetta. I know he hurt you. And it's unforgivable," he said with such heartfelt tones that Vanetta believed him. "You deserved better."

"I did. You aren't responsible for Matthew's actions." Just saying his name sent a crack through her heart. "But I'm not sure about a room."

"Just to talk. There are people milling around here. There's no privacy. We could go for a walk in the garden if you prefer. There are seats out there. Or we can walk along the water's edge, only the temperature has dropped, and it's getting cold. It's your choice."

Stressing out around a bunch of nosy people was the last thing Vanetta wanted. On the island, she lived in a fishbowl. Every move she made was talked about.

"Okay. Let's get a room."

"Wait here. I'll be right back."

While he was gone, Vanetta gazed at the people milling around. She didn't recognize any of them, and she relaxed a little. The last thing she needed was people saying she'd shacked up with Curtis so soon after Matthew's death.

Vanetta looked so desolate, Curtis thought when he returned with a key. "I got the key to the owner's suite. It's a two-bedroom suite with a living room. It has two bathrooms," he said, leading her to the elevator.

The elevator quickly whisked them to the third floor, and they strolled silently down the carpeted hallway to the owner's suite near the end of the hall.

"Make yourself comfortable. I've ordered something to eat, but if you have a taste for something specific, I can order it for you."

"I don't care." Obviously, food wasn't front and center in her thoughts.

Vanetta went into the bathroom to run water over her face. When she came out, several packages were on the coffee table.

"I had them bring up slippers for you and some comfortable things. I hope it was all right."

"You don't know my size," she said.

"I guessed."

Vanetta opened packages. There was a long lounging dress—her size. She peered at the shoe size on the box, and they were exactly her size. Her gaze touched Curtis's, and he raised an eyebrow. She slipped the soft slippers on her feet. Her toes wiggled in relief as she settled comfortably on the couch.

This was crazy. Her family would want her back on the island. She should call them to tell them where she was. She should go back to the island, but she didn't want to. And she didn't want them tracking her down.

Vanetta desperately needed to get away.

She dug her cell phone from her purse and pressed the automatic dial for Lisa.

"Lisa, I'm going away for the night. I'll be back sometime tomorrow," Vanetta said and disconnected before her sister could respond. Lisa would understand, even if her mother didn't. Now that they knew she was away, there was no need for them to worry. Of course, her mother would worry anyway, but Vanetta couldn't control that. She needed a night for herself.

She glanced at Curtis. They'd always had a special friendship connection, even when he was a senior in high school and she was a wet behind the ears student teacher, teaching kids who were far worldlier in some areas than she. He'd never judged her.

Curtis smiled and Vanetta gathered up the packages and went to the bedroom to change, closing the door firmly behind her.

Alyssa's meeting was over in less than an hour. Lisa, Regina, and Gabrielle stayed behind to help her clean up and to talk.

"I haven't had a chance to ask you about the honeymoon," Alyssa asked Gabrielle. They sat on the sun porch with glasses of lemonade.

Gabrielle sighed with a dopey, lovesick grin. "Hawaii

was wonderful. We took a helicopter ride to view the volcano, saw the coffee fields, pineapple fields, went to a luau. I will not recommend poi, but you should at least try it once," she said. "Cornell rented this open jeep, the crazy fool, and the wind almost blew us away. I lost my hat the first day."

"I hope you took some time for loving," Lisa said.

"We did that, too."

"I'm jealous," Lisa said. "I'd give anything to go there."

"Has your mother left for Philly yet?" Alyssa asked.

"She left with Dad the day after the funeral."

The women visited for a few more minutes before they left. It was Saturday night, and everyone had plans. Alyssa walked outside with them and saw them off. One car was heading up the lane as they drove away. Seconds later, Jordan parked in her yard.

Her heart leaped, but by the serious expression on his face, romance wasn't on his mind.

"Sorry I had to work all day. How was your day?"

With a frown, he paused in front of her. "I found a house Matthew purchased recently."

"Where?"

"In Virginia Beach. I have a key. Since you haven't found the scene of the crime, I thought you'd want to go in with me when I check it tomorrow."

"Of course. Did he buy it as a fixer-upper for resale?" she asked as they went back inside.

"It's practically new. Like I said, I haven't been inside. And it was news to Vanetta, too."

"What's the address?"

"An upscale area," Alyssa said when he gave it to her.

"Matthew only brought the best."

"I'll say."

"It has a large parking area that seems overdone for a single-family home."

Alyssa frowned as she thought back to Shana's revelation that Vicky went swinging. Could this place have been used for that purpose? Alyssa glanced at her watch. It wasn't too late to check it out. They'd come up with zilch so far.

"Let's go," she said, and when they got outside, she said, "We'll drive separate cars."

"For what? I'm coming back here tonight, and I know you are. I'll drive, he said, sliding into the driver's seat.

They made the trek to the Virginia Beach ferry and continued on to the house. The imposing brick Colonial stretched before them.

"Since the halogen light is on, the electricity must be on," Alyssa said as she climbed out.

"If not, I have my flashlight." He handed it over and started to go inside with Alyssa.

"Jordan, please stay outside. If it's a crime scene, I don't want it compromised."

"You don't know what you're walking in on."

She gave him the eye roll. "I'm not one of your little marshmallow groupies," she said sarcastically. "I'm the professional here." She slid covers over her shoes before she went in. Alyssa turned the light on and flashed the beam around the room until it hit a light switch. Odors of stale liquor and cigarettes permeated the place. She flicked the switch, and light flooded the room. Turning off the flashlight, she took in the huge foyer. It resembled the ones from Colonial days when foyers were used as receiving rooms. It boasted a pristine black and white marble floor with long padded benches strategically placed along the walls. There was also a huge barlike structure with a tall chair behind it, as if it was used for a reception area to admit customers and collect fees.

To the right was a living room. With a cursory glance, Alyssa observed several groupings of chairs. To the left was the dining room, but instead of a table, it also had groupings of chairs and a sofa table. Upstairs were several bedrooms, set up as such. All the rooms were neat and clean.

In the basement were pool tables, slot machines, and blackjack tables, as well as a bar and liquor cabinets with shelves filled to brimming with every type of whisky, wine, and rum imaginable.

"Guess the Virginia ABC didn't know about this, or the local police," she muttered to herself. They usually didn't know about swinging clubs. With gambling, it would be shut down for sure. Alyssa made notes as she progressed through the rooms.

She went back up to the first floor. Turning in the direction of the garage she remembered seeing from the outside, she walked down the hallway, passing a bedroom, then a bathroom and laundry room. She went back to the living room and flicked on the lamp. The back of a sofa faced her. She went further into the room and stood where she could see everything by swiveling in a circle.

Blood soaked a beige sofa.

Alyssa took out her cell phone and called a detective she knew. She was out of her jurisdiction. Virginia Beach PD would have to process the scene, and she'd have to play second fiddle to them.

It was late by the time everyone left.

"Come on. I'll drive you to the club. You can sleep there," Jordan said to her as the cars pulled away. She nodded off on the way there.

Jordan turned the music on low. He gazed at Alyssa and smiled warmly. His hellcat. Alyssa in action was something to behold. She may not have been the officer in charge, but you couldn't tell that by the way she conducted herself. He was thoroughly impressed. The only thing his mother had been right about was that she *was* unlike any woman he'd dated. That other stuff was a bunch of crap.

Twenty minutes later, he pulled under his club's awning and cut the motor. She was sleeping so peacefully, he hated to awaken her. She must have sensed the change in motion because she awakened on her own.

"Your castle awaits you," he said softly, as if he were some prince.

Alyssa emitted a tired chuckle. A doorman met them and took Jordan's keys. "Good evening, Mr. Ellis. Will you be going out again?"

"You can park it for the evening," Jordan told him.

"Very elaborate," Alyssa said as the doorman left.

"With one word, it can all be yours."

Alyssa gave him the eye. She could see them as a couple. She, the hard-edged detective and he, the polished businessman. As the doorman opened the door and they stepped into the old-world lobby, Alyssa thought, *This place suited him.*

"Are the clubs you're opening in California and New Orleans anything like this?"

"The one in California has more of the adobe look, and the one in New Orleans has a French Quarter style with latticework iron balconies and floor-to-ceiling windows, but both are upscale. I'll take you to see both one day. Why don't you sit while I get us a room?" He moved toward the desk.

Alyssa didn't sit; instead she gazed around the lavish lobby. She felt grungy in its pristine opulence. She felt as if the blood and gore of the crime scene was all over her.

In minutes, Jordan was back. He pressed his hand in the small of her back as he led her to the elevator. The whispered ride to the third floor, the highest floor, was swift.

"I know I can't impress you with the view," he said. "Yours is ten times better than any I could give you here."

"I won't be looking at the view. And I imagine any room

in this place is lovely," she said. "If given the choice, I'd conduct business here any day."

"Your wish is my command," Jordan said, only half-joking. He paused by a door, using the keycard to open it.

He let Alyssa precede him into the room. Alyssa entered an upscale suite with a kitchen and living area.

"I don't need all this. I'm leaving first thing in the morning."

"You're here now," he said, closing the door after them. "There are two bedrooms." He stared straight into her eyes. "Do we need the second one?"

Alyssa swallowed hard. Her stomach dipped as those eyes impaled her. "No," she said, knowing she wanted him every bit as much as his gaze revealed he wanted her. "But I have to shower first," she said.

"So do I. I want to see you this time, Alyssa. The last time was a dream come true, but it was in the dark and I have only mental images of your body. And while they're fantastic, I've been dying to see every inch of you. Because looking at you has to be as fulfilling as feeling you.

She didn't need to hear that. She heated up as if a blaze roared in her.

"Ah, the shower first," she said and made a beeline to the bathroom.

She had been under the spray no more than three minutes, thinking about the case, when the door opened. A nude Jordan entered the shower with her. It was a huge space. There was plenty of room left over even with the two of them, but the space suddenly seemed cramped.

She watched as he washed himself completely, then his gaze sought hers. He was always watching her. But the naked desire this time sent butterflies twittering in her stomach.

"There're two showers in the suite," he said, placing a soft kiss on her neck. "But two seemed excessive."

"A little late asking, isn't it?" Alyssa traced her hands over his slick shoulders, enjoying the texture of his skin.

"Don't you agree?" His tongue slid along her collarbone.

All Alyssa could moan was, "Ummm." And then he squirted soap into his hands and laved it over her, starting with her neck. She inhaled sharply when he slid a palm over her dark nipples and drifted downward. He stood beneath the spray, and his skin glistened as the drops cascaded down his beautiful body.

With light strokes, he brushed her thighs, and Alyssa emitted a deep moan. "You're an expert at this."

"At many things," he said.

"And just a little too smooth," she said, gliding her hand down his torso to the coarse, dark hair. He hissed sharply when she gathered him in her hand. He captured her lips with a ferocity that left her breathless and dizzy. His body molded against hers, and her breasts pressed into his chest, making her tingle with desire.

He moaned, donning a condom. "Not smooth enough," he said, lifting her against the wall. "I need you. Now."

She needed him, she thought as he pressed her legs apart, positioned himself, and sank deeply into her. She arched to meet him thrust for thrust. She wrapped her legs around his waist, and Alyssa thought it impossible for him to burry himself any deeper, but he did, increasing the pleasurable sensations tenfold. She turned her head and kissed him on the neck.

Among sighs and moans, they moved in rhythmic accord until their bodies surged over a steep precipice into pure ecstasy.

Seconds later, Alyssa's feet eased to the floor, but Jordan continued to lean into her, his arms tightly wrapped around her until they drifted back to reality.

* * *

When they were finally beneath the covers, all Alyssa could moan was, "I'm exhausted. I need sleep."

Jordan sucked in a breath. "Who needs sleep on a night like this?" But they didn't make love again. After a sweet kiss filled with tomorrow's promises, he gathered her into his arms.

Feeling contented, Alyssa snuggled against him. This felt right, she thought. She'd never felt this comforted with a man, not even with Reginald. She hated to admit it, but for once, Melinda knew what she was talking about. It was both soothing and frightening to place her trust in a man.

Chapter 12

Alyssa got exactly two hours of sleep before the wake-up call came through. Seconds later, a bell sounded at the door.

"Do all your rooms have doorbells?" Alyssa asked around a yawn.

"No, just the suites. Without it, you might not hear a knock." Jordan answered the door, and Alyssa, without a stitch on, traipsed to the bathroom.

Jordan was back just as she finished brushing her teeth and washing her face. She had just enough time to don the terrycloth robe before he led her to the deck where the table was set with a beautiful bouquet and two place settings. Covered dishes sat in the center, along with three different juices.

"Breakfast is served, madam," he said as he pulled out the chair for her.

But she didn't sit. "Jordan . . ."

"What is it, sweetheart?"

"You're spoiling me." Alyssa wasn't sentimental, and although she wasn't delicate, she loved pretty and delicate things. People thought she didn't because of her choice of career and because she was an outdoor person. They forgot that she was still a woman and that she liked the romantic touch.

"I want to spoil you in every possible way," he said. He'd lost the smile as he bent and kissed her. And although they'd made love last night before she fell into an exhausted sleep, her body flamed with desire.

"Do you like it?" he asked.

"Very much." She wrestled to keep the tears back, although she wasn't usually given to teary emotions. He slid a piece of fresh mango between her lips and licked the juice on her lips. Instead of sitting across the café table from her, he pulled his chair beside hers.

He was everything she could possibly want in a man. Because she was capable, tall, and strong, men tended to forget she was a woman with warm feelings. A man had never treated her delicately before, or made her feel so special, especially not Reginald. She wasn't saying she wanted a man to make decisions for her or treat her as if she were helpless because she wasn't.

"My next acquisition will be a boat," Jordan said as he fed her a strawberry, "so we can come and go as we please. Do you go boating much, Alyssa?"

"Not as often as I'd like. But I love taking my little motor boat out."

"I used to take Matthew's yacht out. In the last year or so, he rarely used it."

"I wonder if Vanetta will sell it now. She doesn't boat at all, except to go out with him."

"It's a nice sloop," he said. "But I don't want to waste the little time we have this morning talking about boats."

"Me, either," Alyssa said as she picked up a melon slice and fed it to him. His lips captured the fruit and her fingers. Alyssa laughed and settled in for a long, enjoyable breakfast.

* * *

After breakfast, Alyssa showered and dressed. Jordan ordered up clothes for her, producing an aqua skirt and blouse that looked absolutely gorgeous on her. He even remembered to include several samples of perfume. Alyssa selected one and dabbed it on before she slipped her feet into her shoes.

Jordan was on the phone when she came out of the bedroom, dressed and poised to leave.

He wore a designer golf shirt and linen slacks. The breadth of his shoulders still amazed her. Her hands had been all over those shoulders last night, and she knew the texture of his skin and the hardness of his muscles.

"I have a few loose ends I have to tie up before I can leave town," he said to the person on the other end. "It should take no more than a week or two for me to finalize things. Send my apologies to the Novaks, and tell Thomas I'll get back to him soon. In the meantime, send them a bottle of Chardonnay." He named a special vintage. "You know where to order it. It's his favorite. It's going to cost a fortune, but it's worth it to appease Thomas."

He was silent as he listened to something the other person said, then said a hasty good-bye and hung up.

Alyssa retrieved her earrings from the sofa table and clipped them on.

"Come here," Jordan said, and Alyssa went over to him, leaned down, and kissed him fully on the lips.

"What is it?"

He gently tugged her into his lap, and Alyssa squealed as she fell fully on him. She laughed until he stopped her with a kiss.

"I have something for you," he said, his breath brushing her face.

"Yeah, what?"

"This," he said, placing a small jeweler's box in her hand.

Slowly, Alyssa opened the box, revealing a diamond tennis bracelet. She had no doubt it was real.

Alyssa didn't want to come off as one of those women who blew everything out of proportion, but a cold chill seeped steadily through her body.

"The bracelet is beautiful, and so are the flowers," she said, "but what did I do to deserve them?"

He gently squeezed her. "Honey, last night was worth ten times this. Next time, I'll buy you a necklace to match."

Please, no, she entreated as she came off his lap, hurt and confusion piercing her insides. The time she spent with him was so special; she thought he'd felt the same, not that she was just another notch on his belt or some rich man's possession to take out and discard at his leisure.

The bracelet was expensive. Jordan had money, lots of it. Men of his financial status were way out of her league. She should have considered that before she gave in to the desire she'd fought for months. She should have known better than to surrender to her weakness.

She was a small town girl from a place where people were down-home and direct. If they hated you, they said so. If they loved you, they acted stupid. But at least you knew where you stood. There wasn't this slick reading between the lines. You didn't jump into something without a parachute to catch you.

This was all new to her, and obviously, she didn't know the rules of the game. Alyssa had to clear her throat twice before she could speak.

"What is this? Payment for services rendered?"

"It's just a gift."

"Why? What have I done to deserve this expensive gift?" The single strand of diamonds sparkled brilliantly, mocking her. "How many thousand did this cost? Is this the going rate for prostitution these days?"

"You're blowing this all out of proportion—"

"Like hell I am. I went to bed with you because I wanted to." Her voice cracked. Her chest hurt. "I thought there was something here that was worth taking a risk on, not because I want to be your mistress who's available at the snap of your finger."

"I never called you . . ."

"You're treating me like one."

"You women are a piece of work," he said angrily, standing across from her now. They were paired off like combatants. "If I don't buy you the bling, you'll cry I'm cheap. You can't cry foul when I play the game you women designed."

"I don't know what kind of women you're used to. But from where I come, we give from the heart. Your jewels can't buy what I gave you, even if you'd spent a million dollars." She shoved the bracelet at his chest so hard he rocked back on his heels. The jewelry bounced off his chest and fell to the floor.

"Damn it, Alyssa"—he reached up to catch her arm, but she snatched it back as if she would sock him if he touched her.

"If I'm one of the 'loose ends' you have to tie up, consider it done. And you can take your jewels and your flowers and stick them up your ass. This relationship, if you can call it that, was no more than another successful business deal to you. I'll find my own way home." She grabbed her purse and slammed out the door.

Her first stop was the gift shop to pay for the clothes Jordan had ordered up for her. The woman started to balk when Alyssa insisted on knowing the cost, but the don't-mess-with-me look on her face brought forth a price. Alyssa whipped out her credit card to pay for it. She could have bought a whole new wardrobe for what they charged for a few simple items here.

After she signed the credit card receipt, she headed to the door. Alyssa hadn't seen any taxis hanging around last night, but she could always call one.

Wade stopped Alyssa before she could get through the door. "Get out of my way," she said through gritted teeth.

"I have a car waiting for you," he said.

"I'll find my own way, thank you."

"Please. I don't want to lose my job."

"He threatened your job?" she asked incredulously, sickened by the way Jordan could throw around his power.

Wade swallowed, the Adam's apple in his throat visible. He was clearly afraid, and Alyssa wasn't going to be responsible for anyone losing a job, especially over a personal matter that didn't involve him. "A driver will take you home," he said. "This way."

Alyssa sighed. She had to get home, didn't she? She followed him outside. Disgusted, she stopped when she saw the car. "Damn it."

"Please," Wade said, taking her elbow and guiding her into the tan stretch limo. She slid onto the plush seat. Wade closed the door, and the car took off immediately.

"Good morning, Ms. Claxton," the driver said. "There's a fully stocked bar with snacks and drinks for your enjoyment," he said.

"Thank you," Alyssa said, but she'd starve before she touched any of it. He closed the glass partition between them, and she settled back in the seat, seething.

The ride was smooth as they sailed toward the ferry. She stayed where she was when they parked and journeyed across. The driver didn't ask for directions but drove directly to her door.

Alyssa fished out five twenties from her purse and handed it to him.

"Ma'am, I can't accept this," he said.

She ignored him and marched to the house. She didn't take a complete breath until she heard the car leaving.

She needed a change of clothes, she thought, moving on autopilot. She'd use work to get her through the day. She ignored the stabbing pain in her chest as she mentally listed what needed to be done.

She hung the beautiful aqua outfit in the depths of her closet so it didn't mock her every time she opened the door.

The whore. They'd spent the night together. He'd watched them drive on the ferry together in Jordan's car. He still couldn't get over her deception.

If he was a betting man, he would have laid money on the fact that she'd never fall for the wealthy, self-centered type. But women were easily turned on by money. He'd thought better of Alyssa, but she was like the rest of them. Money-grabbing whores, the lot of them.

Jordan had a smile on his face as he drove onto the ferry.

He knew something was up. Vanetta's car wasn't in her mother's yard when he passed by the night before. And it wasn't at her house, either. Where was she?

He'd been watching Alyssa for some time, waiting for a time he could get to her. Although he had the mousy other woman, just watching Alyssa stirred his blood. And he hated himself for it. She was bold like Vicky. Although she'd never do the things in bed that Vicky did, she could be taught to please him. He'd dreamed about her. When he was making love with the other women, it was always Alyssa's face he saw.

And she was trying to find him to lock him up. She'd be his before she had a clue of what he was capable of.

He rubbed his expanding privates. He'd just love to

tame her beneath his hands. He wouldn't kill her. No, he couldn't do that, but he'd have to render her immobile. She was a strong woman, and she'd come out swinging. He couldn't walk through town with a black eye or scratches on his face. Once she was subdued, she'd be his forever. They would live their lives out together.

To think of having a woman like Alyssa at his beck and call gave him an erection, the likes of which he'd never had before.

Vanetta came awake slowly. Strong arms were wrapped around her shoulders. She turned her head. Curtis was watching her. He smiled. Vanetta hopped up from the sofa so quickly the blood rushed to her head.

"Take it easy," Curtis said. "Nothing happened. We fell asleep late last night."

She was fully clothed, thank God. Now she remembered how she'd sobbed on his shoulders. She felt like a fool for spilling her guts to him. He was a surgeon, for chrissakes, not a psychologist for mixed-up women.

He picked up the phone. "What would you like for breakfast? You can shower while we wait."

"Don't you have to get to work?"

"It's Sunday. I don't have anything scheduled today. Go shower, and I'll order breakfast. What would you like?"

"Do I smell that bad?"

"Actually, you seem nervous. I wanted to give you a chance to pull yourself together."

"All right. I can't eat much. A glass of juice and tea will do."

He nodded. "I'll order a change of clothing from the dress shop downstairs."

"You have everything here."

"Sometimes airlines lose suitcases or guests neglect to

pack everything they need. We're a full-service club. Everything a business person needs can be found here. How is it that you know so little about a business you own?"

"My husband owned it."

"You were his wife. You majored in finance as well as education. People think you're an expert."

Vanetta rubbed her eyes. "I don't know about expert."

"Look how you're helping the artists on the island build their businesses. It's just about to take off."

"All this mess I'm going through is holding everything up." She sighed. "How can I go on when I have all this crap of Matthew's to sort out? And now, Alyssa thinks I killed him."

"I doubt it. You have every reason to be angry. Just because you're angry doesn't mean you'll kill. I trust you, Vanetta."

"Who knows what a person will do in a fit of anger? What if I'd found them together that night? What would I have done?"

"You didn't find them, so it's unimportant. Stop second-guessing yourself." He captured her shoulders and turned her toward the bathroom. "Now, go take a shower, and I'll order breakfast."

Vanetta escaped to the bathroom. She felt comfortable talking to Curtis, but she couldn't tell him the entire truth. In the past, she'd always had strange feelings around him. As if he expected her to be more than a casual acquaintance, or at least *wanted* more. Maybe it was she who had those feelings. Maybe it was why she'd turned a blind eye to Matthew's absences and the stagnation of their marriage for so long. She'd had questions, but she hadn't sought answers. Was it because she just hadn't cared anymore?

She couldn't deal with that. Vanetta squirted soap on the washcloth to wash her face. She was probably imagining things anyway, she thought as she discarded her clothing to take a shower. The warm water felt great streaming down her body.

When she finished, she dried off with a fluffy heated towel, then wrapped the towel around her.

"There are clothes on the bed," Curtis called out. "I'll be out on the deck."

"Thank you." Footsteps retreated, and when she heard the outer door close, she opened the door a crack to make sure he was gone. Then she approached the bed. He had women's underwear, slacks, a blouse, and a jacket with a scarf. It was as if he was her personal buyer. And of course, they were all the correct size. She picked up the skimpy panties and blushed.

Alyssa dressed quickly and activated the remote to the garage. She glanced at the bike she hadn't touched since her ride with Melinda. She could certainly use a ride with the wind rushing against her, she thought. She shook her head and climbed into the Crown Vic. If only they could spring for an SUV, she thought as she backed out of the garage and headed to police headquarters. Harper's car was already there.

"Tell me what's going on," Harper said when she entered his office. "Even as we speak, the news crews are on their way." John Aldridge was in the office, too, along with Harper's assistant.

Alyssa filled him in on what she knew.

"How did you find the house?" he asked.

"Jordan found a paper trail and told me about it."

Lisa's mother was having a hissy fit. Had the whole family in an uproar because she couldn't find Vanetta.

"She said she was going to spend the night out of town.

She could be in Virginia Beach, or Norfolk, or even Williamsburg. She just needed to clear her head, Mama," Lisa said.

"But she's depressed. She's got enough weight on her shoulders to make a linebacker break," Dorothy said.

"Vanetta's levelheaded, Mama. I'll keep trying her cell phone, but she already told me she wouldn't be home. She turned it off because she didn't want to be bothered."

"I had your dad and some of the cousins drive around the island. But they didn't see her car anywhere. And that murderer is still out there."

"If anything, she'd hide out to keep from being charged with murder."

"Now that's the last thing you need to say, Lisa. Why would you worry your mama like that?" her father asked.

"It was just a thought."

Her dad shook his head. Lisa was back in his mental doghouse.

"Maybe we should call Alyssa."

"No," her mother said, shaking her head. "She might arrest Vanetta for leaving the island. Don't say a word to her."

"Try her cell phone again," her father said. But when there was no answer, the worry increased.

"She said she was going out of town," Lisa repeated weakly, knowing nobody was listening to her. When she didn't get a response, she sighed. They didn't worry about her that way.

Jordan was still smarting about Alyssa's attack over a simple bracelet exactly like the ones he'd handed out to any number of women. None of them had gone off the deep end. But she acted like he'd insulted her. It was a gift, for crissakes. Didn't she know how to accept a gift graciously?

Wade stuck his head in the office. "She gave the driver a hundred bucks."

"Tell him it's his tip," Jordan said between gritted teeth. "You have a minute?"

"Sure. What's up?"

"Have a seat," Jordan said slowly. "You knew Matthew pretty well, didn't you?"

Wade nodded. "Sure."

"He has a house in Virginia Beach. Do you know what it was used for?"

"News to me," Wade said immediately.

"We need to know whatever you know. Two people were murdered there."

"Are you sure it isn't an investment property?"

"I'm not sure of anything," Jordan said.

"I have to get back to the island. My family must be going crazy," Vanetta said. The battery had run low on her cell phone, and she'd turned it off.

"Are you going to stay with your parents?"

"No. For the last couple of days, I've been writing thank-you letters. I didn't realize we had so many kind friends. But now that that's done, I feel like life is drifting by, and I should dive into the artist project."

"You always have so many irons in the fire with your charity work. You do so much for the hospital, and for the art community. We all appreciate you."

"I'm letting everyone down now," she said.

"You aren't letting anyone down. You're entitled to some time," he said. "Tell your mother you're going to spend one more night in Virginia Beach. I promise not to take advantage of you."

Vanetta chuckled. "I know. Last night meant the world to me. So much was bottled inside, and I couldn't let it out.

I needed the release." She smiled shyly. "I appreciate you letting me cry on your shoulder. I don't usually come unglued like that. You must have thought I was a basket case."

"You just discovered you're human like the rest of us. Of course, when you were student teaching, I thought the sun rose and set with you."

Vanetta blushed. "You were the smartest student in my class. I still think you're smart. And your success only proves it. I always wondered why you stayed here. You could work in D.C., or Boston, or New York and become an internationally known surgeon."

"I wouldn't have any of this if it wasn't for you, Vanetta. I owe you a lot."

Vanetta shook her head. "Your success is your own. You don't owe me anything."

"You have no idea what my life was like growing up. And then someone like you, pure and innocent, came along. I couldn't believe it when you just gave me the money to pay off my mother's debt and then wouldn't take the money back later when I tried to pay you."

"I'm no saint. Besides, I didn't need it."

He slid his hands in his pockets. "You have a generous heart."

"Stop, please. Somebody break out the violin." She laughed, and he laughed, too. He had a nice laugh, she thought. For the first time since Matthew died, she actually laughed and felt it in her heart. It felt good. She'd thought she'd forgotten how.

"Seriously, thank you for this reprieve," she said. "For this special time. I have to get back to the island before my family sends out the Marines."

"If you ever need me, even just to talk, call." He slipped a card into her hand, but she didn't look at it. "Anytime, day or night." He took her chin in his hand. "I'm serious,"

he said and planted a soft kiss on her cheek. Such an innocent kiss.

Vanetta nodded and slid into her car, and he shut her
door. She pulled away from the curb. When she glanced in
her rearview mirror, he was watching her.

Her stomach was literally roiling. What did it all mean?
Curtis was a confirmed bachelor. She'd often wondered
why he'd never married.

She knew he'd be there for her, but she wouldn't call. It
was time for her to begin the healing process by herself
and to move on with her life. And the first step in that direction was to go through Matthew's office. She wasn't
going to her mother's house. Her family was going to have
a fit, but she had things to do.

Once home, Vanetta headed straight to the office.
Matthew had a flat-screen TV across from the desk. It
could easily be seen from his desk or from the easy chair
and hassock. Sometimes when he came in late, he fell
asleep in the chair. She'd find him there in the morning
with some stupid infomercial running. She always went to
bed early, so she was an early riser.

The room held paintings by local artists that she'd
chosen. Matthew had wanted her to choose paintings from
galleries in New York or D.C., but with an artist colony
right here, that had made no sense. Matthew had berated
her with, "We aren't poor. We can afford quality art."
Vanetta had rebutted that, noting that artists on the island
created quality work that rivaled any big city gallery.

When she sat in front of Matthew's desk, she realized
Jordan still had the keys. Her lips tightened. The lack of
keys wasn't going to stop her. And she wasn't going to
wait until Jordan returned them. She was sick of people
trying to protect her. She stormed to the garage and found

a large screwdriver. Behind the desk again, she hacked until that damn drawer came open. So much for the expensive piece of furniture. She would have it fixed and auctioned for charity.

Vanetta went through every slip of paper, every file in every drawer. It took her two hours. She didn't find anything useful, except insurance and business papers. She set the ones aside she'd need to go over later.

Vanetta glanced around the room. The closet. She'd attack that next. Adrenaline raced through her. The phone rang, and she jumped a foot. It wasn't until the third ring that she picked it up.

"I've been calling and calling your cell phone," her mother said. "I was just about to call Alyssa for her to put a search out on you."

"Don't even consider it, Mama."

"What are you doing home, girl?"

"I had some things to do."

"Nothing that can't wait."

"This can't wait."

"I understand you've been dealt a blow. A hard blow. Honey, let your family help you through this."

"I have things only I can do," Vanetta murmured.

"Well, I'll come over and help you."

"I don't want help. I have to do this myself. But I appreciate your concern, Mama. I really do."

She hung up.

Lisa was cleaning the last room in the B&B when her cell phone rang. Gabrielle didn't like her talking on the cell at work. Thought it was bad for the B&B's image, but it was her mother.

"Yeah, Mama."

"The more I teach you, the worse you get. Is that any way to answer the phone?"

"Mama, I'm not supposed to be on the phone."

"This is important family business."

"What's wrong?" Lisa asked, closing the door. There was a group there for the week, and the B&B was full. But thank goodness, the guests were out, and she was going to take a quick break. She went to the hallway window seat.

"Something's going on with your sister. She's home when she should be here. She shouldn't be in that rambling house alone. It's way too big, with too many memories."

"Why did she go back?"

"She said she had things to do."

"Maybe she does," Lisa said. "Give her a break. She's not a child. She's a grown woman."

"Vanetta was always delicate. She's not in her right mind."

"Vanetta's stronger than you think," Lisa said.

"Can you go over there?"

Lisa sighed. "I'm almost finished here. As soon as I'm through, I'll drive there."

"And stay the night."

"Are you sure she's not coming back to your place?"

"Knowing her, no."

Lisa sighed. "Let me finish up here so I can leave."

Chapter 13

Lisa wished she could take a bath. She felt sticky and dirty. She lived in an apartment over her parents' garage, and if she drove home, her mother would sail out of the house to get her moving to Vanetta's place before she could park. She saved herself the trouble.

She'd shower at Vanetta's. They were almost the same size.

Lisa had a key to her sister's house. She used it to let herself in and called out, "Van!"

"Back here," Vanetta called back.

"What are you doing?" Lisa asked, following the direction of Vanetta's voice. In the office, Vanetta was attacking things like she was on a vengeance.

"Going through this stuff."

"It can't wait?"

"No."

First, her sister spends the night in Virginia Beach. Then she returns late in the day. Now she's desperate to go through Matthew's things. Something was going on.

"What happened?" Lisa asked.

"It's time I found out a few things about my husband."

Vanetta was hacking at the closet door.

"Wait a minute. There has to be an easier way to get in there."

"He has a dead bolt on this door. It's not like a regular house door where you can use one of those tiny screw-drivers to unlock it."

"Get a credit card. That should open it."

Vanetta glanced around. Then she went to the desk and retrieved a card from a drawer.

In a minute, Lisa had the door open.

There were DVDs in there, as well as files and maga-zines. Vanetta placed one DVD in the player. They could tell almost before it started playing that it was porn.

"Did the two of you watch these together?" Lisa asked. "A lot of couples learn new tricks watching these things."

"I've never seen it before. Obviously, he closed himself off in here to watch it alone."

"Only one shelf? You'd think he'd have a whole closet full if this was the way he got his kicks." Lisa wondered if he'd ever watched them with Vicky or his flavor of the moment. If he cheated with Vicky, it went without saying he probably had cheated all along. Her sister was so inno-cent. But she couldn't talk, either. Her own track record with men was batting zero.

Vanetta quickly lost interest in the tape.

"I guess you found what you were searching for," Lisa said.

But Vanetta was digging into the files, flipping through stuff in the folders. She pulled one that was out of place, turned back the cover, and stopped.

"What?"

"It's a picture of Aunt Anna's bowl."

"What?"

"The heirloom bowl Grandma's worrying everyone to death about finding," Vanetta said, frowning.

"How did he get it? Even better, why does he have this picture?"

"I don't know, but I'm going to find out."

When Jordan picked up the phone to answer his mother's call, he realized he'd worked the day away. Nothing like a woman pissing you off to get you to plow through a lot of paperwork that needed doing.

"Invite Alyssa over to dinner Tuesday night," she said. I'd like to see her again before I leave."

"She's busy."

"I understand she works. If Tuesday doesn't work, find out which night will."

"She's busy all week."

"All week?" she asked. "You didn't even ask her."

"She's working a murder case."

"She has to eat, doesn't she? She can't work night and day." She was silent, then said, "What did you do?"

Jordan sighed. "Nothing."

"Yes, you did. I can hear it in your voice. It goes higher when you've done something you have no business doing. You messed up, didn't you? You might as well tell me."

Jordan smothered a curse. "I have another call coming in."

"It can wait. It's Sunday. As much as the Lord has blessed you, you shouldn't be working on Sunday. You should at least take one day for Him. I bet you didn't go to church today," his mother scolded.

Jordan remembered how his father was a quiet man. "Did Dad ever get a word in with you?" he asked.

"This isn't about your daddy. This is about Alyssa, who is the first decent woman you've dated since college, and you can't hold on to her for a week? What's the matter with you? What did you do? You may as well tell me."

Jordan sighed again. "I gave her a gift, all right. She took it the wrong way."

"No, she didn't. She knew exactly what you meant. Did you listen to anything I said the other day? Hmm? I told you to remember what you learned from home, not what some trashy man who tossed up a different skirt every day in the back room of that store taught you. That man had no couth, and you know it. No decency at all. So I don't blame Alyssa. I wouldn't take just anything off a man, either. If you want to be the king of your castle, then you better act like one. If you want to keep this one, than you have to consider her feelings. You have to give instead of taking."

"I always give."

"Platinum and diamonds. When the shit hits the fan, they don't count for much. They can't hold your hand when you're hurting. They can't love you unconditionally. They can't soothe your brow when you're sick. They can't give you children. They can't make you happy, and they can't make your house a home. A woman like Alyssa wants the man. When you figure out what that means, maybe, just maybe, she'll forgive you in ten years." She slammed the phone in his ear.

He could have gone all day without her lecture. What did a woman who married her high school sweetheart a month after graduation, lived in the same place for most of her life, and only ventured out enough to visit him and her sister know about how things worked in the modern world?

His mother wasn't stupid. But today's world was far more sophisticated than it had been in her day. She didn't understand that.

But he'd lost Alyssa, hadn't he?

He said, "Come in," to the knock on his door.

Curtis strolled in, whistling.

"What're you so happy about?"

Curtis shrugged.

"Did Vanetta get back home okay last night?"

"This afternoon," Curtis said.

"She spent the night here?"

Curtis raised his hands. "Strictly platonic. She needed a new environment. Your mother invited me to dinner. Are you going to join us?"

"No."

"Going to see Alyssa?"

"Christ, no."

"Why not?"

"She's not speaking to me. And if you say one word, one word, I'll lay you flat, and you won't get up for a week." No more. Jordan had taken enough sass from his mother to last a lifetime.

"As long as you don't touch the hand, man. You're a man. You know what you have to do to get her back."

"Who said I did anything?"

"Nobody," Curtis said cautiously. "So, what did you do?"

"Damn it. Get out."

"All I asked was . . ."

Jordan stood, pointed an imperial finger at the door. "Now."

"All right, already. I'm sure you know how to fix it," Curtis said, backing toward the door. "That is, if she's the one. And I have no doubt that she is. I mean, you've been after her since February. A shame to let a little dustup ruin it all." He reached the doorjamb. "And do it now rather than later, okay? Before you hurt somebody."

Jordan growled, and Curtis deserted the field.

It was dark when Alyssa parked the Crown Vic. The fog had rolled in quickly, making it difficult to see more than a few feet in front of her. She should have left a yard light on, but in the fog, it would only cast weird images.

She started walking up the steps to the door and had stuck the key in the lock when someone grabbed her from behind. Damn it. Someone had snuck in as stealthily as the encroaching fog.

She kicked back. He placed a cloth over her nose. She whiffed chloroform. If she breathed as deeply as she wanted to, it would render her helpless. She elbowed him in the side and jerked away. He grunted. She kicked again, bent forward to toss him, but he must have been expecting it since he didn't go flying over her head.

How did someone get close enough to attack her without her knowing? She was always cautious. It crossed her mind that her attacker might be the murderer.

She glimpsed his face. It was covered with something, making him look like some otherworldly creature creeping in with the fog. She reached for the mask; he knocked her hand away. She grabbed for her gun at the same time as she struck out at him.

A sharp chop sent her flying. Pain exploded through her, and when she went down, her head hit the wooden steps, dazing her. For a moment, she couldn't move, and before she could shake the lethargy off, he was on her. He'd retrieved the rag and aimed for her face. Her half-dazed mind functioned enough for her to move. She kicked out hard, connecting with something. He screamed, "Bitch," before he released her and limped off. Pulling her gun out of its holster, Alyssa started to fire after him, but she didn't have him in her sights. She gulped in deep breaths of air, trying to pull herself together while keeping an eye on her surroundings in case he came back.

Shaking her head, she staggered after him around the corner of her house. He was hidden someplace. She was dizzy. She'd better get to safety.

Still watching all around her, she struggled to the front of the house and up the stairs to the porch before she twisted the key still embedded in the lock. Once inside, she closed and locked the door solidly behind her. Out back, she heard a motorboat roar.

Pulling out her cell phone, Alyssa called the station. She should have chased him, but her head was too woozy. She shook her head again, trying to clear it. She couldn't believe how out of it she was.

Sneaky bastard. Somehow, he'd drugged Matthew— maybe the same way.

Damn it. She should have been more careful. What was her connection to Vicky and Matthew, other than that Vicky was her best friend's sister and Matthew was her cousin's husband? She knew of no other connection. Why had he attacked her? And why were the bodies left near her house?

He hit the wheel. "Bitch. Bitch. Bitch." His leg throbbed. He was nearly blind from pain. He had to get away fast. They'd soon have boats out searching for him. But he had to do something about the pain. He slowed at the water's edge, near the cover of trees, and idled long enough to dig out and swallow three pills. He needed something stronger, but these would have to do for now. He started going over the water again, so fast, in fact, the little boat was skipping across the waves.

He concentrated on getting to his hiding place. It took several more minutes before he activated the door opener, slid his boat neatly into place, and closed the door behind him. To the naked eye, it looked like an aging boathouse that needed to be knocked down and rebuilt. But in fact, it was quite sturdy. He wanted to give the illusion that the area was deserted.

He cut the motor and leaned back in the seat, emitting a tired sigh. Cold sweat beaded on his skin.

He'd never get her alone now. He shouldn't have waited so long, but at first, one of her giant brothers was always there. Then she started whoring around with Mr. Money.

Now somebody was always going to be with her. Either a police officer or her family, or Christ, worse, both would be dogging her footsteps every moment of the day.

They had no right. He'd waited so long. She was his. Damn it. She was his! He rubbed his aching leg. He would have her. And he'd teach her a lesson she wouldn't forget.

But first, he had to fix this mess. He couldn't have them knocking on his door, thinking he was anything but the upstanding citizen whose image he projected.

He left the boat and headed to the old rundown barn hidden in the trees. He had some stronger stuff there that would wipe the pain away.

He dragged himself from the boathouse, through the bushes to the sturdy barn door. Even before he reached it, he heard moaning. Rage bit through him. She was supposed to lay docile, waiting for him to return.

Pain forgotten, he exploded through the door. Her glazed eyes saw him immediately.

"Please," she entreated. "Why are you . . . No!"

He hit her hard, knocked her out, and unzipped his pants.

Although Alyssa assumed this intruder had murdered Vicky and Matthew, she had no way of knowing that. Getting mugged outside your door wasn't an everyday occurrence on the island. Besides, the man hadn't reached for her purse. He was after her. He had tried to render her immobile.

It took almost fifteen minutes for her fellow officers to

arrive at Alyssa's house. Practically every officer on the island—and her family, as well—arrived around the same time. Her mother kept a police scanner running in her house, and if they didn't have company, she kept the staticky signal buzzing. Her dad came charging up the lane ahead of Harper's cruiser. At the speed he was going, he was itching for a ticket.

Alyssa opened the door and tucked the gun back into the holster. Her head had cleared up somewhat, but it was pounding like a hammer, and she was still a little dizzy.

Her mother and father bounded up the steps ahead of Harper and the officers.

After one look, her mother called the town's only doctor and browbeat her into making a house call.

"Which way did he go?" Harper asked.

"On the ocean side. His boat is long gone," she said.

"Hope he left some footprints." Alyssa saw him direct the officers. She wanted to be a part of this.

"I've got equipment in my car," she told Harper.

"So do I. Sit before you fall on your face."

Alyssa was glad to ease into a chair, even though she felt useless.

"You look like hell," her mother said.

"Thank you."

"Can you describe him?" Harper asked.

She shook her head. "It was too dark. The fog had rolled in. And his face was covered with a mask. Around my height. He should have a limp and a few bruises. Weighed about one-ninety."

"That could describe most of the men on the island," Harper said and went outside. She saw lights flashing around the house.

"Not to mention those off the island," Alyssa said almost to herself.

"I told you to get one of those yard lights," her mother

scolded. "I'm ordering four—one on each side—first thing Monday morning."

"Lights don't help in the fog, Mom."

"We don't have fog every night, do we?" her mother asked.

Alyssa liked the night sky without the lights. Lights were intrusive. And her mother would flood the place with them. "Don't bother. I'll order them." She'd put one on the garage side so that she'd still have her night view on the ocean sides. Alyssa had moved to the middle of nowhere for a reason.

Alyssa could see the lights on the beach and the officers working. Probably trying to make casts of a clear footprint in the sand before the tide washed it away. When she went to the kitchen for a glass of water, she saw headlights coming up the lane. Probably one of her brothers. She rubbed her head. A lump had formed where she'd hit the steps. She hoped it was the doctor.

Jordan didn't know what Alyssa expected of him. He was dating her, wasn't he? Couldn't buy her gifts, that's for sure. So what did she want? He wasn't even thinking about the M word, but he knew he wasn't ready to give up on her yet, he thought as he finally made it to the island.

He felt like an idiot, but he'd put too much into this for it to end over a stupid tennis bracelet. If she didn't want jewelry, he wouldn't buy her any. She hadn't balked over the clothes. He'd chosen the color because he'd thought it would match well with her complexion. When he'd seen her in that outfit, he wanted to strip her and make love with her all over again.

And she'd thanked him by paying for it herself. He'd had the amount refunded to her charge card. A man had some say, didn't he?

It was late. He didn't have a little speedboat to jet across the water to Alyssa's house. He drove around the long way, and by the time he made it there, dark had set in. He understood why Alyssa used the boat sometimes, although she hadn't lately.

The presence of several police cars in Alyssa's yard scared the wits out of him. Uniformed officers were everywhere. What the hell was going on?

He bounded out of the car and ran to the house, throwing the door open.

"What happened?" he asked. "Jesus." Alyssa looked whipped and bruised. He wanted to get his hands on the bastard who had done this.

"Someone was waiting for me when I arrived home."

"Who?" he asked, grabbing her and holding her close to his chest. He didn't care that she was angry with him.

"He wore a mask."

"I'm taking you to the doctor."

"Too late. Mom already called her, and she's on her way. You shouldn't be here. I want you to leave."

"After we talk," he said.

"We have nothing to discuss." She tried to pull away, but he held her tighter.

"I can't leave, Alyssa. So stop fighting me."

"I don't have the energy to fight you right now."

"Then don't."

The doctor came, finishing their argument.

Alyssa had a concussion, the doctor said. And soon after the diagnosis, other relatives arrived.

Great. That's all she needed. A party in her house.

John was stretched out on Alyssa's living room sofa. She'd offered the bed, but he'd assured her he was going to keep watch from the living room. Twenty minutes later, she heard an occasional snore.

Her brother took up residence in her guest bedroom.

Jordan and Alyssa sat in the sunroom with a movie on, but they weren't really watching the tube. She was snuggled under a blanket, her head resting on his shoulder. The doctor wanted her to be awakened every few hours.

"Nobody's running away with you but me," Jordan said with conviction.

"Umm, you're very territorial for someone in the doghouse."

"Damn right."

"If you think we're making love, you're wasting your time."

"I'm not here for that."

"You shouldn't be here at all."

"Rest, Alyssa," Jordan said.

"I can't."

He tugged her into his arms.

"He'll be back. And he'll attack again when you aren't prepared. This man is dangerous."

"I know that. But better me than someone who's totally incapable of fighting back."

His only response was a tired sigh.

Her family worried about her, but it was totally different having a man concerned about her job. The married guys on the force talked about it all the time.

Since neither of them was watching the tube, he flicked it off. Dark settled in. Soon, their eyes adjusted. Overhead, the fog had rolled in so thick they were cocooned.

This would make a great vacation home, Jordan thought. He liked the way the water surrounded it on three sides. The kids would love it here. They'd have to get rid of the phones, though. No one to disturb their sanctuary.

Alyssa yawned and fell asleep, only to be awakened a

couple of hours later. Jordan popped the lamp on and looked at her eyes. Asked her asinine questions, like how many fingers he held up. That damn watch of his was bugging her.

He reset the alarm on his watch and popped out the light. And since Alyssa was wide awake, they talked before they fell asleep.

It was late that night when he drove to Smithfield to pick April up from the bus stop. He'd have to forget Alyssa until after things relaxed. They'd think she'd frightened him off like some scared rabbit. Little did they know, he was a patient man. A month, maybe two, from now, he'd be back. And he'd be more prepared.

He drove slowly along the road. He'd given April enough money to catch cabs and then some, but he knew she'd save it for her car. Maybe he'd buy her a car. He'd enjoyed himself with her the last time, although she hadn't enjoyed it. She wasn't a faker like Vicky. Vicky was good at faking that she liked what he did to her body . . . until she'd turned on him. But this one wasn't a good actress. Much wasn't required of her. He even got turned on a little by her fear and reticence. She was one uptight sister.

He wondered when she'd turn on him. Eventually, they all did.

He sighed deeply. These women needed to be taught lessons. They weren't afraid of anything. There was something to be said for boldness. But at the end, Vicky was frightened. She showed him the proper respect.

He pulled up beside April and lowered the window. She quickened her steps, moving further from the road, and he rolled along slowly as she continued to walk. She was scared to death, hoping danger would hold off until she could get that car.

"What did I tell you about walking this time of night?" he asked.

This time, she glanced at him a little uncertainly. "I didn't know you were coming," she said, approaching the car.

"Climb in."

She hesitated a second, then got in. He could tell something was going on in her mind.

"Want to talk about it?" he asked softly, trying to ease her fears. He hadn't hurt her, after all. He'd left her several hundred dollars. What did she have to be upset about? Many women looked forward to not having to put out to men—to touch them, to satisfy their different whims. He did all the work.

She sighed. "We'll talk when we get to my house."

Dread settled in his stomach. Then anger quickly consumed him. He drove to her house in silence. He deliberately kept the music off. He wanted her to feel uncomfortable.

They were all cheating whores. She was no different.

"Have you told anyone about us?" he asked.

"Who would I tell?" she asked.

"Women talk."

"I wouldn't tell *anyone* about this," April said disdainfully. As if he was some creep or something. She'd be sorry for talking to him like that. He didn't take crap from any woman. He was as sane as the next man. Even more so.

He parked in front of her house. It was supposed to rain later on tonight. That was good. It would smear his tracks. He wouldn't want his tire tracks in her yard.

"May I come in?" he asked.

"I don't think so."

"We don't have to do anything. Just talk. I just need to talk."

After hesitating, she said, "Just for a little while. I have to work tomorrow."

They both opened their doors at the same time and

walked up the creaky steps to the house. She fiddled with the key, almost dropped it, but he didn't offer to help her. It was obvious she was nervous. She should be.

They were finally in the house. She shut the door and stood there.

"I'm not going to bite you," he said around a laugh.

She emitted a nervous laugh before taking off her jacket, hanging it in the foyer closet, and stashing her purse on the shelf. He made himself comfortable on her old, faded couch.

"You deserve nice things," he said. "I'd like to buy you gifts."

She focused on her hands. "I work two jobs for my needs."

"You shouldn't have to."

"I like to work. Nothing's free in life," she said, tilting her chin. "That's why the arrangement we have won't work. I don't feel good about doing that."

"I care about you," he said. "I'm not just any man."

"But it's not right. I wasn't brought up that way." She shook her head. "I think you should leave."

"That's the way you want it? There's no changing your mind?"

She tilted her chin again. "It's not for me."

He stood and approached her, giving her a warm smile. "I respect you for your decision," he said, trying to stem the anger boiling inside of him. He held her by the shoulders. "Just a little kiss good-bye."

He pulled her close. Tilted her chin and kissed her. When she began to pull back, he held firm. She began to struggle, but he wouldn't let her go. It was time he taught her she wasn't running the show.

"Stop it!" she mumbled against his lips. He bit her tongue. She screamed. He slapped her hard.

She fell back. "Get out. Now!" she screamed, holding her cheek while scrambling to get away.

But he didn't leave. He advanced on her.

She backed up, stumbled over a chair, then scrambled to the hallway. Before she could shuffle more than a couple of feet, he caught her and laid his considerable weight on her. She tried to claw his face, but he knocked her hand away and punched her in the face again and again until she fell and was too dazed to move. He pinned her hands with one of his own and choked her until she stopped struggling. Her meager struggles were nothing against his power.

Breathing hard, he knelt on the floor and gazed down at her. He ripped her panties off and tied her hands. He glanced around him. There wasn't too much damage. Using the remote, he opened his trunk, carried her to his car, and carefully laid her in the pristine trunk. Then he shut it.

Back inside, he tidied the place and grabbed her purse and jacket. He took a couple of minutes to wipe off his fingerprints before he turned off the lights. The phone rang, jolting him. His heart thundered in his chest. He closed the door behind him, careful to wipe the doorknob before he strolled to his car and drove away.

He could keep her for a while and play out all his wildest fantasies until he had Alyssa. He wouldn't need April then.

Chapter 14

Reginald had promised to cut Melinda's grass Monday morning. He would have done it Saturday, but he had two funerals to direct.

Melinda had told him she was used to cutting her own grass, but he made such a big deal out of it, she let him do it. She watched him come up her sidewalk with labored steps. She opened the door for him and leaned back in shock.

"What happened to you?" she asked.

"Step broke. Fell down, hit my head. I feel like the walking wounded."

"You look like it, too. And so does Alyssa. She was attacked last night."

"What? How is she?"

"Got a concussion, but other than that, she's okay. I went over there for a little while. It was pretty late, so I didn't stay long. I talked to Mrs. Naomi for a few minutes."

"Who attacked her?" he asked, clearly concerned.

"The man wore a mask."

"I told her over and over not to buy that place. It's too isolated."

"My house is just as isolated."

"You have other houses close by. Not like hers."

Melinda thought he'd gotten over Alyssa after their kiss, but now, she wasn't so sure. If he was really in love with her, it wouldn't clear his heart so easily. Her own heart sank. She'd been in love with him forever, and he'd never noticed.

"Jordan was there."

"Why was he hanging around?"

"They're dating," Melinda said.

"Humph. It's not going to last."

"What do you know?" Melinda asked. "I'll just cut my own grass."

"Why do you think I'm here? I told you I was going to cut it, and that's what I'm going to do."

"You really want to visit Alyssa."

"Of course I do. We're still friends."

Melinda made a rude noise. "You're still in love with her like a sick puppy."

"What the hell is this all about?"

"Nothing." She all but slammed the door in his face.

He shook his head and retrieved the lawn mower from the garage.

Melinda knew he didn't have a freaking clue about what was as annoying to her as sand in a shoe. Men were so dense.

He was clearly in pain, yet being a man, he had to cut the grass anyway, knowing very well she could do the job. What was he trying to prove? Alyssa wasn't there to see his heroic gesture.

Melinda rubbed her forehead. Alyssa was her very best friend. Why was she getting bent out of shape because Reginald loved her? She could understand his infatuation. Alyssa thought every man saw her as the Amazon woman. But they actually saw a strong, aggressive female who turned them on. So how could she blame Reginald for the way he felt?

Melinda poured a glass of iced tea and carried it out-side. It was painful to watch him limp up and down the rows as if his life depended on cutting the blasted grass. She had a large yard. She watched until she couldn't stand it any longer, then with a glass of chilled tea, she deter-minedly tread across the lawn until she reached him. He hadn't cut long enough to be thirsty, but she thrust the glass at him anyway. With a smile, he took it from her.

The motor was still running, and while he swallowed, Melinda grasped the mower's handle and started pushing it. When she made it to the end and turned around, he was glaring at her.

"Go in the house and sit down," she yelled. "I'll be in soon."

Lisa wore one of Vanetta's silk nightgowns. It was pure luxury to sleep in a soft fabric like that. Vanetta gave her fine garments for gifts, but Lisa always felt she had to save them for special occasions. Besides, you had to dry-clean silk. She could never wrap her mind around dry-cleaning something she slept in. And if she washed it herself, it was the devil to iron. But Vanetta didn't have to worry about ironing her clothes. She had help to do all that for her.

Lisa smelled coffee just before Vanetta came into her room with two cups. She sat up in bed, and Vanetta handed her a cup. Lisa blew on it, then took a heavenly sip. Vanetta bought the good stuff—Blue Mountain from the islands.

"That hit the spot. Did you get much sleep last night?" Lisa asked.

"I haven't gotten much sleep since Matthew died."

"What do you think is the significance of the picture of the bowl?"

"At this point, I don't have a clue."

"Are you going to tell Alyssa about it?"

"Probably. She was attacked last night. Mama thinks it might be Matthew's killer."

"Oh, my Lord. Is she okay?"

"Yeah." Vanetta sighed. "She's pretty good at taking care of herself. She has a concussion and some bruises. I'll call her today."

"I think I'll drive by her place."

"As angry as she's made me, I still don't want anything to happen to her," Vanetta said.

"It's the job," Lisa said. "It's not you."

"Anyway, I don't want to talk about all this right now. My head is swimming. When I called this morning, Jordan answered the phone. Alyssa was still sleeping."

"Jordan Ellis? He stays at the B&B sometimes. I just can't picture them together," Lisa said.

"Why not?"

"He seems to prefer the cheerleader type. The perfect little wife who does the social thing." She looked at Vanetta. "Like you, actually."

Vanetta rolled her eyes. "I wasn't a cheerleader."

"You could have been."

"Jordan's a really nice guy. He's down to earth, and I think he and Alyssa are a very good match."

"Well, if they marry, she'll be moving into that monstrosity of a house he's building. It's the largest on the island. About twice the size of yours."

"It is going to be nice, isn't it? I'm glad mine is smaller. What would I do running around alone in a place that large?" Tears shimmered in her eyes.

"I could think of a million things to do with it. Especially if I had that kind of money. It'll take ten maids to clean it."

"You should start your own cleaning service," Vanetta said, wiping her eyes. "You're so good."

"What do I know about business?"

"You could learn. I'll teach you what you need to know, or you could always take courses. There are enough colleges around here."

"Hmm."

"Jordan would be the first one to hire you. He's not going to clean it. And there are several islanders who'd love to have someone to do the cleaning. Ever thought about that?"

Lisa shrugged. "Not really." Then she could forget about vacations. People who worked for themselves worked themselves half to death. She wasn't ready to settle down that much.

"Do you want to talk about it?"

"I don't think I can."

"I don't want to pressure you, but I'm here if you want me to help you make a business plan."

"You are way ahead of me now."

"Lisa, you're your own worst enemy. You always put yourself down. You are very capable. You can do more than you think you can. What makes you think God gave everybody else gifts and didn't give you any? It's a matter of using what the Lord gave you. You know your strengths and weaknesses. Figure out what your gifts are, and go with it." She nudged her in the side. "I'll be your first customer."

Lisa chuckled. "I couldn't charge my own sister."

Vanetta raised her gaze to the ceiling. "I have a lot to teach you."

Lisa smiled. Graham Smith had told her to stop putting herself down, too. He'd come to the island to rob them of the golden bowl and doubloons. He even thought Aunt Anna had stashed away jewels and gold bars.

He'd befriended her. Lisa had always chosen the wrong kind of man to date. None of her relationships worked out.

So she'd taken a break from relationships. She just couldn't go through another emotional upheaval. So he'd asked if he could just be a friend.

He was an assistant professor, and she wondered why some educated guy like that would want to be her friend. But he'd told her to stop looking down on herself. He was so convincing, and she'd believed him—until he kidnapped her and held her for ransom. Then she'd known it was all a lie. That he was only using her. But in the end, he'd died for her. He'd taken the bullet his partner had meant to kill her with.

It shook Lisa up that someone had died to save her. Grandma said you were supposed to learn by life's failures. And often, she tried to decide what the lesson had been. The only thing she'd been able to come up with so far was that she was still a bad judge of character. She couldn't trust herself around men. She couldn't even pick friends, much less decent dates.

But sometimes, she considered that maybe she should at least do something worthwhile with her life. After all, Graham had thought she was worth saving. But for the life of her, she didn't know what her purpose was.

Oh, crap. This was just too much thinking. She glanced at her sister. Vanetta was always doing good deeds. After what had happened, Lisa was doing the best she could to put one foot in front of the other.

Alyssa slept until nine. When she got up, Jordan was in the kitchen talking to her brother. She stretched, and her muscles screamed in pain. A hot shower should help, she thought and escaped to the bathroom. Her head was still pounding, but not as bad as the night before. She brushed her teeth, then turned on the shower. The warm spray felt good on her body. She stayed in longer than usual, before drying off and dressing.

She smelled food as she went down the hallway. Someone had fixed breakfast. John and her brother were already eating. Alyssa sat, and Jordan set a plate in front of her with a sweet kiss.

She gave him the eye.

"As soon as you finish breakfast, I'm going to run you by the clinic." The only medical facility on the island was the clinic. "Doc worked you into her schedule. She wants to see you. And you can't drive."

"For chrissakes, I'm not an invalid." She focused on John. "After breakfast, we need to discuss this case and decide if the break-in is connected to Matthew and Vicky in any way."

"After you get the okay from the clinic," Jordan said, glancing at his watch. "Get a move on. We leave in a few minutes."

"Listen, I've been running into nothing but dead ends. For the first time, we have a lead. And I'm not about to pass it up."

"After the visit to the clinic," he repeated.

"You're beginning to be a pain in the ass."

"I can live with that," Jordan said.

John and her useless brother grinned at each other. No help from that quarter.

"Then you'll be so kind as to drop me by Shana's after the appointment." She shoved her chair back and stood. Suddenly dizzy, she wished she'd taken things more slowly. Jordan caught her arm.

"I'm okay now. Let's go."

John and Jordan went with her to the clinic. She was told not to return to work until Tuesday, but Alyssa couldn't sit around her house twiddling her thumbs. "Let's stop by Shana's, then we'll go back home."

"The doctor said . . ."

"If you are going to bitch about it, I can drive myself."

Jordan pressed his lips together. "Where does she live?"

John gave him directions, and Alyssa studied her notes from her previous interview. Shana's car was still in the yard when they drove up. Evidently, she wasn't going to work. She was out of the car and at the door before the men had time to take full breaths.

When Shana answered the bell, she seemed shocked to see her. "Thank you. I'll come in," Alyssa said.

"Oh, sure. How are you? I heard about your accident."

"It wasn't an accident." John caught the door before it slammed. He must have convinced Jordan to wait for them since it was official police business.

"And I've had all the bullshit I'm going to put up with," Alyssa said. "What was going on with Victoria? She would have told you, if no one else."

Shana ran her tongue over her lips. "I don't know where she was, honest."

"We know where she died. We don't know why she was there or who's so freaking frightened they want to kill me."

"I don't know that, either."

"I want to know what you know, Shana."

"Just that she found out somebody had deliberately spread that rumor about her husband, and she was going to make him pay. But I don't know how that's going to help you because she wouldn't tell me any names. I told her to be careful."

"Is that why she was with Matthew?" The only people who would benefit from the funeral business were Reginald and Stanley. They had already opened a funeral parlor in Norfolk and were getting good business there. Reginald had agreed to continue working for Brit on a part-time basis until the Norfolk business grew enough to support both Stanley and him.

That had all occurred while Alyssa was working in Baltimore to get experience as a detective. By the time she returned, Brit had sold his business to Stanley and Reginald.

If Vicky knew something, why hadn't she come to her?

She needed to talk to Reginald.

"Have you told me everything?"

"Vicky mentioned that precious bowl your grandmother's always talking about."

"What about it?"

"I don't know. Honest to God, I've told you everything. I don't know anything else."

"Listen, I've heard the last lie from you. You better come clean with everything."

"That's all I know. She wouldn't tell me anymore."

"If you get any additional information, I had better hear about it. Do you understand me, Shana? No more holding out on me."

Alyssa left, and John followed her to the car.

"Do you think she was blackmailing Reginald?" he asked. "Or maybe Stanley?"

Alyssa's first thought was that Reginald wasn't a murderer. Then she remembered how he'd refused to go on the trip with her because of a service Stanley could easily have directed. But Reginald wasn't a murderer. She'd known him forever. He was still her friend. She needed answers to questions though.

She trusted Reginald. She didn't know Stanley as well. Could Vicky have been blackmailing Stanley? She needed to talk with both men, but first, Reginald. Pick his brain and see what he knew.

When John opened the door, she realized he was still waiting for an answer. "I don't know," she said. "Let's go to Reginald's," she said to Jordan.

"One stop, remember?"

"This is important."

"Visiting your old boyfriend?" His mouth almost twisted in a sneer.

"Strictly business."

He stared at her a moment before he realized something was going on. "Can you talk about it?"

"Not yet."

He started the motor and drove away. Reginald wasn't at home. Alyssa dialed Reginald's cell number. He answered quickly.

"Hi, I need to talk to you. Where are you?" she asked.

"At Melinda's. I just heard about your attack. Are you okay?"

"Yes. Stay there. I'll be right over."

Melinda finished with the grass and pushed the lawn mower back to the garage. She felt hot and sweaty while Reginald, her hero, looked cool and comfortable. She nodded toward the phone. "Do you have to go into the office?"

"No. That was Alyssa. She wants to talk with me. She's on her way over."

Did his eyes light up, or was her imagination on overdrive?

"What does she want to talk to you about?"

He shrugged. "Beats me."

Melinda could have hit him. He was just too clueless to live. "I'm going inside to clean up."

"Sure. The tea's good."

As far as he was concerned, she didn't exist. Melinda tore into the house, slamming the door behind her, leaving Reginald wondering what the heck was wrong with her.

He'd agreed to cut the grass, hadn't he? And hadn't he

come here on his day off to do that very chore? She didn't have to do it. Stubborn woman. He couldn't get that kiss or the feel of her lush curves against his body out of his mind.

When the car pulled into the gravel driveway, Reginald was sitting on the steps nursing a drink. Alyssa and John got out of the car, and so did Jordan this time. He leaned beside the car while Alyssa and John approached Reginald, John walking ahead of Alyssa.

"What happened to you?" John asked him.

"Steps broke. I fell down them."

"Your steps?" John asked, a note of surprise in his voice. "More than one broke at the same time?"

"It was the damnedest thing. Never happened before. It was a clean cut, too. Like somebody took a saw to it and cut it nearly clean through. Why would somebody do that?"

John glanced at Alyssa.

"It's funny," John said. "Alyssa beat the crap out of somebody last night. You look like you tangled with a wildcat like Alyssa here."

Alyssa realized she should be interrogating Reginald, but John was asking appropriate questions.

Reginald stood, then winced in pain. "You think I attacked Alyssa?"

"I don't know," John said. "You tell me."

"You're an idiot if you think that, John." He leveled his gaze on Alyssa. "Alyssa, you can't believe for a moment that I would attack you. Not after all we've meant to each other."

"I'm asking the questions now," John said, even shocking Alyssa that he was taking the lead this way.

"Are you arresting me? Do I need to contact a lawyer?"

"We're just asking questions? Do you have anything to hide?"

"No." Reginald's mouth was pinched in outrage.

"According to Vicky, the tales about her husband's involvement in necrophilia were lies, and she discovered who spread them and why," Alyssa asked. "You were working with Brit at the time. Did she talk to you, or do you have suspicions about who that person might be?"

"No. I hope you find out who did it because it ruined that man's business."

"But you benefitted from it, at least you and Stanley did," John said.

"I would never have done anything to hurt Brit. He gave me my first job in the funeral business. I repeat, I have no idea who spread the rumors, and I never believed them. I've never seen him do anything like that and never thought he would."

"How dare you," Melinda came out the house like an avenging angel. "How dare you question Reginald about those murders?"

"Nobody's blaming—" Alyssa started, surprised at Melinda's change of opinion about Reginald.

"Or for hurting you. You know he loves you. He'd never hurt you, Alyssa."

"I didn't say—"

"But you think he'd kill Vicky or Matthew? You of all people know better."

"Melinda"—John approached her with his hands outstretched—"we have to question everyone. We have to get the necessary information so we can find the killer."

"Trying to pin it on Reginald isn't going to get your killer."

Alyssa glanced at Reginald. "You might want to go to the clinic."

"I'll be fine."

"Fix that step," Alyssa said.

John glanced at Reginald before they left. "Mind if we take a look at that step?"

"Knock yourselves out," Reginald said, and John and Alyssa left for the car.

"Where to?" Jordan asked, settling behind the wheel and knowing very well they weren't going home.

"I want to get a look at that step," Alyssa said. "I don't like the way this is going, John."

"Hmm."

Jordan knew the way to Reginald's house.

"Melinda, I didn't . . ." Reginald started.

"I know," she said.

"Why do you trust me?" Reginald asked her. "I'd expect you to be the first in line ready to string me from a rope."

"Vicky was my sister. If I thought for one second that you were responsible for her death, you're right—I'd be at the head of the line."

Reginald stared at her.

"But you're no murderer. It's not in you. I've never met a more considerate, gentle man."

He continued to stare at Melinda for so long she began to fidget. "What?" she asked.

"I've been looking at the wrong woman, haven't I?"

Melinda grunted. "What else is new?"

"It's crazy. After . . . well, suddenly I was spending more time with you and started feeling these . . . and it seemed weird. I thought it was because of what I was going through with Alyssa, then I started to realize it had nothing to do with her. I just never expected . . ."

"Like I said, men are so dense."

"Thank you." Reginald cleared his throat. "How long?"

"It's not important." She wasn't going to play dumb. But she wasn't going to tell him she'd been in love with him forever, either.

"To me, it is."

"You know now. Isn't that enough? Do I have to give you my life history?"

"I already know your history. You're as bad in choosing men as I've been in choosing women."

"I never expected anything out of my relationships."

"I'm not a no strings attached kind of guy," he said.

"I know that," Melinda said.

"So what if after I'm out of all this mess, I take you out?"

"I'd say that's the most sensible thing you've done in years."

"Years?"

"Yes, years. So why does it have to be after this is over? The one thing my sister's death has taught me is not to put life on hold. We aren't promised a future."

"Vicky didn't live her life thinking that. And she wouldn't want you to live yours like that, either."

"Alyssa! Alyssa!"

Patience Kingsley went staggering across the parking lot, trying to get to Alyssa.

"Patience, come back here," her husband Stanley said. "You shouldn't have driven in your condition. You could have hurt someone or yourself."

"Just get away from me!" she shouted. "Alyssa! Help me."

Alyssa rushed over to the clearly distraught woman. "What is it, Patience?"

"She's having a reaction to the alcohol, that's all," Stanley said.

"No, I'm not." Her words were slurred.

"Honey, you can barely stand on your feet. Let me take you home." He looked at Alyssa. "It's Reginald. She's been overset since he was questioned." He guided Patience firmly toward the car.

Patience looked back at Alyssa with fear in her eyes.

"Stanley, one moment, please." Alyssa approached them and pulled Patience aside. "What did you want to talk to me about?" she asked.

"My brother didn't kill anybody. You've got to believe me. You know him. You've been friends . . ."

"I know."

"Then don't pin the murders on him. And somebody tried to hurt him."

"Are you okay?" Alyssa asked her gently.

"Don't worry about me. I'm worried about Reg."

"He'll be okay. Just take care of yourself. No more driving in your condition. Stanley, take her keys away. She's already lost her license. Next time, she'll get locked up."

"He's not home most of the time. I have to get around."

"Not in this condition. You should consider hiring someone to stay with her when you're away," Alyssa said to Stanley.

"I don't drive. I get someone to bring me down here. There she is." Patience pointed to her cleaning lady. "Yoo-hoo," Patience called out. "I'm going to visit my brother." Patience rushed to the car.

"Stanley, you have to get help for her."

"We can't just lock people up these days without their consent, but I'll try."

The next day, Alyssa was feeling better so she met with Harper and John.

"You can't be objective about this, Alyssa. Reginald's your friend."

"He's not a murderer. Someone sawed through his step."

"I don't want to hear any crap about women's intuit—"

"Damn it, Harper, this has nothing to do with women's intuition or *professional* intuition. It's about knowing a person inside out. Knowing his likes, dislikes, and what he is and is not capable of doing. And I'm telling you, Reginald didn't kill them." Alyssa paced the room and glared at Harper.

"You don't know what a person is capable of doing until he's backed against the wall. Vicky could have tied his balls in a knot, and he came out swinging."

"This murder was well-planned, not the work of someone who was acting on instinct. Matthew was drugged. That had to be planned in advance. Who the heck walks around with roofies just in case he'll happen to need them to drug someone?"

"How do you know Reginald isn't taking drugs?"

"I know the man. He doesn't touch drugs."

"The man is as bruised as if he'd gone six rounds with you, for crissakes. He's our prime suspect." Harper jabbed a finger in her direction. "If he takes a leak outside that house, I want to know about it."

"We can clear him quickly." Alyssa sat back in her seat with a satisfied smirk. "They own a limousine service in Norfolk. Reginald and Stanley drive company cars. All their vehicles have a GPS tracking device. They have records on his whereabouts. Reginald only drives one car, the company car, and he drives it everywhere. So there's a record of his movements."

"That can prove helpful, but the person who attacked you got away in a boat."

"The person who murdered Matthew and Vicky drove a car. If you're assuming Reginald committed the murders, then the GPS tracking will weed him out."

"All right. Let's get a warrant for their records. Don't be disappointed if it doesn't go the way you expect. Be ready to deal with the situation if he's our man."

"I can handle it."

"I don't give a damn about what you believe about Reginald. I want you to do your job."

"Don't I always?" Alyssa slammed out of Harper's office and went into her own. Shutting the door, she stood there, gathering herself. It was her job to muddle through the garbage to the truth. And she would.

She rubbed the knot on her head. The swelling had gone down somewhat, but she still suffered from headaches. She pulled the drawer open and shook out two aspirins. Opening a bottle of water, she downed the pills.

Her gaze went to the paper on her desk. The front page news featured two women who were missing. One in Norfolk, the other in Smithfield. Over the last few years, Alyssa had developed a strong belief in following her instincts. They had kept her alive on Baltimore's streets.

She glanced at the article again and began to read about the women who both had disappeared in the dead of night, as if they'd walked off the face of the earth. None of their clothes were missing. It was as if they had left their homes to go to the mall or to work and never returned. Did they leave with someone they knew and trusted? Had they been drugged as Matthew had been?

The information on the funeral home's cars was kept in Norfolk. They had to do the paperwork to get evidence out of their jurisdiction, which took longer.

Jordan received a call from Vanetta a few minutes before he was due to leave for the island.

"I'm sorry to bother you, but I wanted to ask if Matthew had ever discussed my grandmother's golden bowl with you. I found a picture of it in his office."

"No, he didn't." Jordan leaned back in his seat. At some point, Alyssa had mentioned a missing family heirloom, but he hadn't paid too much attention to it. "Is there some significance?"

"I'm not sure. I don't know where he would have gotten

the picture. Things are so crazy . . . maybe I'm making too much out of nothing."

"I'll check into it," Jordan said, although he didn't see what he could do. He knew nothing of a bowl or why Matthew had the picture. Jordan felt as if the world had turned upside down in his absence.

Matthew would have trusted Curtis, and Jordan didn't believe he'd told Curtis any more than he'd revealed to Jordan or Wade. He buzzed Wade and asked him to come in.

"Are you aware of the Claxtons' golden heirloom bowl?" he asked.

"Matthew mentioned it," Wade said.

"Well, it's missing. What did Matt say?"

"Nothing much, just what you said. It's missing. About how that family had it for a few hundred years. Why do you keep questioning me? He talked to you more than he talked to me."

"I haven't been here lately, remember?"

He nodded. "Is it that valuable?"

"I don't know the assessed value. I would imagine since it's from the 1600s, it's pretty valuable."

"Hmm."

"I'm headed to the island," Jordan said. "See you in the morning."

Wade nodded and left.

Okay, Jordan thought. He'd gotten through the last two nights with Alyssa, but she was feeling better now, so he'd better come up with a reason for her to keep him around.

An hour later, he arrived at her house. She pulled in right after he arrived.

"What are you doing here?" she asked.

"Where else would I be?"

"Help me understand this. I'm not willing to put up with the kind of relationship you're obviously accustomed to. So I don't understand why you're still coming around."

Jordan dug his hands into his pockets. "Because I care for you. I admit I made a mistake in giving you the jewelry. It wasn't meant as payment for our intimacy. Maybe I said the wrong thing."

"I don't know. I'm not comfortable with this relationship."

"Do you always hold a mistake against a guy forever?"

"Do you trust your business acquaintances so easily again?" Alyssa asked.

"It depends. I'm used to playing by a different set of rules."

"And that's what worries me. Your mother called."

Jordan smothered a curse. "I'm sure she gave you an earful."

"She wished me well. She's leaving soon and wants me to visit before she does."

"I'll be happy to take you."

"We come from different worlds."

"That's where you're wrong. Actually, we come from the same background," Jordan said.

"When a man gives me a gift, I want it to be from the heart, not something you ordered up by the dozen to fit the girlfriend of the moment."

"It may not have seemed like it, but the gift was from the heart. I was truly happy, and it wasn't just sex. Being with you is different. It satisfies something that's missing in my soul."

Alyssa sighed. "We'll take it a day at a time."

"For now," Jordan said.

Chapter 15

The next day, Alyssa sat beside the technician at the funeral home studying the pages of data detailing the routes of each vehicle. They were focused on tracking Reginald's movements.

"See here," he said. "This shows every place he drove yesterday.

Nothing interesting there. It clearly pinpointed him as being at Melinda's house, even revealing the street names. As they perused data from several days, Alyssa saw that he visited Melinda every day. Had he visited her daily since Vicky's death? Was a romance cooking there? Alyssa tried to picture Reginald and Melinda together. She couldn't see it, but what did she know?

She gave the technician the date of the murders and asked him to give her Reginald's car route. It started out as a normal day. He drove to the B&B, more than likely for breakfast. She wondered if he had eaten alone or with someone—why the heck did she care? Except he was trying to court her at the time. He drove to the funeral home in Norfolk and was there for a few hours. Then he went to the church and graveyard for the burial before driving back to the island. That night before, he had driven home around

seven and went to several places there, including the bar. His
car left again around eleven for Virginia Beach. It looked as
though he had driven . . . Alyssa stared at the screen. He'd
driven to Matthew's place in Virginia Beach, the place where
the murders had taken place around midnight.

Alyssa couldn't believe it. He was there for nearly an
hour before he left and drove to the dock. His car was
parked there for several hours. It wasn't moved again until
a few minutes before six the next morning, and it was clear
he'd taken the first ferry back to the island.

Sitting back in her seat, she glanced at John, who stared
back at her.

"The man who attacked you left in a boat," was all he
said.

With the damning evidence staring her in the face, she
still couldn't believe Reginald would attack her.

"There's got to be an explanation for this."

"You'll have time to figure it out after we arrest him,"
John said.

Alyssa saw no way around it. Harper was going to
demand it.

There was nothing worse than having to arrest your best
friend, especially when the evidence indicated someone
was a far stretch from the man she knew. Reginald was
home waiting for them when they arrived, and so was
Melinda. The tech must have called him.

John Mirandized him, but he rode in the back seat of
Alyssa's car to the station. Alyssa took her time driving
there, traveling below the speed limit. And he was silent.

As kids, Alyssa was always dragging Reginald into
trouble. She'd convinced him to go ino the ocean with her
for a swim when her grandmother told them not to go near
the water without adults present. She was the one dragging
him up the street to the store when Naomi told them to

stay in the backyard. And he'd suffered punishments with her when they were caught.

Alyssa always thought of ways to get into mischief. Not Reginald.

"You have to help me here," Alyssa said. "Who, besides your partner, would do this to you?"

"Oh, now you're going to try to stick it to Stanley?"

"You tell me. Who would have access to your car? Tell me what happened to Brit's business? I think all this is tied together."

"You're wrong. Whoever did this isn't connected with the business."

"Who else has access to your car?" Alyssa repeated.

"I don't know. Extra keys are locked up in the office in Norfolk."

Alyssa's radio crackled. "You gonna make it to the station by midnight?" John asked.

She tossed him the finger and swore, then heard his chuckle over the radio. Everyone was feeling good since they'd finally caught the man who had committed the most gruesome murder the island had seen.

"Would any of your other employees steal your car to frame you? Or kill Vicky and Matthew?"

"Everyone liked Vicky."

"Well, someone didn't," Alyssa said.

"Where the hell are you?" Jordan asked.

"On a stakeout."

"Again?"

Alyssa was in a summer house next door to Stanley's. They had a direct view of his driveway. Most of the employees with access to company cars didn't live on the island. A couple did, but who else could have set Reginald up that way? His sister drank so much she didn't know which way was up. Stanley could be out half the night, and she wouldn't know. "Where are you?"

"In your yard waiting for you," Jordan said impatiently.

"You have a key. Go on in," she said. She'd given him a key after the attack.

"What time will you be home?"

"I don't know."

"Who's with you?"

"John," she said impatiently. "What's with the third degree?"

"I'll see you later." He hung up.

"I'm telling you for the twentieth time, we're wasting good sleep," John said.

"If you say it one more time, you're walking home."

"I have my car, remember. You're testy tonight, aren't you?"

Alyssa tapped her fingers on the countertop. She hated stakeouts.

Melinda and Reginald. It had taken some time for her to wrap her mind around the two of them, but they were a match. Opposites in some ways, the same in others. Opposite enough that they wouldn't get bored with each other.

"I haven't had a full night's sleep in three nights," John said, even though he'd snored on her couch.

"Take a nap before I strangle you."

"You're disgruntled because you haven't had any sleep, either."

"Stanley's going to make a mistake, and I'll be right here when he does."

"How can you be so sure it's him? Seems a leap to me."

"Because he has access to Reginald's car," Alyssa said. "The slick bastard."

"He's not the only one with access. The manager of the limousine division has access."

* * *

Two freaking days of surveillance, and they didn't have crap. A stakeout was like watching paint dry, especially at Stanley's house. At seven-thirty A.M., he backed his car out of the garage. When it rounded the corner, John followed him. The first day, Patience made an appearance around noon. Alyssa hadn't seen her yesterday. She waited until eight and wondered why the housekeeper hadn't shown up. Was this her day off? Was Patience all right? She should go over there to make sure Patience was okay. Reginald couldn't check up on her.

Alyssa didn't want Patience to know she was under surveillance so she drove next door to her house.

She rang the doorbell. It took several minutes and several rings before Patience answered. She looked horrible, as if she'd drank the night away. She held on to the edge of the door.

"What do you want?" she asked. "Haven't you done enough?"

"I'd like to talk to you. May I come in?"

"You're going to arrest *me* now? Or are you searching for more incriminating evidence against my brother. I'm not going to help you."

"I just want to talk," Alyssa said.

"I need coffee." Reluctantly, she moved to the side, and Alyssa crossed the threshold into a beautiful, spacious home. Patience led the way to the formal living room.

"Can I fix you a cup of coffee?" Alyssa asked.

"I'm sorry. I should have offered you a cup. Stanley always leaves me some."

"I'll pour us a cup," Alyssa said.

Patience led the way to the kitchen. "The coffee's over there." She pointed beneath a cabinet. "But there's plenty in the pot. If it's not enough, more coffee is in the cabinet above it. I'll freshen up while you pour," she said and left the room.

Indeed, there was already coffee brewed—enough for both

of them to have a cup each, and Alyssa searched the cabinets for cups. She found them after the third cabinet. Beautiful floral china cups. No mugs for Patience. Alyssa retrieved two with their matching saucers. She started to pour. When the cup was half-full, she stopped pouring and gazed at that coffee as if she was in a trance. The perp had drugged Matthew.

Alyssa stared for several seconds. Stanley wasn't necessarily the perp. They'd followed him for two full days, and he had done nothing out of character. He spent most of his day at the office, returning around five. And there he usually stayed unless they were holding a body or he visited a family. There was really no reason for her to be here or for John and her to watch his house, except that she believed Reginald was innocent. And even believing in Reginald didn't make Stanley guilty. There were others at the funeral home who could have taken the key and used Reginald's car. Except Stanley's proximity to Reginald's house was too convenient to ignore. And maybe that was the reason the perp had chosen Reginald—he knew that with Reginald being her friend, she'd look at Stanley next.

A little devil in the back of her mind shouted that Reginald could be the perp. That there was a little evil demon in him she'd never seen. Didn't many serial killers lead normal lives? Didn't they attend church, have families who never knew of their deviant behavior?

Stanley might very well be innocent, but she wasn't taking any chances. She started to toss the coffee out, then stopped in midpour. She should at least test her theory. If nothing more, she'd know he wasn't using coffee to drug Patience. The poor woman was always out of it. Was he giving her drugs on top of the alcohol? She set the half-cupful aside to cool and tossed the remains from the pot. After washing out the pot, she started a fresh pot brewing before she went out to her car for a collection bag.

Alyssa glanced around the room. The kitchen was easily three times the size of hers with every state-of-the-art and top-of-the-line appliance you could think of, right down to the expensive coffee maker with its timer set to go off in the morning so you'd have a nice cup of coffee waiting for you when you came downstairs. Alyssa had debated getting one of those.

And the garden in the backyard was a gardener's dream. Fall flowers were in full bloom.

By the time Patience returned, Alyssa had two cups of coffee filled.

"Cream or sugar?" she asked Patience as if she was the lady of the manor.

"I'll get it." Patience selected a silver serving tray and put a silver creamer and sugar bowl on it with the two cups of coffee. There wasn't any tarnish on that silver. Who kept their silver pristine that way? A woman with help, Alyssa thought.

"It's warm out today. And you have a lovely garden out back. Let's sit there."

"It's my favorite spot," Patience said.

Alyssa carried the tray to the little iron bistro table and set the coffee and fixings there, placing the server on a side table. For a few minutes, she and Patience put sugar and cream into their coffee and savored a couple of sips while listening to the birds and enjoying the garden's view.

"You make great coffee," Patience said.

"Who can go wrong using your very expensive Blue Mountain brand? This is really worth the money."

"You get my brother off, and I'll send you a year's supply."

"Not necessary," Alyssa said. "I'll do my best for him."

Patience's gaze clouded. "You can't believe he killed anyone."

"I believe he's being framed. And whoever set this up did a very good job."

"Why would anyone involve him? He's never hurt anyone."

"I don't know. You know more about their employees than I do. Does he have any enemies?"

Patience rubbed her forehead. Her hands trembled, and tears slid down her cheeks. "I don't know anything. I'm so mixed up. The drink has affected my mind so much that I even have drunken dreams. I know it's my fault. I've tried to stop. Sometimes I don't even remember drinking, yet half the bottle of booze is gone in the morning, and I'm so out of it. This is the first morning I've been even halfway coherent."

"Do you have memory lapses often?"

Patience nodded. "I know I have to do better. By now, there's probably some permanent danger. Reg is so worried about that."

"Could Stanley be drugging you?" Alyssa asked.

"Why would he do that?" Patience asked, puzzled. "He's always trying to get me to quit drinking."

"Vicky said she knew who spread the lies about her husband being a necrophiliac, and I think she was blackmailing that person. I'm not saying Stanley spread the lies. Only that I'm looking at all the options. There are two major players in Brit losing his funeral business. Reginald worked for him, and both Reg and Stanley bought in at a substantially reduced rate. Locals refused to use his funeral home. Could Vicky have been blackmailing Stanley? Or do you believe she was blackmailing Reg?"

"But why? The mortuary business is booming. Even at that time, their business in Norfolk was enough to sustain both of them. Reginald was only working there to help Brit. He didn't need to work the office here any longer. The money they get from the island business is minimal compared to Norfolk."

Alyssa nodded. "Vicky also mentioned my aunt's golden bowl. It's missing. Stanley visited her often when her dementia worsened."

"Lots of people did. People cared about her. You know that. Even I visited her."

"Where did they get the money to buy out Brit?"

"I assumed they got a loan."

"Vicky's autopsy showed signs of sexual penetration after she died. Has Stanley ever dabbled in necrophilia? Or has he ever shown signs of unusual sexual habits?"

"No . . . I mean he likes to be in control, but nothing like . . . that's sick." Patience wouldn't meet Alyssa's eyes.

"What?" Alyssa said.

Patience stood. "It's time for you to go. You haven't convinced me that Stanley is involved. And Reginald certainly isn't."

"Two women are missing. One from Norfolk, the other from Smithfield. If someone has those women, it might not be too late to save them."

"Please leave."

"Your brother's future lies in whether I can find the person who did this. The GPS on his car puts him at one of women's house around the time she went missing. If you help me, I might be able to save her. But if you don't, she's going to die. Do you think all the drink in the world is going to let you live with that? Do you believe Reginald is innocent? If so, he doesn't deserve this."

Patience pointed a finger at Alyssa. "*You* arrested him."

"Because all the evidence points to Reginald, but you and I both know he couldn't have done it. Someone set him up. I had no choice, and if you don't help me, he might be accused of four murders. Virginia is a capital punishment state. Do you want him to get the lethal injection?"

"Stop it!" Patience put her hands to her ears.

"You can't close your mind to this, Patience, the way you've closed your eyes to your husband's sexual . . ."

"We don't sleep in the same bedroom."

"Because you hate his sexual habits? Am I right? Does he go to other women to satisfy his needs? And do you close your eyes to this because you don't want him touching you? Is this why you're drinking? You feel as if you have to stay with him because he's in business with Reginald and you don't want to upset the cart?"

Tears rolled down Patience's cheeks, but she didn't respond.

"There are options. You don't have to stay in this marriage and take it if you're unhappy. I'm not saying Stanley killed Vicky and Matthew, but someone did. With your help, I might be able to eliminate both Reginald and Stanley. Maybe one of the employees is responsible. But whoever did this kills people."

"Even if he has unusual habits, it doesn't make him a murderer."

"You're right. But we can't ignore questions. Such as, Vicky worked in the funeral home. If she caught Stanley with one of the corpses, she could have blackmailed him. And if she did, Stanley had to get rid of her. But she must have told Matthew. Because the murderer killed two people and left them in a suggestive pose. Why? Talk to me, please."

"Oh, God. Even if Stanley did all that, I don't know where he would put those women. I don't know how he could have framed my brother."

"Did the two of you ever go riding in isolated places when you were courting or just out for a drive?"

"Nowhere a body could be dumped."

"Do you have land that isn't being used?"

Patience shook her head. "No. I mean . . . maybe."

"Where?" Alyssa asked.

"There's nothing there. I haven't been there in years. There was an old barn, but Stanley said it had fallen down. And there was an old dock there, but that's probably rotted away. It's my uncle's place. He died a few years ago, and his children live in California. Since Reginald runs both the funeral homes, he doesn't have the time to deal with the land. Stanley has the grass cut sometimes, so it won't grow too wild. Reginald said he was going to offer to buy it since my cousins never come here, but he never got around to it."

"Where is it?"

"It's off Ocean Trail Road. The old barn used to sit back in the woods. It was small as barns go."

"Thanks, Patience. I want to pack my coffee to go," Alyssa said. "I don't get to drink the good stuff often." She was still taking the cooling coffee to analyze.

"Just give me a minute. I'll put it in a Styrofoam cup."

Alyssa carried the tray to the kitchen, and while Patience went to the bathroom, she poured the cooled coffee in a heavy duty plastic bag.

Alyssa tucked the bag in her jacket pocket.

"On second thought, I'm going to get moving," Alyssa called out. "Thanks."

As soon as Alyssa went outside, she called headquarters to ask for backup at Ocean Trail Road. "I'm going to check it out," she said. "John, can you meet me there?"

In the car, she carefully took the bag out of her pocket and tucked it in her cup holder. Then she drove toward Ocean Trail Road.

It took her fifteen minutes to reach the property. There were no fresh tire tracks there. The path was overgrown, as if it was rarely used. A dilapidated, weathered dock nearby was barely standing. The first storm would flatten it. A bunch of trees and bushes nearly hid a structure straight ahead.

Alyssa stopped a hundred feet from the barn. She took her gun out of her holster and released the safety. Stealthily, glancing all around her, she approached the barn—the barn that was supposed to have fallen down. A branch shivered. She ducked behind a tree and waited. A squirrel disappeared up a tree.

Releasing a breath, Alyssa glanced around again before she continued her progress to the barn.

She listened at the door but heard nothing inside. None of the other cruisers had arrived yet, but some instinct told her to go on. Stanley was probably in his office.

A lock secured the weather-beaten door. Stepping to the

side, Alyssa gently knocked and listened. She did not hear footsteps approaching. After a moment, she went to the back of the barn, but there wasn't an entrance there.

It was a small barn as barns went, just as Patience had mentioned. Just enough to hold some equipment, a little hay. She started back to the front when she saw what looked like a fresh . . . oh, my Lord. The fresh mound was the size of a grave.

She returned to the front and started kicking the door. Harper was going to have her ass for this, but two women were missing, and if a woman was in there, it was worth the destruction. She was still kicking when John approached her.

"I have a crowbar in my car," he said. "That'll pluck that lock right off."

He came back quickly with the crowbar and pried the lock off.

A woman was tied on the table, her legs dangling off the edge. She was completely naked. The place smelled rancid.

"No . . ." Alyssa moaned. They approached the body.

The woman's head moved.

"She's alive. Call it in," Alyssa said, recognizing her as April from her picture in the paper. Alyssa glanced around for something to cover the woman with, but found nothing. She quickly discarded her jacket and placed it over the woman. It was cool in the barn.

"April, do you hear me?"

She only moaned. "Please . . . no." April's voice croaked barely above a whisper. Her legs had to be uncomfortable, dangling like that.

"Help me move her," Alyssa said. "Make her more comfortable." Had the SOB kept her on the table like that for days?

Gently, she and John moved her.

"Where the heck is that ambulance?"

John disappeared. He came back with a bottle of water. "See if she can drink this."

He held April's head up while Alyssa tipped the bottle to her lips. She gulped some of the water too quickly and coughed.

"Try a little more, April," Alyssa said after she had stopped.

April licked her lips before she drank more water and coughed again.

"That SOB starved her."

Finally, they heard sirens in the distance. Harper arrived first, and the ambulance a few minutes later.

April had been airlifted to a hospital in Norfolk. They spent several hours at the scene processing it.

"Finding April doesn't clear Reginald," Harper said, coming up a hill.

"We'll see what she says when she revives."

"You're assuming two things. First, that she actually saw his face, and second, that she will survive."

"I'm hoping we find some DNA in our collected evidence."

There was an APB out for Stanley. He'd left work while they were at the barn, and he hadn't been seen since. They tried to track his car, but it had been found in some isolated area parked near the water.

"That boathouse can withstand a hurricane," Harper said, nodding toward the ocean. "He stored the boat in there." His gaze covered the horizon. "He could be anywhere."

"That boathouse doesn't look very sturdy from here," Alyssa said.

"It has supports beneath the outer covering."

A deputy had uncovered a woman's body in the shallow grave in back of the barn. Several other hills dotted the property. They had been forced to call in the area-wide task force, and a team was on its way to help with the search. The property was nearly sixty acres. There was no telling how many bodies were buried on it, or how long he'd been burying them. With a cursory glance, they'd already found four fairly recent graves, but the other sites were much older.

The next morning Alice was coherent, if still the worse for wear. Alyssa went in with the Norfolk PD to question her. The doctor was only letting them question her for a couple of minutes. An officer sat outside her door for her protection.

Alyssa approached the bed. "Hello, April."

April stared at her. An IV dripped nutrients and medication into her system. "I remember you," she said through dry, cracked lips. "I thought you were a dream."

"I'm Alyssa Claxton. We found you yesterday. Can you tell us who kidnapped you?"

"It was Stanley Kingsley. Did you say your name was Alyssa?"

"Yes."

"He always . . . when he rapes me, he always calls your name."

Alyssa couldn't let April see how much that unnerved her.

"Can you tell me what happened?" Alyssa asked gently.

Tears ran down Alice's face. "I met him though a friend. I'd seen him several times. I thought he was . . . nice." She broke into tears.

"I'm sorry. That's enough for today," the doctor said.

Alyssa wanted to argue, but the woman clearly wasn't in any condition to answer more questions. Alyssa patted her hand and left. In the hallway, April's anxious family was standing by. Thank God she had family to help her through this. She talked with them a few minutes before she left.

A car was posted at Stanley's house and at each of his

businesses, but it seemed Stanley had disappeared into thin air.

And since they knew Stanley had attacked her, John had taken up a post at Alyssa's house each evening. She was rarely alone these days.

The two of them drove back to the island.

"God, this area is so huge. There are a million places a person can get lost in," she said.

"If he's still here," John added. "I don't understand how Matthew fit in all this."

"Except to throw us off."

"I'm going home," Alyssa said to Jordan that evening.

"Is John with you?"

"He'll be there soon. He had to run to the office."

"Then you need to go there with him. I'm leaving the office in a few minutes. I don't want you there alone. How is April?"

"She has a long way to go, but they think she's going to pull through."

"I'm glad of that. But if you don't want to hang out at the office, go by your parents' place until someone is free."

"Oh, for heaven's sake. Stanley is long gone from here. Everyone's searching for him."

"You are one hardheaded woman. I love you, Alyssa. Do this for my peace of mind."

"Tell you what. I'm home. I'll continue to talk to you until I'm inside and the doors are locked." She carefully glanced around her and unhooked her gun before she left the car.

"You're going to be the death of me, you know that?" Jordan said.

"Of course not. You have to learn to relax and realize that I can take care of myself." He'd said he loved her.

"Are you in the house yet?"

"Almost."

"What's happening with those yard lights?"

"I . . . A car is coming up the lane."

"Get in the house, Alyssa."

"I'm in, and the door is locked." She went to the kitchen window. She didn't like this. She had never worried before. "It's Cleve."

"Thank God. Stanley has to be pretty ticked off with you."

Alyssa shuddered and went to the door to let her brother in.

"You're getting to be a pain in the ass, you know that?" Cleve said.

"Thank you so much."

"You go home alone, knowing that sick bastard is still out there. What's the matter with you?"

"I am not ten any longer. I can kick ass with the best of them. Hello to you, too. I need a walk and with your attitude, so do you."

He ignored her and went to the kitchen. "What do you have to eat? I was on my way to Cornell's place when I got the word."

"Nothing. I just got here. But feel free to fix anything you like."

"It's time Paradise got delivery. You'd think at least one pizza joint would offer the service."

"Wait another two decades."

Cleve was still searching the fridge. "Oh, you've got food."

"I do?"

She shoved him aside. Sure enough, there was fried chicken and a pasta salad. "Grandma was here."

"Bless her."

He dug into the depths of her fridge and pulled them out.

"I'm sure she brought greens over, too."

"Who cares about the greens?"

Alyssa found the kale her grandmother had prepared

and took the container out. "There's this thing I have about well-balanced meals. But first the walk and then chicken."

After a longing gaze at the food, Cleve went for his duffle bag. "Meet me in five."

It felt so good being outside in the cool air and hearing the waves rush against the shore beside her.

"Jordan. We need to talk about him," her brother said after they jogged about half a mile. The sun was sinking, and the stars were beginning to shine. The sunset was absolutely spectacular.

"No, we don't," Alyssa said.

"What are his intentions?" He slowed his steps to keep pace with her, but not by much.

"I just started dating the guy."

"Has he mentioned marriage? Or do you plan to live in sin?"

"It's too soon. How would you like it if I drilled you on your dates?"

"That's different."

"Mind your business," Alyssa told him.

"Mama hasn't made any announcements yet. And if you were engaged, she would shout it from the rooftop. You need to do something so she'll get off my back."

"You have to fight your own battles."

"How do you feel about him? The fact that he's in your house says a lot."

"It's a nice sunset," Alyssa said, unwilling to tackle her feelings or, at least, to voice them to her brother.

Chapter 16

Gazing through his binoculars, Stanley watched Alyssa and Cleve run. Rage zipped through him like a sizzle of electricity. She'd messed everything up. He knew she was the one. Nobody else could have put it all together. She had a way of getting information no one wanted to divulge. Even his own wife had betrayed him. No one else knew about that little spit of land. Reginald never would have thought he was using it.

He'd escaped capture by the skin of his teeth. The only thing that had saved him was seeing so many people there as he was arriving. Good thing he'd taken a look through his binoculars from far enough away before going to shore. In his boat, he was anonymous among the pleasure seekers and fishing boats.

They'd made it further down the path. They thought they could protect her from him, but they couldn't. Maybe it was a good thing he was found out. Now he could concentrate all his efforts on Alyssa. She was his. And she'd know soon enough.

When he captured her, he'd take her away.

He set the field glasses down. Opening up a compartment, he glanced at the bundle of money he'd stored there.

He'd started stashing it away just in case he needed to flee one day. Good thing, too, because he couldn't go to the bank now. Vicky had dipped into his savings considerably, what with all the money she'd demanded to keep her mouth shut.

But this little stash should be enough for Alyssa and him to make a fresh start.

Alyssa was beyond frustrated. An entire week had passed, and although Stanley's picture had run in the newspaper and the evening news, there hadn't been one definite sighting. He could be across the country, or even out of the country, by now.

On the other hand, he could be as close as the island. There were dozens of places he could be hiding. And since everyone believed he attacked Alyssa, there was no rest from her family.

She didn't understand why he was fixated on her. Why did he call her name when he raped other women?

Was he even now raping some other woman while he waited to capture her? She was never alone these days.

Jordan had been thinking about the bowl for some time, wondering why Matthew had a picture of it. Nothing unusual about having a picture of a family heirloom. Unless, of course, your reputation was suspect. Then people became suspicious of everything you did. He might have tracked down the people who'd stolen it. Jordan dialed Vanetta's number.

"Vanetta, was there anything else with the picture of the bowl?" he asked.

"It was in a folder with some papers, but I didn't pay much attention to them."

"Mind if I drop by to take a look?" he asked.

"I'll be here," she said.

Jordan was already on the island, so he drove directly to Vanetta's house.

She opened the door while he was coming up the walk and ushered him into Matthew's den.

"I took the folder out. It has four names and addresses in it."

The addresses were for various places all over the country—one in Philly, Denver, Raleigh, and Virginia Beach.

"Do you have a copier? May I make a copy of these?" Jordan asked.

"Of course."

John and Jordan were walking to Alyssa's house when she and Cleve returned from their run.

Jordan had taken off his suit jacket and carried it across his arm. John wore comfortable jeans and a shirt.

"I hope you're as hungry as I am. Grandma stocked my fridge," Alyssa said when they approached.

John rubbed his hands together. "Your grandmother is a great cook."

Alyssa left the men talking while she showered. By the time she was through, the smell of food drew her toward the kitchen. The oven was on, and the men had gathered in the kitchen. Everyone helped set the table, and they were soon seated, the aromatic food in the center.

"We got the toxicology report back," John said. "The coffee was drugged."

"With Rohypnol?"

"Yes."

"No wonder Patience was incoherent most of the time. With the combination of the drug and alcohol, she was

always stoned out of her mind. She's lucky to be alive."
Alyssa sighed. "I'll tell her tomorrow."

"If I were her, I'd throw out every edible item in the
house," Jordan said.

"She also needs to see a doctor," Alyssa said. "I'll mention it to Reginald. He'll see that she goes. No telling what
the damage from the drug–alcohol combination has been."

Naomi got Hoyt to drive her to Alyssa's place after
dinner. Everyone thanked her for the food.

"I'll bring over more tomorrow," she said.

"Grandma, you don't have to cook every day. I can cook
or pick up something," Alyssa countered.

"You've got your hands full."

"Sure are plenty of people here," her grandfather said.
"Don't come home alone. You can always stay at our
place."

"I know. Thanks, Grandpa. I'm glad you're here. We're
booking the two of you on a cruise. I need you to pick out
a date."

Her grandfather shook his head. "I can't leave right
now," he said.

"I have enough relatives on this island if I need someplace to go," Alyssa assured them, knowing they were
using her as an excuse to put their vacation on hold.

"I don't like to fly," Naomi said.

"You won't have to. We're going to book you on a cruise
from Norfolk. And you can't turn it down. It's your birthday gift from your grandchildren. It's already done," Alyssa added.

"What are we going to do on a cruise?" Hoyt said.

"Have fun. Take tours at the ports. You'll have a great
time," Alyssa said. "You'll feel like newlyweds again."

Naomi rolled her eyes.

"You want to go on the cruise?" Hoyt asked her.

"It's my birthday present. What do you think I'm going to do?"

"Well, it's all settled. The only thing left is for you to choose a date."

After her grandparents left and everyone had gone to bed, Jordan and Alyssa talked in the sunroom.

"You don't have to come here every night. Someone is always here with me."

"Do you really think I could sleep, knowing that creep is out there?"

Alyssa sighed.

In his office the next day, Jordan pulled out the pages he'd copied at Vanetta's. Phone numbers and addresses were listed for each name. He called the first one, but the man was in a meeting. He left a message and hoped the guy would return his call.

Jordan spoke to the second person and was told there had been an auction for the bowl, but he'd lost the bid. Jordan also contacted the third person, who related the same information. The last person was out of the country indefinitely. Jordan left a message, but it was anyone's guess when the call would be returned.

He called Alyssa at the office, but was told she was out on a call.

Stanley was tired of waiting for Alyssa. There had to be some way of getting her alone. Somebody was dogging her every hour of the day. He was an intelligent man, and Alyssa was equally intelligent. What a match they'd make.

He'd given the situation lots of thought. The only way Alyssa had figured out it wasn't Reginald was because she knew him too well. She knew very well he didn't have the balls to pull off what Stanley had done. Stanley realized he hadn't left any clues leading to himself. He'd planned well.

Ah, the difficulties of small town life. In the city, Reginald would have been easily convicted. The lead investigator wouldn't have known him personally, wouldn't have known he was too weak to pull off these heroic feats.

A thought surfaced, and Stanley snapped his fingers. God, he was smart. He steered his boat to a shore, went to a payphone, and dialed the island's police station.

"May I speak to Detective Claxton, please," he asked in a high-pitched female voice.

"One moment, please."

"Hello?" she answered after a few seconds. Her voice was music to his ears.

"I . . . I" He swallowed audibly as if he was nervous.

"How may I help you?" she asked.

"I saw the news report about those women on TV, you know, those women that awful man took to Paradise Island. That's why I'm calling you," he said. "I . . . I think I saw the man you're looking for a couple of hours ago. I saw my girlfriend get in his car that night. I don't want to get into any trouble," he said.

"Where did you see him?" she asked.

"In Norfolk. Near Church Street. He was cruising the streets, trying to pick up another girl. He asked me to get in his car, but I ran away. What if he gets someone? I called because, oh my God! What he did gives me nightmares."

"What kind of car was he driving?"

"A black Honda. I have to go. I don't want to get into trouble." He hung up.

She'd come to Norfolk. He was sure of that. And she wouldn't be as well guarded. Everyone would be searching for him. And it was easier to get lost in Norfolk than on the island. He smiled. He'd take her to his boat, and they'd sail away together.

"I got a lead on Stanley in Norfolk," Alyssa called out while dialing her contact there. "Let's get ready to roll," she said to John. When the detective came on the line, she described the call, then she and John headed to her car.

"Do you think it was him or another false lead?"

"We have to check it out either way. She seemed to have more details about where the dead woman was abducted. She said she was a friend of the woman."

John nodded.

Church Street was not a safe place. Drug dealers were selling their wares. It was raining, and dirty puddles glistened with God knew what.

Norfolk PD was combing the area. Alyssa and John went down a side street.

"There he is," she said. She pointed at someone who looked like Stanley, wearing an old jacket. He looked unkempt, a complete turn from his usual self. Barber shops were nearby. A few people were hanging out, and it was a residential area. But the person they tracked down wasn't Stanley.

Alyssa and John separated. Alyssa went one way, and John the other. She saw a woman lying near a trash can in a pool of blood. Was this Stanley's work? Was it the woman who had called her? Had he put her up to it?

Alyssa took out her phone to call for backup when suddenly, something hit her, and she fell to the ground. Felt like an electric shock blasted through her. A taser. She'd felt it before, only this time the voltage was a heck of a lot stronger and longer. Then she felt the pinprick of a needle in her arm. Panic hit her as she started to lose consciousness.

Before she could gather herself, her mouth and hands were taped, and she was dragged into the backseat of a car and covered.

Am I smart or what? Stanley thought. Half the damn Norfolk PD was there, and he'd still managed to get Alyssa and drive out without anyone being the wiser. He drove down Church Street to Granby St., and he made sure to stay near the speed limit. He even passed that wuss John, who was probably searching for Alyssa by now.

The Granby Street Bridge was straight ahead. He turned right before the bridge and parked the car near where he'd anchored his boat. He looked around. Usually, a few people were fishing on the pier, but not today. The weather was foul.

With one quick look to make sure the coast was clear, he opened the backdoor and hauled Alyssa out. He'd forgotten how heavy she'd be. He should have expected it with her height. He wasn't a big man like Jordan. No matter. He could handle this bundle.

Struggling under her weight, he dragged her aboard his boat and below deck, using her own handcuffs to tether her to the bed. Then he went above, weighed anchor, and sailed off.

"Oh, gad." Alyssa felt sick to her stomach. She was going to throw up. She turned her head to the side and heaved into a bucket. When she finished, she tried to get up, but her arm was cuffed to the bed.

Memory came back slowly. The asshole had used her own cuffs to immobilize her.

She needed to wash her mouth out, but then she thought of the condition she'd found April in. Chills wracked her body. She remembered the graves behind the barn. Hers would be a watery grave. She felt movement from the boat. They were sailing somewhere.

She'd never realized how sick Stanley was. He'd always seemed so sane. She wondered what she'd encounter when he made an appearance.

She heard footsteps on the stairs, and then he came through the cabin door.

"Oh, you're up. How are you feeling, dear?"

"Sick," Alyssa said.

"It will wear off." He handed her a cup. "Drink this. You'll feel better."

Stanley had drugged his victims. He'd drugged his wife. "I can't eat or drink. It'll come back up."

"Alyssa, Alyssa. I'll have to teach you to obey me." He set the cup on a table and sat in a chair facing her.

"We're going to be together for the rest of our lives."

He actually looked sane when he said that.

"Why did you kill them?" Alyssa asked. "Vicky and Matthew."

"Vicky betrayed me. We were having an affair, but she caught me at the funeral home one night and started blackmailing me. She realized I started the rumor about Brit being the necrophiliac when it was actually me."

"You had a successful business in Norfolk. The island mortuary is nothing in comparison."

"I wanted it. Brit was too deeply rooted, and he wouldn't sell. The island couldn't support both of us. Besides, I wanted to be seen as a pillar in the community. Vicky threatened all I had achieved. I had to get rid of her."

"Why Matthew? Was Vicky having an affair with him?"

"He was having an affair with Vicky, with Racine. He spread his seed around."

"Racine!"

"Are you shocked? Racine goes to bed with anyone with money. She didn't get very much out of her ex, so she was making out with Matthew to . . . let's see . . . make ends meet.

"Lucky for me Vicky and Matthew were both there that night. I couldn't have my reputation tarnished could I? I needed to be close to you, my love."

"What are you going to do with me?"

"Don't you know? I've worshiped you from afar for years. But now, it's our time. We're going to spend the rest of our lives together."

Alyssa gawked at him. He was freaking serious. He was crazy.

He caressed the side of her face. Alyssa turned away from his touch. He smacked her hard on the cheek, then grabbed her chin in his hand, hurting her. "You'll learn to obey me," he said with conviction. "You *will* enjoy my touch."

If she was free, she could help herself, but handcuffed to the bed, movement was constricted. Chills crawled through Alyssa as he caressed her cheek while holding her chin with his other hand.

Did anyone even know Stanley had captured her? Someone must have figured it out by now. But they wouldn't have a clue where to look. When they were searching just for him, police from all over Hampton Roads hadn't been able to find him.

She thought of the condition she'd found April in and started sweating. There was no way she could get her hands out of the cuffs.

"I've been very displeased by your actions lately. Maybe I left you alone too long. I should have taken you away years ago. I am most displeased with the way you carried on with Jordan."

"How was I to know you liked me?" Alyssa asked, trying another tactic. "You never said a word. You were married to Patience. You can't blame me for not knowing."

He thought for a moment. "Maybe I'll forgive you then. I'll have to think about it." He kissed her forehead, and Alyssa tried not to shudder. Tried not to think about this man making love to corpses. "We have the rest of our lives to make up for lost time," he said before he injected her with heaven knew what.

Jordan got the word Alyssa was missing later that afternoon.

"What the heck happened? What are you doing to find her?" He paced in Harper's office until Harper threw him out.

He went into full panic mode then. He couldn't sit around twiddling his thumbs. He called a couple of old friends from Norfolk, and he borrowed Matthew's boat.

Chapter 17

Patience had paced the floor and fought the bottle half the night, but the more she thought about what Stanley had done to her, the angrier she got. All this time, he was drugging her. He'd gone to bed with corpses then come to bed with her afterward. And she didn't know any of it.

Oh, God. The morning she woke up with worms and dirt on her. What had he done while she was unconscious? Had he covered her with them and had sex with her? He liked for her to lie still when they made love. Not to move a muscle. She knew it was weird, but she'd never equated that with having sex with corpses.

It made sense, though. Corpses couldn't move. They didn't talk back. They didn't demand that he satisfy them. Of course, Stanley would always satisfy her needs before he saw to his own. And he was a skilled lover. In the beginning of their relationship when they first began to make love, he'd ask her what pleased her. She was a little shy about revealing her desires, but he'd touched her, asked her if she liked what he was doing. She'd had her first orgasm with Stanley. He patiently stoked all her desires. And he made sure that she was satisfied first.

It was months after they had become intimate that he'd

revealed his secret desires. She remembered the time vividly. After he'd brought her to a powerful orgasm, he'd asked so sweetly if she'd do something for him. She was feeling so relaxed and grateful. And of course, she'd said yes. How could she not after the way he'd so lovingly taken care of her needs?

He'd asked her if she'd lie still, not move a muscle or talk while he made love to her. And she did. It wasn't as nice as the way he'd pleasured her before, but loving was give and take. He pleasured her, and she was willing to go out of her way to please him. As fetishes went, having to lie completely immobile during the act wasn't asking a whole lot.

But later, things began going downhill when he wanted her to lie naked in the garden dirt on cold nights, her body wracked with chills.

She couldn't remember when she started drinking.

Trembling wracked her body, forcing her to take a nip—just enough to soothe her soul. But one nip led to another. She was pretty toasted by the time she fell into a drunken slumber with her clothes on.

Patience woke up the next morning with a tipped over glass beside her pillow, a soaked spot on her bed smelling of liquor, and a giant-sized headache.

She had to do better than this. She needed to check herself into a treatment center because as long as she was home, she'd find a bottle.

She stumbled to the bathroom and dressed for the day. In the kitchen, she remembered the coffee machine was still on the timer and fresh coffee was already brewed, but she couldn't bear to drink any. The housekeeper must have set it up as she always did. Patience took a Pepsi out of the fridge for a burst of caffeine and poured some gin into the glass along with it to take the edge off her hangover.

She felt a little guilty. Hadn't she promised to stop? But

every time she thought of the things Stanley had done to her, her nerves got tangled up. Besides, she needed one more drink before she started the program. Lord knows, they wouldn't have anything there for her to drink. God, she hoped they had Valium or Xanax or something to knock her out so she wouldn't be able to think.

After she drank the alcohol, she sighed. She felt loads better. At least Reginald was off the hook. She wanted to hear his voice. Sitting down by the phone in the kitchen, she called him.

"Hi, darling. How are you?" Patience asked.

"Did you hear? Stanley took Alyssa. God knows what he's going to do with her."

"You're kidding."

"He'll probably kill her," Reginald said in a panic. He and Alyssa had always been great friends. Patience wondered if his feelings were more than mere friendship.

"When did this happen?" she asked, the news wiping her euphoria away.

"Yesterday. They got a tip about Stanley being near Church Street, and she went there with some other officers. Then she just disappeared. A woman was found dead a couple of blocks away, and they think Stanley did it."

"I just can't believe it." Reginald was a man now, but Patience had always been protective of her younger brother. Whatever hurt him hurt her, too. And the last few years, she hadn't been there for him at all. She didn't know what was going on in his life. She couldn't bear for Stanley to take Alyssa from Reginald.

That cheating SOB. Patience found herself back at the bar. She'd drink another Pepsi to make herself more coherent. But her hands were shaking so badly, she again spiked it with gin.

"Well, I'm going to prep the body of the woman Stanley killed free of charge. The family can't afford a big funeral and . . . I just can't believe it," Reginald said.

"That's kind of you." Patience hadn't thought of that. And people were probably going to start suing his estate soon. That meant they'd sue her, too. She'd be left flat broke, she thought, getting more upset.

"I'll talk to you later," Patience said and hung up. She had some thinking to do. The one thing she knew was that Stanley kept all his funds pretty liquid. She had wondered why he didn't invest in stocks. He always said it was because he didn't like putting his money places where he couldn't get to it immediately. But she now believed he wanted a way to get to his money if it was necessary to leave town on the run.

She wondered if he'd cleaned out their accounts. She was a victim, too. She deserved something out of this ordeal. If the money was still there, she was going to get it.

Patience headed to the bedroom Stanley had turned into his home office. One thing she could say about him was that he was a creature of habit. Patience grabbed their checkbooks and a briefcase, then she grabbed a big black garbage bag.

They'd taken her driver's license away, but she still had keys. She drove to the ferry, then to Virginia Beach. There was a small amount in the island bank, but the bulk of their money was kept elsewhere.

They had started out with joint accounts, but no telling what he'd done in the last couple of years. He could have transferred everything to his individual accounts.

Patience had found checkbooks to five banks in Stanley's office. At the first bank, she discovered the account was still open and held a huge amount. When she told the clerk she wanted to close the account and wanted cash, the woman looked at her as if she had suddenly sprouted a second head. She got the manager on duty to work with her, but Patience got her money—in cash—and put it into the briefcase.

In the car, Patience dumped everything into the garbage bag and moved on to the second bank. After she'd cleaned out the last account, she parked beside the river to think. God, she needed a drink. But she hadn't thought to bring any alcohol. The last thing she needed was to stop by an ABC store this time of day. She needed to think.

First, she took the heavy black bag and locked it in the trunk. Then she sat behind the wheel again and rolled the windows down. It was cool outside, but she needed the cool air to help clear her head.

Alyssa. She called the police station to find out if they'd found her yet. The dispatcher, who had gone to school with Patience told her no, but she wouldn't take the time to talk to her, because she was getting a million calls. Patience hit the wheel so hard she bounced on her seat. Something rolled by her ankles.

"A bottle. Thank God!" Uncorking the bottle, she took a long drink. She could always think better with a little drink, but she couldn't drink too much, else she wouldn't be able to think at all. Alyssa's life depended on her staying sober. She had to save Alyssa for Reginald.

Where would Stanley take her? Patience thought of several places she and Stanley had been over the years. He always liked the out-of-the-way places. Dank, wet, and country. It was the reason he liked the island so much.

She thought of one particular place just over the North Carolina border. Swampy and definitely creepy, it was an old house that sat on the water. She'd jokingly told Stanley she would never stay in a place like that, even for a vacation. But Stanley had thought it would be a nice place to get away from everything. It wasn't far.

Patience took another nip. Even knowing the man her

husband was, she felt a keen sense of betrayal. He was holed up, making love to another woman. She thought of the pleasure she had derived from his touch and went through simultaneous feelings of sickness and fulfillment. The fact that he would give another woman such pleasure made her just as sick.

She'd better stop drinking, she thought yet again. It had to be the drink giving her those mixed emotions.

She picked up the phone and dialed the station again. This time, she asked to speak to Harper.

"Patience, he doesn't have time to talk to you right now, honey," the same woman said.

"But I have . . ."

"I have to go." The phone went dead in her ear.

Jordan was beside himself with worry. His friend from the old neighborhood had acquaintances all over the place who could get information anywhere, anytime. He told him that Alyssa had been abducted from Church Street and got him to see if anyone had seen the vehicle she had been taken in.

Jordan paced the floor while he waited. Fifteen minutes later, he called back.

"It was an old, big blue Buick. Somebody looking like an old lady, but too strong for that. They headed to Granby Street Bridge. The car's parked under there now. He took her away on a boat. I'm waiting to see if anyone knows where he might have gone from there. It was raining earlier. Harder to track," he said.

When Alyssa awakened, the surface beneath her was stable. She wasn't on the water any longer, but in an iron double bed. She was lying on fresh sheets. It was one of those old iron beds and she was handcuffed to the head.

She was also naked. Had he already raped her? But she didn't feel like he'd touched her.

The room smelled freshly painted with a fresh egg shell hue. The sheets were new, as if they were fresh out of the package. At least she wasn't sleeping on some filthy mattress. She still felt woozy.

She smelled food cooking. In a moment, he was back.

"Ah, you're up." Gone was the woman's gray wig, long dress, and support hose. He wore a T-shirt and jeans.

"I know you like men who wear suits, but I'm not going into the office any time soon. I thought we could be more casual."

"May I have my clothes?" Alyssa asked.

"They're soiled. I sponged you down. You're all nice and clean again."

Alyssa's skin crawled, but she had to play along with him so he'd relax and maybe give her some freedom . . . enough so she could get away.

"I have to use the restroom."

"Wait until I bring your food. You can eat first. I've prepared you a lovely dinner. I can cook, you know. Bet you didn't know that. I was in the military, so I can take very good care of us."

Alyssa nodded. He kissed her forehead again before he left.

Ten minutes later, he was back with a tray.

"I need to go to the bathroom before I eat," Alyssa said.

"Can I trust you?"

"Of course."

"Don't disappoint me, Alyssa. You won't like your punishment."

Alyssa wished she was wearing clothes. That her breasts and private parts weren't bare for him to see.

"Did you get some clothes for me?" she asked with a smile.

He returned her smile. "I like you the way you are, but you can wear my shorts and a T-shirt if you'll be more comfortable." He went to the drawer and pulled out a new pair of briefs and a new T-shirt. Obviously, he'd had to purchase clothes after he made his escape.

Alyssa went to the bathroom and closed the door after her.

"Don't lock it," Stanley said.

"Okay." Quickly, Alyssa pulled on the clothes. There was no window. Shit. She searched for a weapon. There was nothing but a bar of soap, towels, and lotion. At least he'd thought of the basics. She opened the cabinet door. There was hairspray. She used the commode, then flushed. She took the hairspray and opened the door. She was too weak for a sustained battle with him, but she could run.

"The food smells delicious."

"My grandmother's special batter-fried fish."

Alyssa cracked the door further. He was standing nearby with the cuffs. She sprayed the hairspray in his face, then kicked out and punched him.

Stanley screamed, clawing at his eyes. He reached out to grab Alyssa, but she hit him once more, tried to grab the cuffs. He fought her. With a diet of drugs and no food, her strength was lagging. She had to get away. She dashed to the door and ran outside. She was in the midst of marshland with tall grass all around. She didn't want to think of the creatures. Mostly snakes out there, no doubt. Anything was safer than Stanley.

She heard him slam out the door after her, and she sprinted toward the woods. The ground was mushy under her feet, and her toes squished in the dark soil. But she was weak. The aftereffects of the injections Stanley had given her. He got close enough to zap her with the stun gun, and she went down screaming.

"No, no," she screamed.

He smacked her upside the head and clapped the cuffs on her. It felt like the charge from the gun would last forever. Thirty seconds was a long time. Finally, the effect started to wear off, and she struck out, but her effort was weak. Roughly, he secured her hands in back of her.

"Get up," he shouted, pulling her by the upper arm. She staggered up, and he dragged her back toward the house.

"Damn whore," he gritted between his teeth. "I knew I couldn't trust you. You're like all the rest. I'll teach you not to betray me."

Dread seeped through Alyssa as her mind's eye went back to April.

Patience knew she was near the turnoff, but all country roads looked the same to her. She'd already taken three wrong turns. She took the bottle from under the seat and took a nip. Screwing the top back on and placing it next to her, she promised herself she wouldn't touch it again. Alyssa needed her.

She drove down a long road that came up against the ocean. Wrong again.

She spied the bottle in the seat. She took a nip and called Reginald.

"Reg, honey, I can't find the right turnoff."

"What are you talking about, Patience?"

"This place at the North Carolina border. Stanley wanted to buy some land there once, but I didn't see any sense in it. It has a little house. I think he has Alyssa there."

"Tell me where you are, and I'll alert the authorities," Reginald said.

"Might be too late. I know it's somewhere out here."

"Patience, have you been drinking?"

She didn't say anything. She hadn't drunk much.

He sighed. "Tell me where you are."

"The place off . . . I forgot the name of the street. There are some lanes that lead to the ocean. You've been here before. They're out here somewhere."

"Listen to me, Patience. I'll call the authorities and come get you. Go to the nearest gas station or store and ask them where you are. Then call me."

"Okay, honey, but I think I can . . ."

"Listen to me, Patience. I'll take care of it."

"Okay." Patience hung up. They all thought she was helpless. A helpless drunk. She'd show them. She could save Alyssa all by herself. Just watch her.

Turning around, she backed into a tree, put the car in drive, and steered toward the main road. God, she'd never find this place before dark. How many little roads could there be in one little town? She knew she had taken the right turnoff.

If it wasn't for the fact that Alyssa didn't deserve what that prick had in store for her, she'd take the money and disappear. Except she couldn't leave her brother. Stanley had nearly ruined his life.

At the main road, she turned right and drove a couple of miles before she saw another turnoff. She nearly missed it, slammed on the brakes and swiveled the car into the lane, just nicking a tree. Her nerves were so torn up—she needed another drink. She took the bottle out again, drank a fortifying swallow, capped it, and placed it under the seat. Last one, she promised herself.

Jordan was beside himself with worry. He'd gotten Matthew's boat from the dock. It was fueled and ready to go. Curtis was with him, along with a friend who knew the ocean.

His cell phone rang.

"They were seen going south. Someone said they saw a

boat pull in just over the North Carolina border." He named the town.

"Where the heck is that?" Jordan asked, giving the details to his friend.

"I know where it is. Let's go," he said, and they pulled away from the shore.

If this was anything like Stanley's other victims, he kept them for a while before he killed them. God, the thought of that piece of scum touching Alyssa, possibly raping her, sent rage through him. He couldn't wait to choke the life out of Stanley.

Stanley threw Alyssa on the bed. "Bitch," he shouted. "Whore."

Alyssa fought back when he tried to tether her to the bed. She'd be helpless if he managed that again. But she was so weak. Whatever he had given her sapped her energy. She kicked him with all her might. He went flying back, hit the wall, and bounced off. She ran. He still had the taser, and if he got close enough to zap her, she was done for. The door was still open, and she ran through, not knowing what good it would do since her hands were bound. But she had to fight. Her life depended on it.

"Come back here, bitch." He was running after her with the taser. Oh God, let her get far enough away.

He zapped her yet again, and she went down screaming. Lightning shot through her, rendering her immobile.

Then she heard a loud bump and felt blessed relief . . . if she could call it that. She still couldn't move.

"Take that, you SOB," she heard, then felt a hand on her. She tried to scream, but couldn't.

"It's me. You're okay."

A female voice. Alyssa felt herself being turned over. Patience leaned over her, wavering. She smelled like day-old alcohol, but at the moment, it was the most pleasant of aromas.

Patience tried to help her up, but fell on her instead. Alyssa didn't have the strength to move. And she didn't know whether she should be afraid or relieved. She was just grateful the taser wasn't sending lightning bolts through her.

But where was Stanley? She moved her head, waiting to see him pop up to zap both of them, but he was near the car, lying on his stomach. Blood was running from his nose. Had Patience run into him? She hoped so.

"Patience?" Alyssa called out. She thought she spotted a snake several yards away, but anything within a mile was too close for her. "Patience . . ."

Patience stirred, moaned, then sat up.

"You have to help me here. Get the keys for the hand-cuffs from Stanley's pockets."

Patience stumbled over to Stanley and shook him. "Are you dead?"

"Don't shake him. Just search his pocket for the keys."

It took forever for Patience to find the key. Alyssa was afraid Stanley would come to and find that taser. She was afraid to ask Patience to get it. She'd more than likely stun herself. Then where would they be?

"Bring it over here." Alyssa positioned herself for Patience to unlock her, but by the time she got the key in, Stanley was coming to. "Hurry," Alyssa said.

Finally, she was free. She handcuffed Stanley before checking him for broken bones. At a guess, he had several. Then she retrieved the taser since she had no idea where Stanley had put her gun.

"Where's your cell phone, Patience?"

"In the car. In my purse, I think."

Alyssa retrieved the cell phone and started to call the

local police when she realized she had no clue where they were.

Patience was leaning over Stanley. "Why don't you try to drug me now?" she said, swaying over the barely conscious man. She glanced at Alyssa. "Are you sure he isn't dead?"

Alyssa shook her head to clear it. "Patience, come over here, please. You have to tell the police where we are. I don't know our location."

"Just press the red OnStar button. It has some kind of locator on it. If you tell them you have an emergency, they'll get the police here."

Alyssa should have known Patience had some kind of service like that. She pushed the emergency button. They told her she was in North Carolina and gave her the name of the road and crossroads.

The police weren't far. They'd gotten calls about a seriously drunk woman driving around and running into trees.

While Alyssa waited, she called Harper.

By the time they checked and discharged Alyssa from the hospital, Harper, Jordan, Reginald and Melinda, and her parents and brothers had arrived.

Stanley had several broken bones. They were going to have to extradite him to get him back to Virginia. But at least he was in police custody. The police were also going to dig on the North Carolina property, so depending on what they found, it might take Stanley years to be tried in Virginia.

Alyssa rode home with Jordan, but there was a gathering at her house when she arrived. Relatives and friends had come from all over.

There was a party going on, although she wasn't in a partying mood. But there was also a sense of home and peace. A sense of gratefulness that she'd come through this alive and whole.

The lagging effects of the injections left her lethargic, although the doctor had said there wouldn't be any lasting harm. She thought about drinking coffee to wake herself up, but she didn't want the nightmare of the last twenty-four hours to live on through the night.

Finally, everyone left, and only she and Jordan remained at the house.

"You scared the heck out of me, you know," Jordan said, steering them into the sunroom, an arm around Alyssa's shoulder.

"I was pretty scared myself for a while." Alyssa was grateful she had showered right after she got home because she didn't have the energy to walk back to her bedroom, much less take a bath.

"Don't frighten me like that again," Jordan said, hugging her close. "You know we're getting married, don't you? And I'm not letting you out of my sight."

"Get real."

He sighed. "At least promise you won't chase people when you're pregnant. I'm serious, Alyssa. I'm not moving into the house alone. I built it for us. After the honeymoon, we'll move in together."

"Jordan, you're acting like all the decisions are yours alone. Nothing's changed. At this stage, you aren't the man I see romping on the floor with children although I think I fell completely in love with you when you set up that scene on the house tour, by the way."

He smiled. "We can set a date then."

"You are such a man."

His chest puffed up.

Alyssa rolled her eyes. "It wasn't a compliment."

He sighed. "I know."

"There's a difference between intimacy and just having

sex. I still see you in smoky rooms with hot babes clipping your Cuban cigars. You still see women as your toys, and I can't live with that. You can buy anything with a price. But you can't buy me."

"Baby, I'm not trying to buy you. I have to admit women have been a convenience. I've been living in this fake world for so long, I forgot the difference in being with a woman who's real. There are no pretenses with you. I like that. I love you, Alyssa."

Now why did he say things like that? She felt herself melting, and she couldn't afford to let her defenses down with Jordan. Dishing out pretty words was easy for him. Could this be real? For once, she was afraid to believe, to let her heart go. "That's easy to say, but . . ."

"You're going to shove my love back in my face?"

"I think you *think* you love me. But I don't think you really know what love is."

"Don't tell me that when I just went through hell, almost lost my mind worrying about you. Don't tell me I don't love you." Now he was angry.

Jordan didn't think there was a woman alive who could hurt him or bedevil him the way Alyssa did. For a moment, he was stymied. What more could he do to make this woman believe in him? Believe in them?

The only light came from the moon and stars above. He glanced down at her. He was getting used to this scene. And he enjoyed it.

Alyssa nestled contentedly in the crook of his arm, but he wanted to shake some sense into her. He kissed her forehead instead. She'd been through a lot. He tightened his arm around her. In her presence, the caveman came out in him. He wanted to whisk her away and protect her in his lair. And she wanted to saddle him with conditions.

"I'll give you until the house is built," he said. "We're moving in there together. That's a promise."

"You've got some nerve," she said around a yawn. "You haven't heard a word I've said."

"I heard every word." He yawned. Guess he would have to turn into his father's son after all. According to his mother, this was the kind of man who appealed to Alyssa. He respected his father, and Alyssa was worth the change. He'd court her slowly and intently. By the time the house was finished, she'd be his unconditionally.

And that was a promise.

Dear Reader,

I hope you enjoyed Alyssa and Jordan's story in the second title of the "Quest for the Golden Bowl" series. The first title, *Golden Night,* featured Gabrielle Long and Cornell Price. The theme of the series is family history, so I hope you're talking to your older family members to gather your family's interesting stories.

Four titles are scheduled for the series. Stay tuned for the third title, featuring Barbara Turner and Harper Porterfield. Harper realizes he has to step it up if he wants to catch Barbara before another suitor snatches her away. Barbara just wants to stay alive long enough to get her grandmother's stolen money back.

Thank you for supporting my stories. Please visit my web page: *www.CandicePoarch.com*. You may contact me at: *readers@CandicePoarch.com*, or write to me at: P.O. Box 291, Springfield, VA 22150.

With warm regards,
Candice Poarch